DOUBLEDAY

New York

London

Toronto

Sydney

Auckland

FROM
THE
TEETH
OF
ANGELS

Jonathan
Carroll

PUBLISHED BY DOUBLEDAY
a division of Bantam Doubleday Dell Publishing
Group, Inc.
1540 Broadway, New York, New York 10036

DOUBLEDAY and the portrayal of an anchor with a
dolphin are trademarks of Doubleday, a division of
Bantam Doubleday Dell Publishing Group, Inc.

Book design by Claire Naylon Vaccaro
Photographs © 1994 Nick Vaccaro

Grateful acknowledgment is made to the following
for permission to reprint previously published
material:

Epigraph from "Godfather Death," *Transformations*
by Anne Sexton. Copyright © 1971 by Anne Sexton.
Reprinted by permission of Houghton Mifflin Co.
All rights reserved.

A Natural History of the Senses © 1990 by Diane
Ackerman. Reprinted by permission of Random
House, Inc.

Excerpt from "Evening Talk" in *The Book of Gods
and Devils,* copyright © 1990 by Charles Simic,
reprinted by permission of Harcourt Brace &
Company.

Library of Congress Cataloging-in-Publication Data

Carroll, Jonathan, 1949–
    From the teeth of angels / Jonathan Carroll. —
1st ed. in the U.S.A.
        p.   cm.
    I. Title.
    PS3553.A7646F76   1993
    813'.54—dc20   93-22997
                                        CIP

ISBN 0-385-46841-5
Copyright © 1994 by Jonathan Carroll
All Rights Reserved
Printed in the United States of America
May 1994
First Edition in the United States of America

10   9   8   7   6   5   4   3   2   1

For Bunny & Charlie—
hands on our faces forever

and for

Richard & Judy Carroll
Rita Wainer
Herb Kornfeld

Hurry, Godfather death,
Mister tyranny,
each message you give
has a dance to it,
a fish twitch,
a little crotch dance.
"Godfather Death," by Anne Sexton

The Gods only know how to compete or echo.
Gilgamesh

FROM

THE

TEETH

OF

ANGELS

Part One

Wyatt

Sophie,

Just returned from Sardinia, where we'd planned to stay two weeks but ended up driving away after only five days because it is one HIDEOUS island, dahling, let me tell you. I'm always suckered by books like *The Sea and Sardinia* or *The Colossus of Maroussi,* where famous writers describe how wonderful it was to be on wild and woolly islands forty years ago when the native women went golden topless and meals cost less than a pack of cigarettes. So, fool that I am, I read those books, pack my bag, and flea (intended) south. Only to see topless women, all right—two-hundred-pound German frau-tanks from Bielefeld with bazooms so enormous they could windsurf on them if they only hoisted a sail, meals that cost more than my new car, and accommodations the likes of which you'd wish on your worst enemy. And then, because I have a limp memory, I always forget the sun in those southern climes is so deceptively hot that it fries you helpless in a quick few hours. Please witness my volcanic red face, thanks.

No, I am past forty and consequently have every right to "just say no" to things like these trips from now on. When we were driving back, I said to Caitlin, "Let's just go to the mountains on our next vacation." Then, lo and behold, we came to an inn below the mountains near Graz, next to a small flickering brook, with the smell of wood smoke and slight dung, red-and-white-checked tablecloths, a bed upstairs that looked down on the brook through swaying chestnut trees, and there were chocolates wrapped in silver foil on our pillows. There's no place like home, Toto.

While we were in Sardinia, we spent a lot of time in a café-bar that was the only nice thing about the place. It was called the Spin Out Bar, and when the owners found out we were American they treated us like heroes. One of them had been to New York years ago and kept pinned on the wall a map of Manhattan with red marks all over it to show anyone who came in where he'd been there.

At night the joint filled up and could be pretty rowdy, but besides the Nordic windsurfers and an overdose of fat people in floral prints, we met a number of interesting characters. Our favorites were a Dutchwoman named Miep who worked in a sunglasses factory in Maastricht. Her companion was an Englishman named McGann and there, my friend, sits this story.

We couldn't figure out why Miep was in Sardinia in the first place, because she said she didn't like a lot of sun and never went in the water. She was happy to leave it at that, but McGann thought it germane to add, "She reads a lot, you know." What does she read about? "Bees. She loves to study bees. Thinks we should study them because *they* know how to make a society work properly." Unfortunately, neither Caitlin's knowledge of bees nor mine extends beyond stings and various kinds of honey we have tasted, but Miep rarely said anything about her books or her bees. In the beginning Miep rarely said anything about anything, leaving it up to her friend to carry the conversation ball. Which he did with alarming gusto.

God knows, the English are good conversationalists and when they're funny they can have you on the floor every five minutes, but McGann talked too much. McGann never *stopped* talking. You got to the point where you'd just tune him out and look at his pretty, silent girlfriend. The sad part was, in between all his words lived an interesting man. He was a travel agent in London and had been to fascinating places—Bhutan, Patagonia, North Yemen. He also told half-good stories, but inevitably in the middle of one about the Silk Road or being trapped by a snowstorm in a Buddhist monastery, you'd realize he'd already spewed out so many extraneous, *bo*-ring details that you'd stopped paying atten-tion six sentences back and were off in your own dream image of a snowbound monastery.

One day we went to the beach and stayed too long—both of us came home with wicked sunburns and bad moods. We complained and snapped at each other until Caitlin had the good idea of going to the bar for dinner because they were having a grill party and had been talking about it since we'd arrived. Grill parties are not my idea of nirvana, especially among strangers, but I knew if we stayed in our barren bun-galow another hour we'd fight, so I agreed to go.

"Hello! There you two are. Miep thought you'd be com-ing, so we saved you places. The food is really quite good. Try the chicken. Lord, look at your sunburns! Were you out all day? I remember the worst sunburn I ever had . . ." was only part of McGann's greeting from across the room when we came in and walked over. We loaded up plates and went to sit with them.

As both the evening and McGann went on, my mood plunged. I didn't want to listen to him, didn't want to be on this burned island, didn't relish the twenty-hour trip back home. Did I mention that when we returned to the mainland on the overnight ferry, there were no more cabins available, so we had to sleep on benches? We did.

Anyway, I could feel myself winding up for one hell of a temper tantrum. When I was three seconds away from throwing it all onto McGann and telling him he was the biggest bore I'd ever met and would he shut up, Miep turned to me and asked, "What was the strangest dream you ever had?" Taken aback both by the question, which was utterly out of left field, and because her boyfriend was in the middle of a ramble about suntan cream, I thought about it. I rarely remember my dreams. When I do, they are either boring or unimaginatively sexy. The only strange one that came to mind was of playing guitar naked in the back seat of a Dodge with Jimi Hendrix. Jimi was naked too and we must have played "Hey Joe" ten times before I woke up with a smile on my face and a real sadness that Hendrix was dead and I would never meet him. I relayed this to Miep, who listened with head cupped in her hands. Then she asked Caitlin. She told that great dream about making the giant omelette for God and going all over the world trying to find enough eggs. Remember how we laughed at that?

After we answered, there was a big silence. Even McGann said nothing. I noticed he was looking at his girlfriend with an anxious, childlike expression. As if he were waiting for her to begin whatever game was to follow.

"Dreams are how Ian and I met. I was in Heathrow waiting to fly back to Holland. He was sitting next to me and saw that I was reading an article on this 'lucid dreaming.' Do you know about it? You teach yourself to be conscious in your night dreams so you can manipulate and use them. We started talking about this idea and he made me very bored. Ian can be very boring. It is something you must get used to if you are going to be with him. I still have trouble, but it is a week now and I am better."

"A week? What do you mean? You've only been together that long?"

"Miep was coming back from a beekeepers' convention in Devon. After our conversation in the airport, she said she would come with me."

"Just like that? You came here with him instead of going home?" Caitlin not only believed this, she was enchanted.

She believes fully in chance encounters, splendid accidents, and loving someone so much right off the bat you can learn to live with their glaring faults. I was more astonished that Miep had come with him yet said openly what a bore he was. Was that how you sealed the bond of love at first sight? Yes, let's fly off together, darling, I love you madly and'll try to get used to how boring you are.

"Yes. After Ian told me about his dreams, I asked if I could come. It was necessary for me."

I said to McGann, "Must have been some kind of powerful dream you had." He looked plain, pleasant, and capable but only in a small way—like an efficient postman who delivers your mail early, or the salesman in a liquor store who can rattle off the names of thirty different brands of beer. I assumed he was a good travel agent, up on his prices and brochures, and a man who could choose a good vacation for someone who didn't have much money. But he wasn't impressive and he talked forever. What kind of dream *had* he had to convince this attractive and nicely mysterious Dutchwoman to drop everything and accompany him to Sardinia?

"It wasn't much really. I dreamed I was working in an office, not where I do work—some other place—but nowhere special. A man walked in I'd known a long time ago who had died. He died of cancer maybe five years before. I saw him and knew for sure that he had come back from the dead to see me. His name was Larry Birmingham. I never really liked this fellow. He was loud and much too sure of himself. But there he was in my dream. I looked up from my desk and said, 'Larry. It's you! You're back from the dead!' He was very calm and said yes, he'd come to see me. I asked if I could ask him questions about it. About Death that is, of course. He smiled, a little too amusedly I realize now, and said yes. About this time in the dream, I think I knew I was dreaming. You know how that happens? But I thought, Go on, see what you can find out. So I asked him questions. What *is* Death like? Should we be afraid? Is it anything like we expect? . . . That sort of thing. He answered, but many of the answers were vague and confusing. I'd ask again and he'd answer in a different way, which at first I thought was clearer, but in the end it wasn't—he had only stated the muddle differently. It wasn't much help, I'll tell you."

"Did you learn anything?"

Ian looked at Miep. Despite her aloofness and his dialogue ten miles long, it was obvious that there was great closeness and regard between these two remarkably dissimilar people. It was a look of love to be sure, but a great deal more than that. More, a look that clearly said there were things they knew about each other already that went to the locus of their beings. Whether they'd known each other a short week or twenty years, the look contained everything we all hope for in our lives with others. She nodded her approval, but after another moment he said, gently, "I . . . I'm afraid I can't tell you."

"Oh, Ian—" She reached across the table and touched her hand to his face. Imagine a beam light going directly across that table, excluding everything but those two. That's what both Caitlin and I felt, watching them. What was most surprising to me was that it was the first time Miep had talked of or shown real feeling for her man. Now, there was suddenly so much feeling that it was embarrassing.

"Ian, you're right. I'm sorry. You're so right." She slipped back into her chair but continued looking at him. He turned to me and said, "I'm sorry to be rude, but you'll understand why I can't tell you anything when I'm finished.

"Excuse me, but before I go on—it's hard for me to tell this, so I'm going to have another drink. Would anyone like a refill?"

None of us did, so he got up and went to the bar. The table was silent while he was gone. Miep never stopped looking at him. Caitlin and I didn't know where to look until he returned.

"Right-o. Tanked up and ready to go. You know what I was just thinking, up there at the bar? That I once drove through Austria and got a case of the giggles when I passed a sign for the town of Mooskirchen. I remember so well thinking to myself that a bonkers translation of that would be

Moose Church. Then I thought, Well, why the hell not—people worship all kinds of things on this earth. Why couldn't there be a church to moose? Or rather, a religion to them. You know?

"I'm rattling on here, aren't I? It's because this is a terribly difficult story for me to tell. The funny thing is, when I'm finished you'll think I'm just as bonkers as my imagined worshippers at the Moose Church, eh, Miep? Won't they think I don't have all my bulbs screwed in?"

"If they understand, they will know you are a hero."

"Yes, well, folks, don't take Miep too seriously. She's quiet but very emotional about things sometimes. Let me go on and you can judge for yourself whether I'm crazy or, ha-ha, a hero.

"The morning after that first dream, I walked to the bathroom and started taking my pajamas off so I could wash up. I was shocked when I saw—"

"Don't tell them, Ian, show them! Show them so they will see for themselves!"

Slowly, shyly, he began to pull his T-shirt over his head. Caitlin saw it first and gasped. When I saw, I guess I gasped too. From his left shoulder down to above his left nipple was a monstrously deep scar. It looked exactly like what my father had down the middle of his chest after open heart surgery. One giant scar wide and obscenely shiny pink. His body's way of saying it would never forgive him for hurting it like that.

"Oh, Ian, what happened?" Sweet Caitlin, the heart of the world, involuntarily reached out to touch him, comfort him. Realizing what she was doing, she pulled her hand back, but the look of sympathy framed her face.

"Nothing happened, Caitlin. I have never been hurt in my life. Never been in the hospital, never had an operation. I asked Death some questions, and when I woke the next morning this was here." He didn't wait for us to examine the scar more closely. The shirt was quickly over his head and down.

"I'm telling you, Ian, maybe it is a kind of gift."

"It's no gift, Miep, if it hurts terribly and I can't move my left arm well anymore! The same with my foot *and* my hand."

"What are you talking about?"

Ian closed his eyes and tried once to continue but couldn't. Instead, he rocked back and forth, his eyes closed.

Miep spoke. "The night before we met, he had another dream and the same thing happened. This Larry came back and Ian asked him more questions about Death. But this time the answers were clearer, although not all of them. He woke up and he says he had begun to understand things that he didn't before. He believes that's why the scar on the inside of his hand is smaller—the more he understands of the dream, the more it leaves him alone. A few nights ago he had another, but he woke with a big cut on his leg. Much bigger than the one on his hand."

Ian spoke again, but his voice was less. Softer and . . . deflated. "It will tell you anything you want to know, but you have to understand it. If you don't . . . it does *this* to you so you'll be careful with your questions. The trouble is, once you've started, you can't stop asking. In the middle of my second dream I told Birmingham I wanted to stop; I was afraid. He said I couldn't.

"The ultimate game of Twenty Questions, eh? Thank God Miep's here. Thank God she believed me! See, it makes me so much *weaker*. Maybe that's the worst part. After the dreams there are the scars, but even worse than that is I'm much weaker and can't do anything about it. I can barely get out of the bed. Most of the time I'm better as the day goes on . . . but I know it's getting worse. And one day I won't . . . I know if Miep weren't here . . . Thank God for you, Miep."

I later convinced him to show us the scar on his hand, which was utterly unlike the one on his chest. This one was white and thin and looked years old. It went diagonally across his palm, and I remember thinking from the first time we'd met how strangely he moved that hand, how much slower and clumsier it was. Now I knew why.

There's more to this, Sis. But what do you do in a situation like that? When half your brain thinks this is mad, but the other half is shaking because maybe it's real? They asked us for nothing, although I doubt there was anything we could do. But after that night whenever I saw or thought of McGann, I liked him enormously. Whatever was wrong with the man, he was afflicted by something terrible. Either insanity or death dreams were clearly out to get him, and he was a goner. But the man remained a bore. A good-natured, good-humored bore who, in the midst of his agony or whatever it was, remained wholly himself, as I assume he'd always been. That's the only real courage. I mean, few of us go into burning buildings to save others. But watching a person face the worst with grace, uncomplainingly, grateful even for the love and help of others . . . That's it, as far as I'm concerned.

Two days later, Caitlin and I decided more or less on the spur of the moment to leave. We'd had enough and weren't getting any pleasure at all from the place. Our bags were packed and the bill was paid within hour and a half. Neither of us likes saying goodbye to people and, as you can imagine, we were spooked by McGann's story. It's not something anyone would be quick to believe, but if you'd been there that night and seen their faces, heard their voices and the conviction in them, you'd know why both of us were uncomfortable in their presence. Then it happened that as we were walking out to the car, we ran right into Miep, who was coming toward the office in a hurry.

Something was clearly wrong. "Miep, are you all right?"

"All right? Oh, well, no. Ian is . . . Ian is not well." She was totally preoccupied and her eyes were going everywhere but to us. A light of memory came on in them, and her whole being slowed. She remembered, I guess, what her man had told us the other night.

"He had another dream today, after he came home from the beach. He lay down and it was only a few minutes, but when he woke—" Instead of continuing, she drew a slow line across the lower part of her stomach. Both Caitlin and I jumped at that and asked what could we do. I think we both also started toward their bungalow, but Miep shouted, really shouted, "No!" and there was nothing we could do to convince her to let us help. If that was possible. More than that though, the thing that struck me hardest was her face. When she realized we weren't going to try to interfere, she looked over our shoulders toward their place, where Ian was, and the expression was both fear and radiance. Was it true? Was he really back there, scarred again by death, scarred again because he hadn't understood its answers to his questions? Who knows?

On the boat back to the mainland, I remembered what he had said that night about the Moose Church and how people should be allowed to worship whatever they want. *That* was the look on his girlfriend's face—the look of one in the presence of what they believe is both the truth and the answer to life. Or death.

Our thoughts,
Jesse

Putting the letter down, I closed my eyes and waited for her to speak.

"Well, what do you think, Wyatt?"

I looked over, but the morning sun sat right on top of her head like a hot yellow crown. I had to squint even to make out the shape of her face.

"I think it's intriguing."

"Whaddya mean, 'intriguing'? Don't you believe it?"

"Sure I do. That's been my problem for years—believing. Sometimes I think it's not leukemia that's killing me, but terminal believing. Terminal hope."

"Wyatt, don't be facetious. This could be *it;* the thing that could save you. Why aren't you more—"

"More what? More excited? Sophie, I have cancer. They've assured me I'm going to die. That I don't have much longer to live. God's doing me a big favor by letting me even be here today. Can you imagine what it's like living with that in your head every minute of the day?

"In the beginning, when I first knew I was sick, there were all kinds of things in me that simply aren't anymore. I woke up every morning and cried. I went through a period where I looked at the world twice as hard because I never knew if I'd see any of it again. Life became a three-D movie; I made everything stand out, stand at attention. But even that goes away after a while, strangely enough.

"I read about a woman in New York who had her purse snatched. That's lousy, right? But know what else the thief did? Started sending things back piece by piece on special occasions in her life. She had a Filofax in her bag where she'd marked her anniversary and kids' birthdays, things like that. So on her first birthday after the purse was stolen, she got her driver's license back in the mail. Along with a greeting card from the guy. Next, he sent back her birth certificate. It went on and on. Such a perverse story, but clever too, you know? The man was into dread. He figured out a perfect way to torment her for years. He didn't want to steal a bag—he wanted to burrow into her life like a tick."

Sophie nodded but smiled too, as if she knew something I didn't. She kept smiling when she spoke. "At the same time, it's almost sexy when you think about it: all that attention and the time he spent at it. How many creeps would go to the trouble of stealing your purse and then sending you a birthday card?"

I knew I could count on my friend to understand. "That's exactly my point. Death is like the purse snatcher and that's what's so goddamned mean. It steals things from you, and then slowly gives some of them back so you start getting confused but hopeful at the same time. If it's going to steal my purse, then just take it and get the hell out of my life. Don't send back old credit cards or a license I've already replaced.

"I read a letter like this, or an article in the paper, saying some doctor in Osaka claims to have found the cure for cancer in a derivative from plum pits . . . I don't *want* to have any more hope. I don't want to believe somewhere in the world is a cure or an answer or a guru who'll be able to take away my fear. I would like to learn how to die now."

She looked at me disgustedly. " 'Your job is to find out what the world is trying to be.' Whatever happened to that, Wyatt? You were the one who gave me that poem. Does learning how to die also mean learning how to stop living?"

"Maybe."

"Then maybe you're full of shit. I don't think that's how God wants us to do it, and I'm not talking about going gently into some good night. I'm not experiencing what you are, granted, so maybe I have no right to talk about it at all, but I'm going to anyway. The only way to defeat the purse snatcher is go find him. Find him, show him your face, and say, 'I've found you and you can't scare me anymore.' If Death keeps torturing you by sending back stuff you thought was gone, then go find Him and tell Him to stop. I think you learn how to die by . . . Oh, shit!"

I hadn't been looking at her as she angrily spoke so I didn't realize she was crying till I looked up at that last word. Her face was wet with tears but her eyes were furious. "The minute I finished reading this letter I called you, I was so excited. If you can find this Ian guy, he could have the answer! But it doesn't interest you?"

"Sure it does, but maybe finding the answer doesn't mean finding a cure for my illness." I picked up the glass of orange juice and took a long, cold drink. Sophie always squeezed her own juice, and it was a delicious treat. Fresh orange juice, tart and full of stringy pulp that burst with its own taste when you nibbled it.

"Wyatt?"

"Hmm?"

"What *is* it like?" From the tone of her voice, it was clear what she meant.

Rolling the glass between my hands, I looked down into its orange swirl. "I met a young woman when I was taking my last treatment. She couldn't have been more than twenty-five. Cancer of the throat that had spread down into her chest . . . the works. She would have fooled me if I hadn't known what to look for, because she'd done a good job of disguising herself. Had all her hair, or at least a very good wig, and lots of natural color in her cheeks. But that's another thing you learn to recognize—what's real and what's makeup, wigs, tanning studios . . . This girl told me the only thing she could do now was wait for the results of her treatments and try to figure out ways of fooling the world into thinking she was one of them. Healthy, whole; a real human being. Because that's one of the things you learn when you get sick.

"What's it like? Get cancer or start to die and you quickly see how people work. It's very different from what you thought all your life, believe me. Anyway, this woman told me something chilling. Said she'd just received her last radiation treatment. There's only so much you can be given before it stops helping and starts to destroy you. They give you so-and-so many doses and then that's it—if all those rads or whatever they're called don't work, you're out of luck. But know what else they told her? Not to get near babies. And certainly don't *touch* any, because she was so full of radiation that she would be dangerous to them."

"No!"

"That's the truth. As if dying's not bad enough, huh? It's that kind of humiliation too. The worry you might throw up in the restaurant if you don't take your medicine at the right time. Or suddenly not being able to lift yourself out of a chair. Or when pain becomes so unbearable that you have to ask a stranger in a voice that won't scare them to call you an ambulance. What's it like? It's like being the radioactive woman. Except you're radioactive to the whole healthy world. Everyone looks at you as if there's something wrong with you. As if you glow, or are infectious, and no matter how many times they're told that's not true, they secretly think it is. But there isn't anything wrong with *you*—it's what entered you that's wrong. There's . . . I'm going in circles. What's it like? It's like being the radioactive girl. You're not living anymore; you're juggling. It's such a mistake to think you can escape."

"This makes me so depressed, I have to eat something. I'm going to the kitchen. Do you want some more orange juice?"

"Yes, that would be very nice."

She got up and jingled her way across the patio, followed by Lulu. Lulu, the black French bulldog who, halfway through her comfy life, grew cataracts on her eyes and went blind. Sophie bought a small tinkly bell which she wore on one of her slippers so that the dog always knew where to find her in the house.

Sophie and Lulu. The three of us spent a great deal of time together. Sophie's late husband, Dick, had owned a rare bookstore in downtown L.A. that was one of my favorite hangouts. He was a man who loved books and taught you how to love them too. I never could figure out which of the two I liked more. When Dick passed away, Sophie and I became close. We talked on the phone almost every day and ate dinner together three or four times a month. She was only in her mid forties when he died and left her both a healthy business and inheritance. But she showed no interest in getting involved with another man. For a while I thought she had fallen in love with a woman who worked in her store, but I was wrong. I asked her about that side of her life one day. She said I was the only other man she had ever really loved, but since I'm gay . . . I said tell the truth. She said that *was* the truth.

"Wyatt! Come in here, you've got to see this!"

"What?"

"Just come in here. Fast!"

I quick-stepped from the baking sunlight into the shade of the eaves. Swung open the screen door and walked up the two steps to her kitchen. First thing I saw was Sophie with her hands on her hips, shaking her head. Then I heard before I saw the frantic clitter of Lulu's toenails on the linoleum. Clickety-stickety-click she spun in panting, snuffling circles, then jumped up against the counters all in a mad rush because she knew something wonderful besides her mistress was in the room.

Something wonderful was a small calico cat sitting on the windowsill above the kitchen sink. It was cleaning its head by licking a paw and then wiping it over its face. I'd not seen the cat before, but it acted with the calm and deliberation of an animal completely at home in its surroundings.

"You gotta see this. It's our daily ritual. That's Roy, the neighbor's cat. He climbs in through the window and sits there, waiting for Lulu to smell that he's here. Since she went blind, her nose has gotten extrasensitive. Once she catches a whiff of him, she proceeds to go nuts and hunt for him as if he's the golden fleece. But she's so stupid because he always does the same thing. In through the window, sit over the sink, wait. Now watch what happens."

The dog became more frantic the closer she got to the cat. Roy seemed bored by her scrabbling and twitching. Perhaps he only saw it as his due for deigning to be there. He kept cleaning his head, with an occasional frozen pause to check on the whereabouts of his fan.

"Every day this happens?"

"Every day. It's like a Noh play—each goes through exactly the same moves, same roles, everything. Wait, though; part two is about to begin. First Lulu has to get tired and give up."

We waited for that to happen and it did a few minutes later. She collapsed in a gasping, exhausted heap on the floor, her head held up high so that she could pull in more air. Roy, finished washing, stared like an indifferent god at her. Lulu had definitely given up.

Slowly His Majesty dropped down from the windowsill to the sink to the floor with nary a sound. But the dog heard; she perked right up again. Roy walked over to her and swatted at her rear end, just barely touching it. She turned, but he was already in front, swatting at her face. Now she went crazy. Like a skilled boxer, the cat leaped and parried and pranced and was wonderful the way he stayed out of harm's way. Sophie and I started laughing because the two of them really got in the most extraordinary workout. After a few more seconds of this leaping and lunging, Lulu now thoroughly out of her mind with excitement and frustration, Roy sprang back up on the sink and right out the window.

"The phantom strikes again."

"And it happens every day?"

"More or less."

"Fabulous. But I think she likes it."

"She loves it! Once by accident she got hold of his paw and was so startled that she didn't know what to do. And you know, I was just thinking. Know what it reminds me of, Wyatt?"

"What?"

"Your thing with hope. What you were just talking about."

"How do you mean?"

"You're like Lulu with the cat. You're blind, but you know it's there. You can smell it and feel it. It keeps tweaking your tail. The closer it gets, the more you whip around and around, trying to catch it. Till now, when you've given up and are down on the floor."

"And whatever it is that'll save my life pokes and torments me to remind me it's there? That's stretching it a bit, Sophie."

"It is not! You and I have been talking about this ever since you got sick. I remember the things you've said. Maybe you *want* to give up hope or think you have now, but I don't believe it. And neither do you because both of us know it's still there. 'Cause that's what hope *is*. We can't really see it, but it keeps brushing its paw past our face close enough so that we feel the breeze. It's always there but sometimes we catch hold of it and having it scares the hell out of us, and we let go. Like dumb Lulu the one time she caught Roy.

"Anyway, here's your orange juice."

For a certain period in every life, a person can do no wrong. That period may last an hour, a month, or much longer, and that is the real unfairness of fate. But length aside, there does come a moment for everyone when he is invincible, infallible, immortal. Even if it lasts only an afternoon.

I was lucky—supremely lucky. For some years, I was the host of a very successful children's show on television. It was not the best time in my life because those years were all rush, deadlines, sprint from here to there, hurry-up-and-get-it-done. But the momentum and energy that came from it were exquisite. Solid gold adrenaline. The best you can hope for is to live in a present so full and all-encompassing that you lose any sense of future or past. For those years I lived in that kind of packed Now, and it was enough.

My roommate was the producer of the show and we thought we had the kind of relationship that could survive Hollywood, success, too much money, not enough time, everyone and his brother coming out of the closet . . . all those things. But it didn't. I fell in dubious love for a couple of weeks with a film critic in New York and had a short frivolous affair with him. I confessed everything over the phone to my friend and partner in Los Angeles, hoping he would understand.

He didn't. When I returned home, he had already moved out. What was worse, afterward he treated me with the same good will and kindness in our working life as he had privately. What is more distressing than being treated well when you know you don't deserve it? I was dismayed, but I was also a STAR, which flattered me into believing for a time that I was allowed to behave badly and get away with it. Hey, all of television land still loved me. They didn't know what I had done.

Not many people know how to be famous, to twist the phrase, and that included me. I behaved atrociously toward someone I genuinely loved, then tried to brush it away like lint off my cashmere sleeve. Instead of atoning, I decided on a spree. Went out and had a ball and *almost* forgot down deep what a shit I was. Drinks on the house! Strike up the band!

Then one day while taping the show, I didn't see a thick cable on the floor and tripped over it. I fell on my arm and got a nasty bruise. Which didn't go away. It was the color of an angry thundercloud, and it stayed around for weeks. Until then, I'd been one of those lucky ones who are rarely, if ever, sick. I went to hospitals to visit others, never to stay. My medicine cabinet contained a bottle of aspirins and an unopened package of cold pills.

The doctor spoke slowly, as if someone were carving his

every word into stone tablets as he pompously enunciated each one.

"We're concerned about these test results, Mr. Leonard."

"But it's only a bruise that's stuck around, doctor."

"Unfortunately, it is more than that."

I tried to shut my eyes but fear wouldn't let me. How quickly we understand the worst. So many simpler things in life we fail to grasp—algebra problems, trip directions, why love failed. But we hear "it is more than that," and our understanding increases a hundred thousand times. More. Take that quick desperate breath that is the only possible first reaction, then say, "What do you mean?"

He explains even more slowly. It is your first lesson in the language of death.

In the hospital the only two interesting people I met were Radioactive Girl and Liver Man. The others were a mixed bag and blur of panic, greed, and resignation. We knew why we were there, but our misery did not love one another's company. It only reminded us of our running clocks and isolation. We wanted to be out of there, away, even without a clean bill of health. Just *out*. Didn't want to walk down those shiny corridors, look out the clean windows into gardens that were too silent and well kept, gardens that reminded you of cemeteries. In a hospital what you miss most is the roll and tumble of real life. A pastrami sandwich served by a surly waiter. Horns honking, people passing in animated conversation . . . And there are really only two facial expressions in a hospital—great fear or calm. Once in a while you see sadness, but people try to hide that; it's either unprofessional or unfair to show it. Hugh called them faces squeezed out of a tube.

Liver Man Hugh Satterlee was all the things I missed outside. Animated and funny, he had, astoundingly, managed to retain his sense of balance throughout a nightmare ordeal that made me cringe just to hear about it.

Years before, they had found a tumor on his liver. It didn't respond to treatment and worsened until he was close to death. Then, miraculously, a donor was found and Satter-lee was given a transplant. He recovered. His wife died. A year and a half later, another tumor was discovered growing on the new liver—in exactly the same place as the old one. Inoperable. Time to die. When I knew Hugh, he was about to be moved to a hospice in Palos Verdes so that he could "at least die with a view."

"Bet you never heard a story like mine. Spooky, isn't it? Maybe I should start a tumor business. Bring me your organs and I'll grow tumors on them for you. Like those surrogate mothers, you know?"

The only thing that distracted me from the omnipresent fear and boredom of hospital life was to ask people for their stories. Some were eager to talk, but others regarded me distrustfully, as if I were trying to take from them the last thing they would ever own—their personal history. Before I was discharged from the hospital the first time, I sat for an afternoon with Hugh and told him some of the stories I'd heard. He was very ill. His eyes were exhausted and blood-shot, although now and then he smiled or chuckled when he heard something he liked. When I was finished, he sighed and wondered out loud if Death was the final pencil sharp-ener.

When I asked what he meant, he said most of the people I'd talked about had probably never once really used their lives, although it was the only thing we ever truly own. Think of it like a pencil, getting duller and duller until finally there's no lead left to write with. Then Death comes along, and if you're lucky, you're given a while before it happens to think things over, put them in their place, whatever. Just like sharpening the pencil so that it can be used again the right way.

Unable to stop a wave of bitterness flooding over and through my voice, I asked, "What good is sharpening it if you're never going to use it again?"

"Because it's back the way it should have been all along, Wyatt. I don't know about you, but I always found sharpen-ing pencils a very pleasant thing to do. And afterward, placing them on the desk ready to go. It didn't matter if I was going to use them then or in a month. Having them there, seeing them clean and sharp . . . that was the real pleasure for me. These stories you've heard? Doesn't it sound as if the people are finally savoring their lives for the first time? It does to me.

"But you know something else I've thought about? I was poor most of my life. Have you ever been poor? I mean really rock-bottom poor, not a dime in your pocket? It's a terrible, terrible place to be. Horrible thing to experience. And you know what? You learn the experience in one second. Know you're poor for ten minutes, and you've learned the lesson for the rest of your life. You don't need to go through years of it, like school. One day, an hour, and you know all about it. Same thing's true with dying. Know for sure you're dying for even ten minutes, and you've learned the lesson forever."

"That contradicts what you just said, Hugh."

"Yes, it does." He closed his eyes.

A week after Sophie showed me the letter from her brother, he disappeared. Jesse Chapman worked for an agency in Vienna that helped refugees from the East Bloc find places to live in the west. Consequently he was often traveling, but this had nothing to do with that. His wife called after he had been missing four days. His employer had no idea where he was. It was not like Jesse to disappear for even twelve hours without letting someone know where he was. He'd gone to work with a briefcase and an overcoat. No luggage, and he did not take his credit cards. At breakfast he'd been calm and talked only about what they were going to do that weekend.

Sophie and Caitlin Chapman had been college roommates and remained close over the years. Caitlin called Sophie first because she was her best friend as well as her husband's sister.

I'd met Jesse a few times when he was in Los Angeles, and he'd struck me as a stable, competent man. His suits were dark; he wore his hair long but carefully cut; while on vacation he still shaved every day. He did not strike me as a passionate man. His letter about the travel agent who dreamed of Death was a surprise because I had never known Jesse to be the witty, observant man who came across in it.

To be fair, I think it's also necessary to say that Jesse Chapman didn't like me. No matter how open our society has become about homosexuality in recent years, there are still a great many intelligent, sensitive people who have real trouble dealing with gays. I am in no way swish, nor do I particularly like those who are. I don't believe in sexuality as theater and am uncomfortable with those who feel compelled to dance across life swinging pink boas behind them, hooting and mincing all the way. But I have never hidden what I am either. I am not sorry and I am not ashamed. Apparently after we met the first time, Jesse asked his sister in a low voice if I was a fairy. When he heard I was, it colored every subsequent conversation we had. He watched and listened to me from a distance. Then one ugly night we got into a stupid argument about boxing, which I know a lot about because I used to do it as a kid. Jesse didn't know a thing, but spoke with the assurance of one who most certainly did. To make matters worse, Sophie kept interrupting to tell her brother he didn't know about boxing; why was he spouting off like this? Which didn't help. I wasn't any better. I knew he was full of baloney and could have let him have his rant and left it at that. But behind his words, I felt, was the distinct connotation that I was gay so how could I know about the sport. So I got pompous, he got defensive, and we ended up being barely civil to each other.

When Sophie called to tell me about his disappearance, I was doing nothing but reading medical textbooks about my disease and wondering what to do next. When there is only so much time left, you become schizophrenic about the last days. On one hand, you feel compelled to try to make every-thing matter—each meal a feast, any conversation full of wit and memorable lines. This might be the last one, so make it matter. Even if it's ending, life is full of treasures and it's wrong not to savor them while you can. That's the feeling when you're positive and hopeful. On the other side of your moon is the despairing cynic who sees no point in getting out of bed in the morning because sooner or later you'll end up flat on your back there till the hopeless end. It is a constant battle between the two. From one moment to the next you never know which will emerge victorious. And whichever one does win, the other is disgusted.

"Wyatt? It's Sophie. I've got some bad trouble and you've got to help me."

The cynic ruled that day. One hand held the telephone to my ear while the other rested on a dull book of densely packed sentences explaining in cruel detail how little hope there was. She had trouble? How dare she even use the word with me!

I listened while she explained what had happened but grew increasingly more impatient as she continued. He had disappeared? What of it? A man had dropped from his life like a pine cone off a tree. Was I expected to get down on my dying knees with the others who really cared about him and search for where he might have fallen? Forget it!

After I'd asked the appropriately sympathetic questions, a large silence dropped over the conversation and each of us waited the other out to see who'd speak first. Sophie finally did. What she said changed the trajectory of the rest of my life.

"You owe me a wish, Wyatt." Said as quiet as a whisper and a final sentence.

I reared back, as if stung by the biggest bee on earth. "No! Sophie, you know you can't ask that now. It's too late. I don't want to hear about it."

"Tough! I don't care what you want to hear. You owe me a wish and I'm using it now. That was the deal. Those are the rules."

"Goddamn you! Then what is it? What do you want?"

"I want you to go with me to Europe to find Jesse."

"Are you *mad?* Europe?"

"You have to. We promised each other."

"Sophie, I've got leukemia, remember? Sometimes I don't even have enough energy to get out of a chair."

"I know, but you're also the world's smartest person in a

crisis. There's nobody I trust as much, either. If you get sicker there, they have good hospitals. Don't worry, I checked. I've been talking on the phone for the last three hours. You're the last call I had to make."

"Where is *there,* by the bye. Where would we be going? Europe is a large place."

"Austria. Home of Mozart, whipped cream, and Nazis."

"Jesus Christ."

"No, he was from Israel."

When Dick died, I made a big mistake. After the initial shock and funeral and the weeks needed to put a dead man's affairs in order, I suggested to Sophie that we go away somewhere together. I used the standard lines: it'll be good for you; being someplace new will take your mind off it . . . I was extremely concerned about her and was convinced a good chunk of time away from home would spark her spirits and help her to start fresh. To my amazement, she liked the idea.

"Where would you want to go?"

Surprised that she hadn't protested, I had no next sentence. I hadn't thought that far in advance because I was so sure the whole conversation would be spent convincing her she should make a trip.

"Go? I don't know. We've got the whole world. You choose. Where would you like to go?"

"Switzerland. I've always wanted to go to Switzerland."

"You never told me that."

"I know, but it's true. I've always wanted to go in winter and be up high in the Alps in a snowbound hotel. The mountains are all around and in the morning you hear big booms because avalanche patrols are dynamiting places they think are dangerous."

"And you smell wood smoke and wear sunglasses because the light off the snow is blinding."

"Right, but only during the day. Around four every afternoon it starts to snow big lazy flakes and everything is quiet."

It was the happiest I'd heard her in weeks, but I had to ask again to make sure. "You really want to go to Switzerland? Because if you do, I'm going to arrange it immediately."

"Are you serious, Wyatt?"

"Yes. I think we could both use a vacation, and Die Schweiz sounds good to me."

" 'Schweiz'? Do you speak German?"

"High school German, but it'd be fun to try it out again."

"Oh, let's go! It's a brilliant idea. You'll arrange it?"

"Every step."

But why oh why did I choose what I did? At the travel bureau I looked through handfuls of brochures and leaflets promising Switzerland the way Sophie wanted it. In the end, I signed us up for a week at a Club Mediterranean in Zims, a ski resort in the Berner Oberland that had a perfect view of the Eiger, Mönch, and Jungfrau mountains. I'd never been to a Club Med but had heard they were bustling, happy places where one ate well, danced at night, and sometimes met interesting people. I checked again with Sophie and luckily she agreed that it sounded like fun, so when we later walked smack into Uh-oh'sville, I didn't feel quite so bad for having steered us into it.

The trip over was a pleasure. We flew into Zürich and then took increasingly smaller trains from there toward the mountains. At Interlaken it began to snow. By the time the little cogwheel chugger slowed to a stop in Zims, the whole world was snow, low clouds, people speaking French and German stomping by with colorful skis over their shoulders. We stood outside an original Art Deco train station breathing in cold clean air. As if on cue, we turned to each other at the same moment and embraced.

"Wyatt, you're a genius! It's perfect."

Uh-huh—for the next half hour.

Club Med owned an immense old resort hotel built in the 1920s that had been one of the main reasons I'd chosen to go there: in the photographs it looked exactly like Sophie's description of her dream getaway hotel.

But about thirty minutes after passing through the front

door, we knew we'd made a serious mistake. Children ran shouting and screeching through the lobby and corridors as if either they or the hotel was on fire. Instructors and staff buzzed around like smiling zombies on methedrine—organizing, directing, telling you what to do, where to go, asking why when you weren't out skiing, sledding, skating, signing up for the many splendid things the Club offered. At all meals they told you where to sit. If you had the unimaginable cheek to say you didn't want to sit there, the smiles slid off their faces in an instant, like slush down a windshield, and they became nasty as only the French can be. The brochures had made it sound good-natured and relaxed. Far too quickly we discovered it was both hyper and vaguely fascistic. By the end of the first day we were calling it Club Dread.

Yet we found our way through the week there because the landscape was stunning and we thoroughly enjoyed being with each other. We hiked, went sledding, watched skiers shush down the sides of white on blue-black mountains. It snowed every day, and every afternoon we walked together a little farther up the trails that led into even deeper snow and silence.

We were resting on a black bench in the middle of a snow field eating tangerines warm from our pockets when Sophie first spoke of the idea.

"Nothing smells up here but the fruit. Did you notice that? Down below you smell the trees and the dung from the barns, but here it's only these. So pungent and out of place, isn't it? I love it when my hands are full of the scent. Dick and I were eating oranges in bed one morning. Before I realized what he was doing, he took up the peels and began rubbing them all over my body. They were cold and smooth. It was delicious. I smelled so wonderful. Then we made love, of course. The whole room was a perfume of sex and oranges. I've never eaten one since without remembering that morning.

"Wyatt, I heard something last night that got me thinking. I wanted to talk to you about it, but held off 'cause I wanted to think it through first. Don't say I'm nuts till I've finished.

"After dinner when I was waiting for you in the lobby, there was a man telling a little girl a story. He was speaking English, so it was kind of hard not to listen. It was the fairy tale about the man who goes fishing and catches a flounder, but it convinces him to throw it back in return for three wishes. Remember that story?"

"Yes, 'The Fisherman and His Wife.' I did it on the show. The wishes ruin their lives.''

"Sure, because it's a fairy tale. They're always so tediously *moral*. Nobody gets away with anything fun and all the interesting people are bad guys.

"But listen, this is different. I started thinking, wouldn't it be wonderful if you had a partner or a friend you could make a pact with: each of you would be granted one wish by the other. No matter what the wish was, the partner would have to do everything in his or her power, short of committing a crime, to make it happen. I wish I'd been able to do it with Dick; he would have loved the idea. What do you think?"

I ran my tongue around the inside of my cheek and watched a bunch of blackbirds flying over the snow. "It sounds like a Sophie Chapman idea. Do you want to do it with me? You're willing to take that chance?"

"You and Dick are the only men I've ever trusted enough to love—besides my brother. But he's blood, and you can't count family. I think this is the kind of promise people wouldn't dream of making today because there's no trust, and let's face it, it's dangerous. Who knows what the other guy'll want?"

"True. And you're serious about this? We pledge to do what we can to make each other's wish come true, short of murder?"

"No! We do *everything* we can to make it come true, not just what we can. That's the difference. Everything."

"One hundred percent serious?"

"A hundred percent."

"I'll tell you truthfully, I like the thought very much, but it does make me nervous."

"Hey, me too! When the idea hit me, I thought about

the people I know. But which ones would I trust to do this with? Only you."

I looked at the birds again. I said yes to her deal because of the birds at that moment more than anything else. More than my love for Sophie, more than our friendship. How the birds dipped and swooped beautifully as one; all consummate faith in one another's movements. Not having to think if going left was correct because going left was the only direction in their one grand mind then. Consummate faith. Sureness that if I ever did have something I wanted desperately, someone would care enough to work hard, perhaps even harder than I myself, to bring it about. Complete faith that they'd not ask me to do something beyond my powers for them. Like birds flying together.

"It's a deal."

As we shook, she craned her head back toward the tin-colored sky and said loudly, "Dick, you're the witness. You heard every word."

We joined hands and walked back down to Club Dread.

In the years since, neither of us had made our formal wish. Thus the moment on the hill sank back into a pleasant snapshot in my mind's photo album. Remember that afternoon? That bench? That's where we made our pact. Just like kids.

Only it wasn't like kids today. Sophie was calling in the IOU, and the tone of her voice said she meant it.

"Look, Wyatt, there are now only three people in the world who matter to me. You, my brother, his wife. If I were to lose Jesse, that would take away a third of the loves I have left. If I don't go over there to look for him, I'll hate myself forever. But I don't trust myself in situations like this. I get crazy and emotional and don't have any calm places inside me to go and think or regroup.

"You do. You're the king of cool and order. I know how sick you are. Believe me, I know. I lived with Dick, remember, right up till the end. I'll take care of you. I swear to God I will, but I need you to go with me. If you do . . . Come on, you can understand."

"I understand, but I don't want to go. You're creating an impossible situation—a choice between our friendship and what's left of my health. I'm dying, and a trip like this will exacerbate things. That's how *I* feel. If you insist, I'll go. But I don't want to and I resent you for it. There's nothing else to say."

Her voice came out as hard and cold as mine. "Fair enough."

I tried on words like *Austria* and *pack your bag* as if they were clothes I was modeling in a mirror. None of them fit. I felt odd and uncomfortable in all of them. How could I do this, friend or not? You're dying, man! People with cancer of the blood do not get up and head for the airport.

Except me.

But indignant and worried as I was, I knew I had nothing else to do. Except die. Die comfortably and safely in familiar surroundings with all the best care in the world. If Sophie hadn't called and made her demand, what would I have planned for the rest of that day? Or week or month? Take my pills and drops as directed? Read a few pages in the book I couldn't get interested in, eat, make some phone calls? Such dreary, dreary stuff. If the last days of my life were so precious, why was I living them indifferently? I didn't want to travel with Sophie because I was afraid of becoming gravely ill in another country, but what difference would that make? I'd recently watched a television biography of the composer Frederick Delius. Told he was going blind, Delius had friends lead him up a favorite hill at daybreak so that he could watch the sun rise for one of the last times in his life. I loved that moment in the show, and whether or not it was true, I believed it. Now I was in much the same situation. Only when I was offered the chance to see great and possibly important things for the last time, I cringed and whined. I wanted *my* bed, my doctor, the dumb book on the living room table that had bored me from the first moment I'd picked it up.

Despising myself for feeling that way, here is what I did to overcome it. I went out for a long ride in the car to think things through. On the way back to my apartment via Hollywood Boulevard, I stopped at a toy store that sold rubber masks. The walls of the place were unfortunately covered with familiar faces made of latex and fake hair. John Kennedy, Elvis, Santa Claus. I could readily decipher who the masks were supposed to portray, except for certain uncelebrated monsters with five eyes or a dwarf arm erupting out of the top of the head. But a number of them were very badly done. That is not what I wanted. For what I had in mind, I needed the face of someone I didn't know.

The man who ran the store was a little bald guy who kept a constant cigarette going in a marvelous silver-and-black holder, à la Franklin D. Roosevelt.

"Can I help you?"

"Yes. I'm looking for a mask, but it's gotta be of someone unfamiliar or unknown. Know what I mean? It can't be Michael Jackson or Arnold Schwarzenegger."

"How about one of Finky Linky?" He pointed to a face on the wall I'd already seen. There I was, in the rubbery flesh. The one-time famous Finky Linky. I smiled at the store owner and we shook hands.

"A very popular mask in its time, and still requested now and then. Very popular. You get your show syndicated and you live forever. This we all know, right? How're you doin', Finky Linky? I just want to tell you, my grandchildren loved your show, and I watched it right along with them a couple of dozen times myself. We miss you! You had the only good kids' show on TV. Now it's only Japanese space kid cartoons and big animals teaching you how to spell.

"But that's another subject, and you got business here. How about Chernenko?" His eyes lit up. He had something cooking.

"Who?"

"I think I still got an Andropov too. Wait. I can probably sell you ten of each, if you want." He began turning to some drawers behind the counter but stopped to ask a final question. "You're not in the party, are you? I mean, I don't do this stuff out of any kind of disrespect, you understand. It's just business. Simply business."

I was totally confused. "What party?"

"The Communist Party, what'd you think? Not that there's much left of it. Here. Here's the Chernenko and heeeere's, yup, here's the Andropov. I thought I still had some of each. Unfortunately. I probably will till the day I die." He brought out masks from the drawers and handed me two old, anonymous faces. Although I didn't know the men, the masks themselves were superb.

"Who are these guys? Are they famous?"

"For about five minutes each, much to my bitter dismay. Each was general secretary of the Communist Party Central Committee. Don't you remember? For about a week apiece. Then each of the sons of bitches had the nerve to drop dead and I got stuck with twenty units I ordered.

"See, when Brezhnev was around, I sold a ton of him. People loved those eyebrows. That one big eyebrow going across the top of his head . . . a winner! When he croaked I sold five that day alone. Collectors. So naturally I thought the next boss of Russia would be a popular item too, and live as long, so I ordered twenty. That was Andropov, right? Or was it Chernenko first? I don't know, I always get them mixed up. No matter. One came in right after the other but they were in charge only a couple of months before they died. Then they elected Gorbachev. And let me tell you, my thinking wasn't so wrong there because I sell a lot of him, even today. A *lot* of Gorby.

"But you want unfamiliar, take your pick from these two old jerks. As I said, I can give you one hell of a deal if you want to buy a few of them. Your special Finky Linky price."

Finky Linky needed only one and chose Chernenko, simply because it was in my hand at the time. After I'd paid and then signed the mask of me so the owner could put it up on his Wall of Fame at home, I left. Two steps out the door, I pulled the mask over my head to see how it felt. My plan was this. If I was going to make this trip, I knew there would be many times when I'd be scared and weak. That's what the mask was for. I would keep it near me at all times and the moment I felt myself weakening or the fear coming, I'd put it on and let myself be scared or whatever. But after a certain time I would tell my fear that's enough—it had to go now because I had other things to do. That seemed a fair deal with fear. Recognize and accept it fully, completely, totally. If it wanted me to shake or cry, so long as I was wearing the mask, I'd do it. But when its time was up, then it had to go away and leave me alone. Dying, I would split myself in two. Traveling, I'd take both me's along and let each have its time of the day. But if I could be strong and a little lucky, then the weak me, Chernenko, would have less and less time. Like a child throwing a fit in the middle of the sidewalk—down flat on the pavement, kicking and screaming for the world's pity and attention—he'd burn himself out in his own furious flames.

"Pardon me asking, but just what the fuck are you doing?"

The policeman was on a motorcycle at the curb in front of the store. Wearing a white helmet and reflective sunglasses, he gave me a smile that wasn't a happy one. It was the smile of a person who has seen almost all and has very little humor or patience left for what he hasn't. "Come here."

I walked over, still wearing Chernenko.

"What were you doing in there, party boy?"

"Buying this mask."

"What? Can't hear you."

"Buying this mask. That's why I'm wearing it."

"Issat right? Take it off."

I took it off, and he wrinkled his forehead, as if somewhere in his macho brain he recognized me. "What else did you do?" He was a big man, whether from fat or muscle I couldn't tell. When he shifted his body, the black leather jacket he wore groaned and complained quietly.

"I just told you, officer, I bought a mask. Go in and ask the man."

"Don't crack wise with me, party boy. Hand it here."

Unlike many Angelenos, I like the Los Angeles police. The majority of them are hard-working, courageous people

who do impossible work pretty well. Yes, they have a reputation for being storm troopers, but I would storm too if I had
to do their job. That's not to say I hadn't had a few unpleas-
ant brushes with troglodytes in uniform like this one: tough
guys who held all the power cards and knew you knew it. A
friend had once challenged one of them and ended up in
L.A. County Hospital with a cracked skull. No, thank you.
I'd give him my mask and let him be King for a Day if that's
what gave him a hard-on. There were more important things
at hand.

"Oh-oh, what's this? Blood?" He was off the bike and
had his gun out so fast I barely had a chance to register what
he'd said. Blood? What? Blood on my mask? From what?
Had I shaved that morning? Suddenly I couldn't remember.
The fear came hard and fast as a cramp across the gut. I
couldn't remember something as simple as whether I'd
shaved that day. Before these thoughts finished going through
my head, he was standing next to me, his pistol against my
temple.

"Move slow, friend. We're gonna go slow back in there.
Pull any shit and you're dead."

I put my hands up and let him push me back toward the
store. Shock, panic, fear, and adrenaline all burst up through
my body like fireworks, making me shake wildly.

"I don't—what—"

"Shut up. Walk straight and don't say another word till I
find out what's going on."

Going on? What *was* going on? I'd bought a mask, had a
little chat with the owner, walked out of the store—

"Open the door. Push it real slow and careful."

I did. There was the body. Starfished in the middle of the
narrow space near the cash register, the owner's body lay in
its final violence. His head was a splattered mess.

Someone had shot him from very close range. I think.
How else could it have looked like that? There were strews
and whip lines of blood on everything—the counter, the cash
register, all over him.

My knees buckled. I couldn't pull any air down my
throat. Thirty seconds. I'd been talking with this man, this

blast of body, thirty seconds ago. What happened? What *could* have happened? When could there have been a holdup? There'd been no gunshot or scream. Standing right out in front, I'd heard nothing.

But look. Look, there's his cigarette holder, a smoking butt still inside. It had lived longer than he had. I'd seen death before, but not this close. Not this foul and obscene and fresh. Fresh was the absolute word for it. I said it aloud. "Fresh."

Then my slammed mind came back to the world and realized the cop's gun was still at my temple.

"Yeah, you freshed him, party boy. Nuked his fucking brains, then you walked out on the street wearing one of his masks. You're a very cool customer, eh? A very cool guy you are, party boy. Get over to the counter, spread your arms and legs, and don't move an inch."

"Officer—"

"Do what I say. It's easier and simpler to shoot you here and tell them I caught you in the act. A lot simpler for me. But do what I say now and I'll try not to. And put that mask on."

"What?"

"Put the mask on. Do it!"

Madness. The cop, the dead man, me standing spread at the counter wearing a rubber mask, about to be arrested for murder.

Your mind goes so fast. Whom could I call? Sophie. I'd call Sophie. Who was my lawyer? I couldn't remember his name. Okay, okay, Sophie would know. What proof did I have? Nothing. Would I die in jail? When would they put me in the police car . . .

"I can't believe it." My mouth, or some part of me, spoke. "I didn't do it! I just bought a—"

"Shut up. And take the mask off now."

"What?" I turned to look at him. He was down on the floor next to the body.

"Take the mask off and face the wall. I'll be done in a minute."

"Why did you want me to put it *on?*" I took it off and

dropped it on the counter. What was this hell? He was a nice man. We chatted. Now he was dead and I was going to jail. Where had it come from? "This is wrong! The whole damned thing is wrong!"

"Does it make any difference without the mask?" The cop's voice was quiet and calm for the first time.

"What? What do you mean?"

"Turn around. Look at me."

I turned. There was no longer a body on the floor, but rather a picnic, all set out. Beautiful food, a white tablecloth, red wine in crystal goblets. Places set for two. No body. The cop had removed his sunglasses and was standing a couple of feet back from the picnic. His face was flat, eyes wide-set. A nondescript, healthy-looking man. That was all. Nothing more.

"Do you feel better without the mask? Does the fear go away? Sit down, Wyatt. Have something to drink."

"What is this?"

"Your mask plan—to put it on only when you're scared? It won't work. See what happened when you took it off just now? You felt exactly the same, right? Ready to piss in your pants. Fear's never friendly or reasonable. I had to tell you that. Then I thought it better to show you. When it's Death and Fear and Worry, all those big words that begin with capital letters, you can't cut a deal with them, make them disappear by taking off a mask. They're too strong and mean. They do what they want.

"You want to know who I am, naturally." He bowed and put a hand on his heart. "Death. Simply Death. Sometimes I come earlier than our appointment so that people can get used to me. But even then it's hard. Don't you want some wine? It's all very good. I have a large expense account!" He smiled. "Only the best. My customer is king." He stuck his index finger into the air.

But it was He. Once He says His name to you, there is no question. It is Death. Death is talking to you now. He has come. He brings calm. You are calm although Death is with you.

He bent over, picked a piece of rolled ham off a plate,

and, dipping it in a little cup of the yellowest mustard, popped it into His mouth. "I'm sorry to disappoint you with your mask, but I wanted to save you valuable time."

"I am going to die. There's no hope? None?"

"None. Yes, you're going to die; so is everyone. Most of them won't get to talk to me about it. Consider yourself lucky on that score."

"Can I ask you questions?" As soon as I said it, I remembered the doomed man in Sardinia. How he had asked Death questions but suffered when he didn't understand the answers. "Forget it! I don't want to ask! Forget it."

The policeman's eyes narrowed and he paused a moment as if considering. He licked his lips, and that dangerous moment between us shivered down to silence. Then his face softened again and he nodded. "Okay, your only warning. But if you ask that again, I'll say yes, and you know the terms." He moved to go.

"Wait! Can I call for you? If I *do* want to ask questions?"

"Yes. Consider this too: it's getting close to your time, Wyatt. Not yet, I can say that. But soon. It might very well be worth it to take the chance. Perhaps you'll understand my answers. There are a surprising number of people who do. Honestly. And once you commit yourself, we can talk about whatever you want." He gestured toward the untouched picnic. "Sometimes it's better to learn through shock than through persuasion. One last thing, if you're interested: the travel agent, McGann? He isn't dead. Let me know if you want to talk."

"Wait! One question. Just one. But no ties, no obligations. Please?"

He nodded. "Ask and I'll let you know if I can answer."

"How I live *till* I die . . . is that my choice? Is there free will?"

"Absolutely. We have no say in that. It's your cruise. We're only the last port." He opened the door of the shop and walked out.

Rose

Most often they ask what she looks like naked. Can you believe the chutzpah? What does your best friend look like with her clothes off. Which is hilarious, because anyone who has seen Arlen Ford's films has seen her as naked as she will ever be. What does she look like in her birthday suit, and what is she *really* like are the two favorite questions. So okay, World, are you ready? Her right breast is slightly larger than her left, and she is almost entirely pleasant. But let's face it, info like that is neither good copy nor ammunition, particularly for journalists. People want to know the dirt, the smudge, where this illustrious woman's secret moles are, and what kind of temper tantrums she has when no one's around to hear.

She has temper tantrums. Who doesn't? The only chocolate she will eat are Godiva "golf balls" at four dollars apiece, and she drives a ridiculously expensive automobile. Is that enough? Because that's about it for scam. That's all the dirt this horse's mouth has to offer the interested. But their problem is, no one knows this woman better than I do, so they keep coming back hoping one day I'll have more or new ugly to give.

I am Rose Cazalet, Arlen Ford's secretary and oldest friend. She refuses to call me her secretary, preferring instead either "adviser" or "companion." Both certainly sound better, but unfortunately these days both words carry a decidedly gay aroma with them, so I prefer plain old "secretary."

Just to keep the records straight, we have known each other ever since we were fifteen at a private girls' school in Connecticut, back when places like that were the rage (and not the plague). We both entered as tenth-graders and were assigned to be roommates. She was smarter than I, but I was better at math, which saved us both. My family had money, but my new friend had already had sex by the time we rolled around to talking about it, so I was entranced. Neither of us wanted to be there. Arlen was a scholarship student from New York who spent the next three years at the school feeling insecure and hopeless among all the money and power that belonged to the families of the Bitsys and Muffys. Arlen liked me because I was the first to point out that Bitsy and Muffy, combined, had the intelligence of a lawn sprinkler.

She was not yet beautiful. Good-looking enough, but not THE FACE people know and worship any chance they get. That all came after her mother died in our senior year. Arlen returned to school stricken by the loss and utterly, overwhelmingly beautiful. Don't ask me how it happened. I believe most people turn into adults when they reach puberty, while others change because of love or adversity. Arlen Ford became the face that launched all the ships because of the death of her mother. I would swear to that. I vividly remember her walking into our dormitory room that Sunday night after returning from the funeral. She was all loss and havoc, sorrow and anger too. But like macabre artistic fingers, those bad things somehow combined to sculpt her face into the one we adore now.

She quit school a month later. So little time to go till graduation, but no matter: one Saturday she packed a bag, gave me a hug, and said she had had it. She was leaving. She's been impulsive as long as I've known her. Trusts her instincts but is also willing to accept any consequences. I like that. I like it in anyone. It ain't how high you jump, it's how you land. No matter how this woman has landed over the years, she has always accepted full responsibility.

She was eighteen, beautiful, and broke. First she went home to her father in Manhattan, but on hearing she'd quit school, he (understandably) hit the roof. They had a vicious fight that ended with her moving out. The first time she called me, she said she'd gotten a job as a saleswoman at Bloomingdale's in the pillow department and was living at the YWCA. I was totally impressed and terrified for her. Selling pillows and living at the Y? She was either crazy or an enviable character straight out of one of those 1940s' screwball comedies: A Barbara Stanwyck or Jean Arthur "gal" who spoke fast and smart and got the job done superbly. But even hearing about this drastic change in her life, I never really doubted she would succeed at what she wanted. She was my best friend and I honestly believed we special ones could do anything. That's the real joy of being young— pure dumb faith. There's no way we're going to fail at what we choose to do with our lives.

By the time I graduated, she had already met and moved in with Nelson Crispi. Isn't that a great name? He worked at the Strand Book Store and wanted to be a playwright. He was the one who got her into books. Before, she'd read only for school and then the occasional mystery novel or thriller while on vacation. Nelson gave her a lasting love and hunger for literature that was invaluable in more ways than one.

When I visited them in their Houston Street walk-up

apartment in New York that summer, we drank Medaglia D'Oro coffee thick as fur which they brewed on their tiny stove in a weirdly shaped coffee pot Nelson had bought in Italy. According to him, it was the only way to make it.

I was so jealous and impressed! We were all about the same age and I had lived with Arlen until only a few months before, but both of them seemed so much older, so sophisticated and in the know. They talked about life in Manhattan and people they knew. Actors, poets, a rich woman who kept a live fox in her apartment. New movies, great cheap restaurants they'd discovered. Fellini, Lermontov, the Second Avenue Delicatessen . . . All the passwords to the other side of life where the glittering secrets were. I wanted to roll this knowledge, these titles and names and places, off my tongue too, like Nelson, like Arlen. They weren't showing off; they didn't need to, because this was only life as they were living it and they were simply describing it to me. I was jealous as hell, of course, yet I loved them for this knowledge and unconscious cool.

Also for the first time in my life I recognized a tangible tightness in the air around them, if I can call it that. And innocent as I was, even I recognized that it was sex. They were crazy for each other, not that they ever made a big show of kissing or touching when I was around. No, I just knew in my quick-study heart that these two were in the middle of a feast and were reveling in it.

What on earth could be better than that? She'd been right to leave school. *I* was the fool. The blindered goody-goody who did what she was told, got good grades, and already woke up in the middle of the night in a fever wondering what to major in at college. The result? In the fall I'd be sitting in a classroom yet again, this time for four more years. Of what? Arlen would be living in wonderful New York doing compelling things, making love at all hours of the day and night with her writer-paramour . . . while I studied verb tenses or geography, or sat in the student center on a Saturday night wishing to God in Heaven that I had a date. A *date!* How could I ever take that nonsense seriously again after seeing this? Here was my best friend with her own lover and apartment and a life that scoffed at vacations and fraternity parties on the weekend.

I returned home both elated and miserable. I would go to college to satisfy my parents, but if it ever pissed me off for one instant, I'd pull an Arlen and *leave*. I knew people in New York now. I carried that knowledge within like a lucky charm in the pocket you can't help touching every few minutes. Arlen was my talisman and example; she was the way life should be.

We kept in close contact. Through those phone calls and, later, our endless letters I heard about her adventures, various lovers, travels, discoveries, and eventually her being discovered.

There has been a lot written about how Arlen Ford was discovered, most of it silly or maliciously wrong. This is how it happened, plain and simple. Nelson read an ad in *The Village Voice* about an open casting for a low-budget film that was going to be shot on the Lower East Side. Talk about the right place at the right time! The film turned out to be Weber Gregston's first, *The Night Is Blond,* and although she'd gone along to it with her boyfriend more as a joke and to see what a movie casting was like, Arlen landed a small role. A few years later in an interview, Gregston said he noticed her because of the way she crossed the room the first time he saw her.

"God knows she was beautiful, but more than that, she was one of those charismatic presences you're *forced* to watch when they enter a room. The magnetism's that strong. They can stand there doing nothing but you've got to watch."

If you know anything about Arlen's life, you know things got better and worse at about the same speed from here on. She began taking drama classes and loving them. Then Nelson went into turbo-boost paranoia-jealousy overdrive about her sudden success. If anyone should have understood what was happening, why the world was suddenly paying attention to his girlfriend, it was this guy, because no one was a greater Arlen fan than Nelson Crispi. But I think by then he was so in love with her that he simply did not want to share her. Which was a very wrong move on his part because she was already way beyond that. She didn't use him as a stepping-stone (as his nasty book on their relationship snivels), but once he became an impossibly annoying whiner and finger-pointer, it wasn't long before the relationship ended.

One winter's day there was an urgent knock on my dormitory door and there she was.

"What are you doing here?"

"I came up for the big game." She opened those miraculous black eyes even wider than usual. "Didn't I? Isn't there one this week? This is college. There's always a big game going on!"

We stayed up late filling in the blanks of our lives for each other and laughing. She'd met so many people in New York and done everything I could imagine doing. But the irony was that, despite all the wonder and excitement of life in New York, she had a terrific time being a plain old college girl with me for a week.

She thought I was amazing because I understood what the instructor was saying in Russian class. She asked me so many whispered questions in art history about the slides of Renaissance paintings that we both got the giggles. The teacher gave me a look that would have frozen lava. Over my protests, Arlen insisted we go to a fraternity party. We didn't have a good time and left quickly, but in the short hour we were there she managed to provoke two high-volume, go-for-the-jugular arguments with two pompous frat brothers. I would have called them fools and marched off after five seconds, but she enjoyed the confrontations and kept goading her opponents. She also held an unfair advantage over them because in each argument, the guy would be halfway into making his points, and then look at her and instantly get lost in her magnificence. All she had to do was give one of her you're-quite-a-guy looks, and he was a goner. Her beauty could vacuum-clean a man's mind in an instant.

Arlen knew this and used it to her full benefit. When we got home later and talked about it, she was cold as an arctic eel on the subject.

"Men want to go to bed, then maybe talk. Women want to talk first—a lot—then maybe go to bed. That much I've learned. So okay, if that's the way of the world, then I'm going to use it my way."

"You sound cold and conniving about it, Arlen. Like there are no nice men on the whole earth."

"Sure there are nice guys. But I'll give you something else to think about, Rosey, that's been bothering me lately. Answer this. How many superb women do you know? I'm talking about intelligent, sensitive women; ones you like spending lots of time with because, among other things, they're great company. They know how to talk, have a good sense of humor, aren't just givers or takers."

"That's a hard question. I need time to think about it—"

"Beep! Time's up. Wrong! You need about one minute because the answer is almost none. Neither of us knows many great women. They're rare birds. Worse, generally speaking, we also know women are ten times more sensitive, thoughtful, et cetera than the male species . . . which leaves us in pretty bad shape when it comes to finding desirable men. How many real winners do you think are out there waiting to sweep us off our feet?"

Despairing, the innocent freshman romantic in me frowned at her. "This conversation is not lifting my spirits, you know. Why are you saying this? All those great times you've been having . . . It sounds as if the only trouble you have is that too many men want to sweep you off *your* feet."

"Yes, into bed. But do you want them in your life the next morning, when your makeup's smeared and maybe you've got gas from the ritzy meal last night? Do you want to spend the rest of the day with this man doing nothing? Just maybe read the paper or take a walk if the weather's nice? Hold his hand or even pinch his ass not for any sexy reason but only because you like him? Or can you imagine spending the same day inside because it's February and snowing outside, but you're both so content and caught up in what you're doing that for long stretches you forget he's there? Except at the same time you know he's there because he adds to the small bliss of the afternoon. It's rare. The only thing I know, Rose, is be careful. Use what you've got, and don't let the man get the upper hand. Not ever. Even when you love him with every cell of your skin, it can go bad really quickly. Even when you think you've got the relationship down pat. Even when you're positive you know all his nooks and crannies."

I couldn't get out of her why she was so damned defensive and skeptical, especially in light of her recent triumphs. But she wouldn't reveal any more, and then our week together was over.

One of the results of her visit was that we became devoted correspondents. Talking on the phone was nice and immediate and we did it often, but both of us loved getting mail and trying to put the best, most insightful, witty parts of ourselves down on paper for the appreciation and approval of the other. Arlen had discovered the letters of Frank Sullivan and sent me a copy of that wonderful book. We read to each other from it, saying how rewarding it would be to go through life with a pen pal like Sullivan. Let's do it. Let's make a vow that at least once a week from now on we'll write to each other and try to make the letters as good as anything in our lives. It is an agreement I have cherished.

Arlen kept working at various jobs, continued her acting lessons and auditions, and finally left for Los Angeles after being invited to join the Swift Swigger Repertory Company. I was depressed that she would be moving so far away, but I'd assumed it would happen sooner or later. Also the sneaky thought existed that if nothing came clear in my mind after graduation, I might go out there and stay with her a while, take a look around, and see if it was the place for me too.

That spring she called to say she'd landed a very good part in a film, which turned out to be *Standing on the Baby's Head*. Is it necessary for me to say more about Arlen Ford's career? From the day the movie opened she was a bona fide star.

I went to see it with none other than Matthew Flaherty, the man I'd been waiting for my whole life and the same fellow who later tried to kill me. Although that sounds dramatic, it is true, but not an important part of this story. Except what Matthew did moved me to L.A. more quickly than I might have gone.

We met in the university library. I had been studying for

an exam and took off to go to the bathroom. When I returned, there was a *most* handsome man holding my Russian history book in his freckled hand, looking at it with complete concentration. He was tall and virile. He worked on the railroad but came to this library whenever he got a chance in his time off to read and think. In his pants pocket was a collection of poetry by someone I had never heard of. Inside were lines like this:

> *I have left my breath with you*
> *It is there, warm and secret,*
> *By your ear, on your collar*
> *against your throat.*

EEYOW! Are you kidding? Bull's eye! I was an indulged little patty-cake college student who thought I knew my way around because I was studying psychology and dark Russian novels. Ergo I was a perfect sucker for this noble railroad savage, who had poetry sticking out of his pocket and an obvious interest in me. That he worked as a laborer and had never gone beyond high school made him all the more alluring and heartbreaking. He was also the first lover I ever had who took care that I liked it and then made me like it more than anyone else had.

Life was rapture for a while. Until he began saying he didn't like any of my friends. To please him, we saw no one else when he was around. Small sacrifice. We stayed locked away together in my place, in bed, or in his car going from wherever he wanted to wherever. I saw nothing wrong with it—we were in love and lust. It was only on the weekends.

The end began in a bar when a man a few stools away kept looking at me. Matthew threw a quart-sized beer mug straight at his head. Blood, broken glass, chaos.

I was so frightened and appalled that I wouldn't talk to him for a month. He left flowers in front of my door, presents; he wrote letters. He tried so hard that, scared as I'd been, I was flattered. I agreed to meet him for coffee. He was the king of charming, sexy, and decorous behavior. And I'd missed him. I longed to reach across the table and touch his mouth.

We started again, but it finished in bed one night a week before I was to graduate. We had made love and it was good. Both of us were tired and we fell asleep immediately. I don't know how much later it was, but I woke to his snoring. It was so loud it made me smile. I gave him a little poke in the arm but it did no good. I whispered, then spoke in a normal voice, then poked harder. Nothing worked. Still smiling, I reached over and gently squeezed his nose with two fingers. He breathed once; his throat choked and blocked. He jerked straight up wide awake. Grabbing my hand, he bent it back till I screamed.

"Don't ever touch me when I'm sleeping," he said, and slapped me full force across the face.

And then he beat me.

Your own bed is where you never need be afraid, if you're lucky. Forget sex. Sleep and exhaustion, the pillow you know, your night light adjusted just so; this is where you can let your guard down completely. Leave it in a corner with the pile of still-warm clothes from today. The Dutch say there's no sound more lovely than the tick of the clock in your own home. You in your own bed is even better. But when it goes wrong, when you've made the primal mistake of inviting the wrong person to join you in sex or sleep, oh, that is the worst nightmare: coming out of the black comfort of sleep in your own bed to terror.

I do not want to talk about it. Forgive me, but I cannot. He hit me till I bled and there were hanks of my hair on my bed, sticking to the front of his T-shirt. I screamed and screamed. My despicable neighbors, the ones I baby-sat for, did nothing for half an hour. Forty-five minutes? I don't know. The police didn't come until a vicious eternity had passed and I was beaten beyond hysteria. When they arrived, Matthew was on his knees in front of me, crying and apologizing. Please please please. I love you so much. Oh, my baby.

Two days later they released him. The first thing he did was return to my apartment. I was there because I had to hide my wrecked face at home. He opened the door with the key I'd given him on the anniversary of our first month together.

"Rose, honey, I'm home! Are you here?"

That is exactly what he called out. As soon as I heard his voice, I started screaming. He ran into the bedroom and caught me by the foot as I tried to climb out the window. This time the neighbors did act fast and called the police, but not fast enough.

In the few minutes it took for them to arrive, my lover had punched me in the throat, torn off my sweatpants, and, forcing me to the floor, started to rape me. Only now there was the shoe. New black high heels I had bought to wear to commencement. I'd been trying them on when he pulled his key from the lock and called my name. I didn't plan to go to graduation, what with my face looking like bad meat, but they were new and I liked trying them on in the safety of my little bedroom.

There was the shoe on the floor. On my back, coughing from a punch, feeling him pump dry into me. His eyes were closed, his expression peaceful. I turned away. Barely able to breathe, I saw the shoe. My hand was already halfway there. Snatching it up, I swung as hard as I could at him—one two three. On the third blow, I felt no resistance when it struck—no hard bone, no bouncy skin. Soft, so soft. He froze, made a terrible strange sound, and flipped off me, roaring. The metal-tipped heel had gone directly into Matthew's right eye, into the delicate jelly that was his perfect vision, and killed it.

God bless the rape victim. Stabbed soul who's seen a face up too close to ever forget it, felt the groping hands, the heat of the breath, known no power and no hope. Who cannot go to the bathroom or welcome a lover there again without remembering, Once my body was not mine. Someone wrong took it and never gave it back. God bless you. I know what you know.

. . . . .

I called Arlen and, genuine friend that she was, she flew east immediately to be with me. Demanded I come back with her, come and sit in the sun and do nothing as long as I liked. She would take care of everything. She described life in Los Angeles as a mix between *The Dating Game* and the greatest meal you ever ate. I didn't understand what she meant by that, but what was the alternative? Graduate, and when the two black eyes had healed again so I wouldn't have to explain anything, go home and live? Everything I knew was finished; what I'd lived and trusted was either over or dead.

Arlen was between movies then and spent too much of her time ferrying me around, showing me the sights, and trying to perk me up. The irony was that, after two weeks in California, my spirits didn't need lifting anymore. I was delighted to be there, eager to know as much about the place as I could and how it worked.

Through a friend of hers, I got a job as a publicist at a movie studio. It was interesting work, frantic and oddly fulfilling. I made friends, worked hard, started dating again.

At Arlen's insistence, I continued living with her. We were entirely comfortable with each other and, as is often the case with people whose careers are meteoric, she liked being with someone who knew her from back when and loved her still.

She made *Lazy Face* and *Mother of Pearl* back to back. The critics dismissed her as one-dimensional and flavor of the year. They said it was easy to mistake her intensity for conviction. They said she was simply lucky; so far she'd worked only with great directors who were able to take her under their wing and show her what to do. Oh, yeah? To the dismay of her agent, Roland Jacobs, she agreed to make *The Kingdom of Jones* with an obscure English director. He thoroughly botched the film, but not her performance. When she came home from shooting on location in Austria, she told me she'd fallen in love with Vienna and, when she had enough money, was going to buy a house there.

One of the few things I could not understand about my best friend was her taste in men. While we lived together we talked endlessly about what made up Mr. Perfect. We were in almost total agreement about his qualities, but then she would become involved with either the strangest or most boring male. Rock stars with more tattoos than brains, actors or executives who looked in the mirror too much and had seizures if there wasn't a telephone nearby. We double-dated a lot, and dinner conversation invariably revolved around new diets or tax shelters, new wonder(ful) drugs or personal gurus. I told her she could do much better than that and she agreed, but then another one would roll up to our door in a vintage Cobra and the *de rigueur* palomino haircut.

While she was filming in Austria, I began going out with her agent, Roland. He was quite a bit older, which made me hesitant at first when things between us went from fun to very nice to something-is-happening-here.

When Arlen returned and I told her what was going on, she hugged me and said she was jealous. I asked if she and Roland had ever gotten together, but she waved it away with a smile. "I wish! No, I made a pass at him a long time ago but in the nicest possible way he said I wasn't his type. You're a lucky girl."

The only story I want to tell about the man I married has to do with the first time we made love. All my life I have had a very irregular period, so irregular that I always carry tampons in my purse. God knows, I would not have finally agreed to join Roland on the horizontal that night if I'd known it was going to arrive. But arrive it did and embarrassed the hell out of me. Normally that sort of thing didn't bother me, even with a new lover. Love me, love my body *and* how it works. But come on; going to bed with anyone the first time is a fragile moment. Multiply that by a hundred when you're going to bed for the first time since you were raped.

Right in the middle of a welcome and wonderful time, both of us suddenly felt wetter than we should. The lights were off. I reached across, turned them on, and screeched. My bed looked like a massacre. Blood was everywhere. I leaped up and ran to the bathroom for a towel or wet sponge or just to get out of there and hide. Standing on the cold white tiles of the clean bathroom floor, I hung my head and chanted, over and over, "I don't believe this. I can't believe this happened *now!*" When I had the courage to return to the bedroom, Roland was already balling up the sheets he'd stripped off the bed and was whistling to himself. When he saw me, he dropped the bundle of white on the floor and spread his arms like an opera singer. "I love dramatic women!"

The next morning he had to leave very early for a meeting. A couple of hours later when I opened the front door to pick up the newspaper, a large empty box of Tide laundry detergent filled to bursting with a hundred red roses was there on the step. The note taped to it bore Roland's abominable handwriting, in a quote from *Anna Karenina,* my favorite novel: "His heart stood still at the nearness of his happiness."

Some months later Arlen asked if I would consider becoming her personal manager, professional adviser, whatever I wanted to title it. The salary would be three times what I was making and the work as she described it would be challenging but not difficult. Much of it was similar to what I was doing at the studio. Still, I was initially hesitant. But I knew, through living with her, that the more famous she became, the more puzzled and disturbed she was by a world that never stood still long enough for her to stop being dizzied by it. From me or someone else, she definitely needed help.

At the dinner where Roland was supposed to help me decide whether or not to take the job, he proposed marriage instead. He said at that particular moment he didn't care about the fate of Arlen Ford; he cared about us, and that was all he wanted to discuss. I said I already knew I wanted to marry him and had for a long time. Which shut him right up. But later, after we had hugged and toasted each other many times with good champagne, I returned to the subject by quoting the adage about choosing your job more carefully than you do a spouse because you'll be spending more time with it.

Of course there were dangers involved, especially now that Roland and I were going to marry and the connection

between the three of us grew even more intimate (or claustrophobic). However, in the end I said yes, for all the obvious
reasons, but mainly because Arlen said she needed me and
meant it. Never for an instant had I forgotten what she'd
done when I needed her most. I would give the job a try. At
the end of six months, if it wasn't working, either of us could
push the ejection button. But she asked for a full six months.
She believed it would take at least half that time for us to get
used to working with each other, then another three months
to get used to working together against the world. Six
months.

It turned into seven years. In that time, among other
gulps and hurrahs, I learned two things. One, be suspicious of
anyone who uses his or her middle name in a professional
capacity: Mark Gary Cohen, Susanne Britanny Marlow, Blah
Blah Smith. For too long it seemed that any time we had
contact with one of these trilogies it came to nothing but
disaster. The doctor who delivered our son had three names
and I almost died because of his incompetence. Poor Arlen
got involved with several three-name producers and the re-
sultant films were debacles or were forgotten in a week.

The other thing I learned was when something drops,
never try to catch it before it hits the ground. Let it fall. If
you don't, you'll catch the wrong part or edge and hurt
yourself. Naturally this applies to both objects and people,
including me. In those seven years, I had an affair and would
not listen to my good husband, who kept trying to catch me
as I fell into dishonesty, ugly silliness, and making those who
loved me suffer. It ended only when I realized I was about to
smash onto a floor of terminal selfishness and desire. I sur-
vived, but didn't deserve to.

So it was ironic that I was the one who kept trying to
catch Arlen as she fell in so many different ways. The movie
world is made up of fabulously successful people who never
believe their victories are genuine. Judging from the enormous and often instantaneous turnover of fates in those high
places, they're right to be unsure.

I particularly remember going with Arlen to a party at
Malibu Colony jam-packed with the famous and powerful.

The biggest shots gravitated to the living room. At first glance it appeared to be a relaxed gathering of the gods in jeans, swapping funny tales about the business. Yet all of them wore a kind of tensed-jaw, ready-to-spring expression. Their stories were great, but each one had to be bigger or funnier than the last. These people weren't listening to one another; they were planning what to say next time they held the floor. It was exhausting to see them all straining for love and attention. It was as if they were trying to suck every bit of air out of the room. I stood up and went outside.

Sadly, Arlen was one of those straining people. She had begun as an actress who made it on talent and beauty. But then the movie community, and later the world, said, That's fine but what else do you have? She was indignant. I've given you everything I am. Where do you get off asking for more? They were silent, but the time came when her new films didn't do so well, and people quickly began talking about her in the past tense.

She panicked, and her personal life began careering around like the ball in a pinball game. There were bad, self-destructive love affairs, which in one case resulted in her spending three weeks in a rehab center for cocaine abuse. And other unbelievably wrong decisions that led to ugly celebrity behavior; she was on the covers of sleazy magazines that cater to the failed, the furious, and the miserable. The photograph of her coming off a plane at Rome airport with an ugly snarl on her face and an arm cocked to punch the photographer . . . Was that really Arlen Ford the movie star? Looking so old and hysterical? The woman we all once wanted to be or have? Falling without trying, she gave them what they wanted. Enough to make them indignant and fascinated with her again, but now for the wrong reasons. She showed she was human, and we're always more comfortable with people than with gods.

The grand finale came not from death or drugs but a tuna fish sandwich. One night after returning from a party, Arlen switched on the light in her living room and discovered a middle-aged woman sitting on the sofa holding a wrapped tuna fish sandwich in one hand and, in the other, the crowbar she'd used to break into the house. "You're so skinny in your films, Arlen. I knew you'd want this. Eat it."

There was no place left to hide, not even her own home. So she luckily did something very smart: dropped out for a year, moved to her beloved Vienna (alone), and went house hunting. She bought an enchanting *Jugendstil* jewel on the outskirts of Weidling, a sleepy little village about six miles from Vienna. Her place sat on a hill in the middle of a vineyard with a panoramic view of the Danube. It was lovely but in appalling condition, and by the time she finished renovating it, Arlen had spent almost as much for the repairs as for the house itself.

Her letters from that time (at the beginning she forbade us from calling unless it was an emergency) were only about rebuilding a house in a foreign country whose language you barely understood. She dyed her hair henna, wore no makeup, and enrolled in a beginner's German Course at Berlitz four days a week. When she wasn't overseeing repairs or studying verb tenses, she drove all around Austria in her new car. Her descriptions of buying wine in small towns on the Hungarian border, with names like Rust and Oggau, were classic. She ate wild boar on a snowy December evening in a Tyrolean restaurant that dated back to the fifteenth century. She floated down the Danube in a kayak past castles and a ruin where Richard the Lion-Hearted had once been held prisoner. She was stopped on narrow mountain roads by horse-drawn hay wagons or farm children leading their herds of fat cattle, bells clanging, slowly across her route. Friends were townspeople, the couple who ran the local *Tabak,* an old man who raised hawks in the Wienerwald.

Some people there knew who she was, most didn't, but from what she wrote, none of them cared. One of the good things about living there was that Austrians were generally unimpressed with celebrities, unless they were famous conductors or opera singers. Leonard Bernstein and Jessye Norman were mobbed for autographs on the street; Arlen Ford was not. She loved that. In one of her letters she said, "Sometimes living here I feel like a child hiding from my parents under the bed covers. I know they'll be angry when they find me, but until then down here it's cozy and safe. I get the feeling if I just stay still and don't move, maybe they never will find me."

Wishful thinking. Her disappearance was quickly noticed, and rumors started flying. After the one about her committing suicide (they hadn't found the body yet), Roland issued a press release saying only that she was very much alive and well and was traveling in Europe. People believed what they wanted. One whisper had it that she was at a rehabilitation center trying to kick a drug habit, another that she was dying of cancer at the Mayo Clinic. One rumor even said she was married and living in Oslo. I sent that clipping. Her response was "At least they got the continent right. Please ask your husband if he thinks married life in Oslo would be a good career move for me." We worried about her, but also believed she was happy far away in her new anonymous life.

While she was gone there was certainly no lack of offers of work. Roland sent innumerable Federal Express letters to Vienna describing the many different roles being offered, not to mention the princely salaries that accompanied them. Her answer was always no. She was too content, too involved in work on the house, not ready to come back yet. One of the few times she called us, I asked point blank if she thought she would ever be ready.

"Don't scold me for being happy, Rose. If you do, you're not my friend."

She was right and I felt contrite, until I realized I hadn't asked the question in a scolding tone. I simply wanted to know if she would ever return to acting. Since Roland had been listening in on an extension, I checked with him to make sure my voice hadn't had anything hard or accusing in it. Agreeing with me, he said he thought her remark came from guilt at having dropped out of a life so many millions of people would love to have.

"Yeah, but that life was destroying her. She didn't have anything left."

He shrugged. "Maybe, maybe not. Don't forget that guilt keeps score. She's happier now in one way, but we both know the woman's talent and potential; no matter how fulfilling it is to repair a door or plant roses, something in her is probably howling to act again. The more talented they are, the more voices are inside disagreeing about what they should be doing."

"That's sick! Why should anyone feel guilty for being happy?"

He came up and put his arms around me. His familiar and beloved smell was suddenly there, as was his heavy chin on my shoulder. "Real happiness doesn't last long. If it goes on any longer than a week or a month, all our bad parts start shouting something's wrong here. Fire! Man overboard! Call the cops!"

I was nose to nose with him. "Do you believe that?"

He kissed me. "Yes, I do. We want happiness, and we work hard to get it. But when it comes, we end up looking over its shoulder for the bill or—"

I hated the thought. He was absolutely right but I hated it. To stop whatever else true and horrible he was about to say, I put a hand over his mouth, then my mouth against my hand. We stood looking at each other until he closed his eyes.

When the repairs on her house were finished, Arlen invited us to spend a few weeks in Austria with her. As usual, Roland was working too hard and said it was impossible for him to leave. I blew my top and gave so many good reasons why we should go that it shamed him into a compromise—a ten-day trip to Europe.

We flew directly to Vienna, where we were met at the airport by a curiously subdued Ms. Ford. Both of us had expected her to be exuberant, full of the lust for life and energy she had lost in California. It was only logical to expect it after reading her sparkling letters from here. But driving back to town, she was quiet and almost monosyllabic when answering a question. I was torn between wanting to see the sights and immediately getting all the news from the new Arlen Ford. I kept looking to see if her face showed any clues. Her hair was a shock and an indication of something. I just couldn't figure out what. She'd cut it short as a man's, and looking at her new profile, for a few beats you really didn't recognize the famous Arlen Ford. The lines on her face hadn't disappeared but had softened, despite the fact she wore little makeup. Lines come from making the same faces a hundred thousand times. Whatever had been happening to her in this European life, she was not making the same faces here as she had in Hollywood. I thought she looked more beautiful than ever.

As we drove along the Danube a few miles from her place, Roland slid forward on the back seat till he was right behind me and said, "You don't sound different, Arlen, but you do look slightly more saintly. Probably from all this spartan living you've been doing."

She glanced at him in the rearview mirror and pursed her lips. "There's so much going on that I have to tell you about. You know how much I love the two of you, but it feels strange having you here. You guys are American and L.A.; this is Vienna. I feel I've been living in a cloister all these months and this is the first day I've been allowed visitors."

"Yeah, to us Hollywood types you're Ford, the movie star. But to Vienna, you're Sister Marie Thérèse in the cloister."

"Exactly! Well, not exactly, because Weber Gregston's at the house. He's been here a few days. Broke into the cloister and pulled me out before you arrived."

"Weber's here? Why?"

"He wants me to be in a new movie."

"And you said no."

"Roland, it might be too good a role to pass up, damn it."

Roland grabbed the back of my neck and gave it a quick squeeze. "Are we going to talk about this now or should we wait till I've finished my seizure?"

"We're going to wait and talk it all over together. I want Weber in on it. He's part of the family too. But not now. Want to see the hospital where Franz Kafka died? It's right near here."

. . . . .

She *was* a completely different person in Vienna from the one I had known. Her house was the first indication. Inside, it was so empty that it gave me the instant one hundred percent creeps. Her home in Los Angeles was full of tsatzkes from everywhere—flea markets, antique stores, the different countries where she'd made films. I loved the way it exuded life and a lovely eccentricity.

By comparison, the Vienna house was stark. A black leather couch and an exquisite black-and-white Chinese carpet, and that was it for the living room. You could have gone bowling in there, it was so empty. But compared to the other rooms, it looked as crowded as a discount furniture showroom. The floors were all gorgeously finished parquet, the walls cloud white. There was a futon in her bedroom, even a television that sat on the floor in a corner squat and lonely. Arlen liked to watch the news to see how much of the German she could pick out. But where were her clothes? The high piles of books that were invariably in any Ford residence? A radio? Pencils? Pots and pans in the kitchen? There was *a* pot, a pan. Where were the other things? The stuff that goes into a day in the life of anyone? I didn't ask, for fear she'd say there weren't any.

When we were finished with the tour, I told her it looked like the set for a documentary about Zen Buddhism. She nodded, with a look on her face that said my remark satisfied her. I couldn't resist asking if she planned on buying any more furniture or maybe even a picture. She said no, this was how she saw the house. More important, this was how she saw her life in this house, and was satisfied. Stripped bare, essentials only.

Luckily Weber walked in at that moment. Otherwise we would have been stuck in a silence that had come too quickly after our arrival. He was barely controlling a long leash attached to a reddish-gold puppy that was all long legs and loud skitter on the slippery wood floors. Before we had a chance to say anything, Weber had unclipped it, and the beast galloped and slid across the room top speed at us. It banged greetings first into Arlen, leaped, turned to me, leaped, then Roland, then Arlen, back to Weber . . . the wild joy only a young dog knows in a room full of new faces. It was Minnie, the Viszla Arlen had bought on the spur of the moment while on a day trip across the border to Sopron, Hungary. My friend's pleasure and the dog's at seeing each other appeared about equal. I don't like animals much, but since most of the rest of the cosmos does, I hold my tongue. I admit, whenever I see someone mooning over a cat or dog or whatever four-legged, I'm indifferent, vaguely repelled, or suspicious of their ardor.

We hadn't seen Weber in ages. Besides being a full-fledged genius (I say that without any hesitation), he's a genuinely good guy. Roland and I were *so* glad he was there. Too often, too damned often in those subsequent days, pauses and silences fell like heavy, deadening snow over our conversations with Arlen. Inevitably, Weber was the one to break them up with a funny story or an insight that brought us back to noise and made breathing easier. Arlen had grown so introverted that it was frightening. I could imagine her being silent for a week if no one was there.

She and Weber had been an item a few years before; surprisingly, not when they were working together, but after. She said he came to visit her on a set one day and that night they'd decided to move in together. I had always hoped the relationship would work because he was such a good soul, but Hollywood is not the best place to work on a relationship, much less its fine points. Not when the partners are high-strung and competitive, creative, and prone to mood swings as grand and terrifying as Tarzan's through the vines. They stayed together almost a year (a record for Arlen) and parted amicably, sort of. Absence made their hearts grow fonder. In the ensuing years they became great telephone pals. They made a deal: either could call anytime, anyplace if they ever needed help or only a sympathetic ear. She'd never made a deal like that with *me* and I indignantly told her so. She answered reasonably that one makes deals with lovers one would never make with anyone else.

When her rising star began to level off, Weber's continued to climb, but they remained close. He kept asking her to be in his films. At first she was still too busy. Later she took

his concern for pity and refused. Weber went so far as to ask
Roland to intervene, but we knew that would never work
with Arlen. She piloted her own ship.

Now we were both excited to hear she was even considering going back to work on his new film. Yet each day went
by without her saying anything about it. Finally Roland got
fed up and dragged Weber and the dog outside, ostensibly for
a walk. He grilled Weber on the project. When they returned
from the great outdoors, my husband wore a smile I'd seen
usually only in bed after good sex. "If she doesn't take this
role, so help me God—"

"So help you God *what?* What will you do, strong-arm
her into it? Hire one of Don Corleone's men to shoot her in
the kneecaps?"

"Rose, what's the matter? What's with the sudden
grumpiness? Wait till you hear about this movie!"

"While you were gone I sat on her sun porch looking at
this whole thing—the river, everything. It's the Danube
down there; you know what I mean? It's the Danube, and
this is Europe . . . It's really a delightful place, save the
monk's quarters. She has a good life here. It's not our life, not
what we want to do, but she's happy. You can tell by the way
she looks and how she talks. What good would it do her to
go back and face all that junk? She has money and is fed up
with fame. Guys gave her diseases; she took too many drugs;
her last films were crummy and she knows it. She's not even
thirty-five but has already lived one whole life. As her friends,
shouldn't we encourage her to go on living here if that's what
pleases her?"

He shook his head. "Look, both of us love the woman
and have never worked against her best interests. If she wants
to retire here sometime to live out her days on the Danube,
studying German and making tortes, fine. It's *not* a bad life; I
never said it was. But it's obvious to me from what she's been
saying that she *isn't* finished with acting yet. I honestly don't
think she's had her fill. Remember what she said the other
night about still wanting to work with Scorsese? Maybe she'll
get fed up after doing this one with Weber. But if she doesn't
do it, she's crazy. It's undoubtedly the best role she's been

offered in years. Oscar stuff. Let me tell you about the film. Your hair will stand up on your head."

On our last day in Austria the four of us, plus Minnie, hiked from Weidling over the Wienerwald to Grinzing, where we spent most of the sunny afternoon in a *Heurigen,* one of Vienna's famous wine gardens. The white wine was new and very strong, the food all delicious heart attack cuisine—roast pork, Schmalzbrot, deep-fried Camembert with Preisselbeeren. Minnie sat at stiff attention next to Arlen's leg, her shiny black nose periodically rising up and over the edge of the table, periscoping where the good smells were. She must have gained three pounds that day from all the treats slipped to her.

After we'd eaten and sat like cats in the sun, we took a taxi back to the house. There, at long last, in her living room full of late afternoon sun, Arlen asked Weber to tell us the plot of his new film, *Wonderful.* We knew everything already because of the secret pow-wow between agent and director, but, described again so soon, the project still sounded irresistible.

For a while.

The problem was Weber. He was a superb director and a bona fide artist, but a lousy describer. Clearly his talent was in his eyes and imagination—not on his tongue. Because he told the story so badly and dully, I was dying to tell him to jump up and dance around, act it out! It's a great story, so tell it great! Give it its due. I looked at Roland and could see from the unhappy set of his mouth that he felt the same. As far as the unsuspecting Arlen knew, this was our introduction to the movie too. But the way the creator-writer-director described it, this once-in-a-lifetime opportunity sounded like a training film for shoe salesmen in Idaho.

Naturally I'd thought a good deal about the story since first hearing it and, as Roland has prophesied, feeling my hair stand on end at the possibilities. Now I was bursting to interrupt with ideas and suggestions, clarifications, adrenaline. But I forced myself to hold back at least until Weber was finished. Otherwise, the target of our affection would realize that the three of us were in cahoots.

Silly me. Stupid me. What we don't understand, we condemn. Halfway through Weber's monotone, *Arlen* interrupted and began to talk. Starting with "No, no, Weber! It's better than *that!*" she impatiently took over the telling as if he weren't even in the room. Her voice began to dip and soar with excitement. She brought this magical story to life with the energy and talent of a person who could hold the attention of a room whenever she wanted. It was a star telling a story she loved, a story as great as her ability to tell it. Unable to do it right sitting down, she stood and began moving around in a growing fever of accents and actions, dialogue and camera angles, fade-outs and back stories that brought it all roaring to life. She made *Wonderful* wonderful.

I was so caught up in her magical account that it took some time to tear my eyes away from her grand performance to see how Weber was taking it. He sat back on the couch with hands locked over a knee, wearing a smile of total triumph. He'd tricked her! Set her up! He'd purposely bored us so as to lure Arlen into taking over and telling his story the way he knew it deserved to be told: with the enthusiasm and delight of a zealous convert, of someone thrilled to see the light and committed to being part of the design.

His scheme worked perfectly. When Arlen was finished, she was the most excited person in the room. She could see the future and it was hers. She ended by describing her role. From the tone of her voice, if the film had been a house for sale, she would already have bought it, moved in, and been reading a magazine in the den.

We sat in charged silence, the three of us in thrall to her performance. Roland was the first to speak. Arlen was still so into what she'd been doing that her head jerked slightly at the sound of his voice.

"I think it's your cup of tea, sweetheart."

Turning to him, her eyes slowly registered what he'd said and what it meant. "It is. I think I have to do it, Roland. If I don't . . . ." She walked to the large window that looked out on the vineyards. "I was going to plant sunflowers over there. Sunflowers and pumpkins over there. I love pumpkins when they've just begun to grow. They remind me of little Japanese lanterns." She stood at the window with her back to us for a long time. It was her moment and she owned it in all of our lives. When she turned, her eyes went right to Weber. "You bastard. I don't know whether to thank or kill you."

"Ah, come on. It's like eating grapefruit—after the first bite it's not sour anymore."

She gave him a false exaggerated smile that was gone in an instant. "Fine, then *you* take the first bite."

I started feeling odd after we returned from Europe. When that moved up to odder, I went to a doctor and found out I was pregnant. Unfortunately, I am one of those women who has to fight their body the whole way to bring a child to term. There was one complication after another. By the time Arlen had returned to America and began filming, I was flat on my back in bed and thus unable to work with her.

Perhaps it was for the best, because from day one, *Wonderful* was plagued by difficulties that had everyone either pulling out his hair or trying to avoid the wrath and roll of studio executives growing ever more ballistic as they watched both the budget and shooting schedule climb into the ionosphere.

No one wanted to upset me because I was having my own tough time, so what little I heard was watered way down. They were having "difficulties"; one of the actors had taken sick (in fact, had had a major stroke), which threw filming off . . . that was what I heard. But then an article appeared in the Calendar section of the *L.A. Times* entitled *"Wonderful* Chaos" which went into delighted gory detail about what was happening on the set, and it scared me good. When I told Roland I'd seen the article and asked what the hell was really going on over there, he sat on our bed and, sighing like a sick old man, *began* by saying it was a catastrophe and he'd be amazed if the movie was ever finished. Weber was renowned for bringing every one of his pictures in on time and under budget, so what was going wrong on this one? My husband, who ain't no dummy when it comes to making movies, shook his head and said, "I honestly don't know. I've never seen anything like it. I get the feeling he's Job with this one. Anything that can go wrong has or will. I gave him a present the other day as a joke—a motorcycle helmet. Know what he did? Didn't smile. Said, "Good idea," put it on, and went right back to work. Worked the whole day wearing a goddamned helmet. And you know what's worse? I don't think anyone on the set laughed when they saw him in it."

One of the people who saved the project was Arlen. Everyone connected with it said she was invaluable. When she wasn't in front of the camera, she was on the sidelines trying either to pep someone up or soothe a savage executive who was threatening for the fifteenth time to shut the picture down. Weber swears that when the head of the studio called him in for the inevitable do-or-die meeting, Arlen insisted on being there. She spoke so logically and compellingly about the film that the cynic in the two-thousand-dollar suit across the table from them said okay, go ahead and finish. Weber won a great many prizes for his work on *Wonderful,* but to his credit each time he gave an acceptance speech he said without Arlen Ford they never would have completed the film.

To be honest, I don't like the movie. I love scenes *in* it, especially the opening. All that hazy snow, silence; then as things start to focus, we realize everything is upside down. Then the roar comes up and we're shown that it's not snow, it's confetti. The world upside down in a snowstorm of confetti. Camera rights itself, changes perspective, pulls back, and there's the little girl being held out a window by her feet in the middle of a ticker-tape parade. I love that. I love many parts of the film, but the story Weber and Arlen told us in Vienna was far warmer and happier than the final result. Real art shows you in great, eye-opening detail that the world is either a good or a bad place. Both are valid, certainly, and it is up to us to decide how we want to fit those unarguable truths into our own experience. I saw *Wonderful* for the first time after I'd fought my body and an incompetent doctor to give birth to a healthy child. I didn't want to be told life is a series of flickering accidents and twists of fate that were here and vivid but finally confusing. I believed important battles *could* be won; that that was so because we possess certain great weapons—commitment, stamina, love—that can even the odds against us.

Admittedly I am old hat and stuck in many of my views. *Wonderful* touched off emotional sirens and loud debates wherever it was shown because, if nothing else, it was a movie you had to see if you wanted to be considered hip or informed. Critics and loudmouths had a field day with it. It was a masterpiece, an insult, an empty diatribe, a cautionary exegesis (honestly, they used that word) that brilliantly illuminated . . . It was a success. A high-brow film that appealed to a wide audience who willingly went back to see it again in case they'd missed something first time around.

To spice up the stew even more, after it had been out a while and begun winning nominations and prizes, Arlen announced at the Berlin Film Festival that she was retiring from acting. Why? Because she'd had enough. She was charming and funny about it and very candid. She admitted that, with the exception of this film, her career had not been successful in recent years. She preferred to retire now, having done the best work of her life, rather than years down the line when she'd be thrilled just to get character roles. "I like to believe I *have* some character, but would rather not think of myself *as* one yet. That comes soon enough. It's just better to go out riding the elephant at the front of the parade. Simple as that."

She continued to promote the film, but even after she was nominated for an Academy Award and the job offers increased to the point where she could have had any role she wanted, she said no. Once when we were alone, I asked why she was going through with it when it really seemed again that the sky was the limit for her career. She said, "I used to think that everything was in acting. Do it right, and all the answers, plus all the rewards you'd ever want in ten lifetimes, would be there at the finish line. You could find your place, you could find a home and peace . . . Then after a couple of bad choices I began realizing it wasn't so. But my life was caving in then too, so I thought maybe that's part of the disillusionment. One of the main reasons I made *Wonderful* was to see if this was true. Those last few films I did before quitting the first time were dogs. Just work to put money in the bank. I was ashamed and embarrassed when I saw them. I thought, Fuck it, I can't do this anymore. I've got to keep some of my soul intact. So I quit. When Weber asked me to be in this, I knew, no matter what, it would end up being a great movie. The best possible environment to work in. But even this one left me genuinely cold, Rose. Like going to bed with someone you once loved but don't anymore. Don't even feel a spark for. No matter what, this'll definitely be my last."

The four of us went to the Oscar ceremony together. Before it began, I told my best friend that if she didn't win I would personally blow up the Academy. I knew she was serious about her plan to stop. There had been a gratuitously cruel article in a national magazine about her that implied nasty untrue things. It concluded by sneering how "timely" it was that Ms. Ford had announced her retirement long before the awards, implying she'd done it to get the sympathy vote. She was the one who gave me the article, saying only, "Here's another good reason for going back to Vienna."

When Weber's name was announced as the winner of the best director award, Arlen put her fingers together and whistled like a doorman. Before going down to accept it, he pulled her up out of her seat and hugged her a long time. She was crying when he let go. Clapping madly, she didn't sit down again until he started his speech, thanking everyone, but her most of all.

It would have been perfect if she'd won for best actress, but she didn't. Instead, some old woman who should have won years before for much better performances wobbled up and thanked the Academy with a wink and a measured smile that said, All of us know I shouldn't be up here for this but—

Crying, I turned to Arlen and said, "It's wrong. You deserve it and everyone here knows that. The whole world knows it, Arlen."

She squeezed my hand and said, "Everything you want in life has teeth."

A week later she moved to Austria for good.

Part Two

Wyatt

"Holy cow, it's Finky Linky! May I have your autograph?"

I love giving autographs, love the fact someone thinks my signature is important enough to want to keep. What astonished me was that people still asked for it years after I'd disappeared from the almighty television eye. It had been so long since I was a celebrity that it seemed like life on another planet. So now when someone came up and recognized me for the being I once was, it was like a phone call from Saturn or Pluto. But a welcome call certainly, one that I was glad to receive.

The only problem was that Sophie and I had just finished a horrendous trip from Los Angeles, one of those flights from hell the modern traveler is subjected to more and more. The ordeal began when our flight was delayed for an hour and we were stuck in the hot packed plane, our freshly pressed clothes and spirits already sinking into wilt. Then, in evil stereo, two unhappy babies traded off shifts of howling around us throughout most of the flight. Round the ride off with a pack of stewardesses so lacking in kindness and professional concern that you were afraid to ask for a glass of water for fear of annoying them.

Twelve hours to Europe, then a three-hour layover, where our jet-lagged and shell-shocked burning eyes watched the frenetic race and flutter of that giant airport. Finally back onto another plane for the flight to Vienna. On arriving we were supposed to have been met by Sophie's sister-in-law Caitlin, but she didn't show up, and we had to figure out how to get from the airport to town in a language that neither of us understood beyond my high school German.

Welcome to Europe. We took a bus to the Hilton, and as I wrestled our bags from here to there, I heard that normally welcome request. I was so tired, stressed, and confused by the rush of what was going on and where we were that I didn't think it strange to be asked for an autograph in Vienna, Austria, where there couldn't have been a whole lot of people who'd seen *The Finky Linky Show,* much less recognized me long after it was off the air.

When I turned to see who was asking, I laughed for the first time in twenty hours. One of the most beautiful and, until a few years before, famous women in the world held out a cheap pen and a scrap of paper for me to sign.

"I'm your biggest fan, Mr. Linky."

"Arlen! My God, how long has it been?"

We embraced. "Too long, Wyatt. Too damned long."

"I completely forgot that you live here. How great! Arlen, this is my friend Sophie." The two women shook hands. Sophie said hello but her face didn't, which was strange because normally she's very open and pleased to meet new people. But it was plain she didn't take to Arlen, who, despite her fame, happened to be one of the nicer people I knew.

The Arlen Ford too, the one who had had the colossal nerve and courage to walk away from her movie star career at its peak. Weber Gregston had introduced us years before, and for a while we saw quite a bit of each other. She was smart and sensitive and great company. Also she had been generous enough to come on my show a couple of times and be silly with us. Judging from the mail we received afterward, she was a big hit with the kids.

We stood around chatting for a while until a man came up behind her and touched her shoulder. She whirled around and, on seeing him, Arlen simply blasted out love and joy. Whoever this fellow was, he owned most of the real estate in *her* heart; nothing could have been plainer. She took his hand and gestured toward us. "Wyatt and Sophie, this is Leland Zivic."

"Hello, Leland. Tell me again how you say your last name."

A warm and friendly smile broke across his face, revealing big white teeth with an interesting gap between the front two. "Ziv-itch. I know, it's a funny one. Part of me is Yugo-slavian."

They were on their way to Italy. When I'd known Arlen in California, she was cool and sophisticated and didn't suffer fools gladly. The same woman now reminded me of a teen-ager in the first throes of love. She couldn't take her eyes off Leland. In Hollywood she'd had the reputation for living close to men who worked out too much or fought too much and wore sunglasses after dark. But from his looks, Zivic was definitely not one of those. Quite tall, he had longish brown hair and a pleasant round face that appeared open and friendly. I think his eyes were a bit small, but it was hard to tell because he wore wire-rimmed glasses with gray-tinted lenses. He had on a brown leather jacket, corduroy pants about the same color, and scruffy white sneakers. Comfort-able clothes. That's all. Everything about him looked com-fortable, even his face. As if he were a living, breathing easy chair you loved to sink into whenever you had the chance. All this took place in no more than five or six minutes, but I came away with the impression that Arlen was madly in love with a plain nice man. I didn't know if I was more delighted or surprised.

She gave me her telephone number and said to be sure to call in a few days so that we could get together for a meal. She made a point of including Sophie in her invitation, but again my friend was merely pleasant in her thanks. The happy couple got onto an airport bus and we went looking for a taxi.

When we'd found one and were in it, Sophie dug her brother's address out of her purse and slowly tried to pronounce the endless German name to the driver. He shook his head, turned in his seat, and gestured for the paper.

"Laimgrubengasse. Okay!"

She sat back and turned to me. "How come every word in German sounds like a command?"

"They've had a lot of practice. Why did you give Arlen the cold shoulder? That's not like you."

"Did I? I guess I'm tired. No, that's not the reason. It's because I never liked her. Every film I saw her in, she gave the feeling she was so very *pleased* with her performance. Like Meryl Streep, another of my least favorite actresses. Gangway for Her Majesty, Queen Drama. Start polishing the Oscars."

"Oh, come on! Did you see her in *Wonderful?* You've got to admit that was a great film."

"Great film, but she wasn't great in it. I clapped when she didn't win the Oscar."

I wasn't in the mood to argue. Sophie was as fixed in her opinions as any stubborn, self-assured person is. Once in a while it was fun trying to argue her out of them, but most of the time it was useless and I had long ago stopped trying. Right at the moment the only thing I wanted to do was sit in a chair larger than an airplane seat, hold a drink in my hand, and feel grateful I didn't have to move for a while.

Out the window, Vienna looked much as I had expected it would. Most of the large European cities I've visited have a solid dignity and timelessness; the buildings have been around long enough to see a good bit of history. I know things over here are as trendy and impermanent as they are anywhere else, but one constantly gets the feeling that these places will stay as they are now, as they have been, for centuries. The impressive streets, wide as airport runways, will be the same when people float down them in hover cars or spaceships or whatever the future invents. Where America is all fresh and flux, Europe is like old wealth: no matter what happens, it will always be there.

When we passed what we later found out was the State Opera House, the driver languidly lifted an arm in its direction and said, *"Opern."* When this information didn't register on either of us, he shook his head at our stupidity and put mad Arabic music on the car stereo, top volume.

"Is this Cairo or Vienna?"

"Should we offer him a big tip if he turns it down?"

Since we would have had to scream to be heard over the snaking and screeching of the music, neither of us said another word for the rest of the ride. Also, it seemed every time I happened to look into the rearview mirror, his eyes were there checking me out.

Laimgrubengasse is a very narrow, short street that slants up sharply and then angles into another small street. A few doors down from the Chapmans' building was a restaurant called Ludwig Van. A plaque on the façade said Beethoven had lived in the house when he was in Vienna.

The cab left us and drove away, music still attacking. I trudged our bags over to the door, where Sophie was already pressing the intercom button. No answer. We looked at each other, clearly the same thought crossing our minds: What now? What do we do if no one's home?

"Is Caitlin dependable?"

"Extremely. Something important or bad must have come up for her not to meet us at the airport. It worries me." Sophie scowled and pressed the button again for several seconds. "I've got to talk to her and find out—"

"Hello?" A small voice came out of the intercom, a woman's, sounding very far away.

"Hello, Caitlin? It's Sophie. Wyatt and I are here!"

"Hi, Sophie, Um. Um."

"What's the matter? Let us in, willya? We've got all these bags."

"I . . . Sophie, I *can't*. There's a big problem here. Look, um, go down the street, Laimgrubengasse, till it meets with Gum-pen-dor-fer-strasse. On Gumpendorf, go left and you'll see a café; it's called the Sperl. Go in and wait for me. I'll come in ten minutes."

Sophie exploded into the speaker. "Are you crazy? We're not going to any café! We just flew a million miles and you're not going to let us *in?*"

Caitlin's voice came back loud and just as angry. "Please do what I tell you! I'll be at the Sperl in ten minutes. Yes, I know you came all this way, Sophie, but you'll understand why I'm asking. Believe me, it's important." The connection broke with a definite electric click. The two of us were left looking at the nondescript apartment building and a black pile of suitcases at our feet that now needed to be lugged again.

I slowly began pulling one up onto my shoulder. "This is the strangest welcome I've ever had to a new city. Don't get me wrong; I'm not complaining. I only wish I were twenty years old and could appreciate it more."

Cross as she was, Sophie came and put her arms around my tired neck. "Do you want to kill me? I want to kill my sister-in-law, so you have every right."

"No, but I do have to sit down soon. I'm very tired and need to take a pill, or there'll be problems."

"Oh, Wyatt, I completely forgot . . . Here, let me take those bags."

"No, I can handle them. Let's find this café and have some beer. Is the beer in Austria as good as it is in Germany?"

"I don't know. I've never been here before. What did she call it, Gumperstorstrada? Laimgrubengasse. How come every street here sounds like a Hungarian recipe?"

The Sperl was not hard to find. Imagine a European café, dust it with age and romance, and there you are. Men played billiards quietly and seriously in a corner, waiters in tuxedoes with white napkins draped over their arms moved gracefully from the kitchen to the tables, where, with dramatic swoops of the arm and little murmurs as to what they were serving, they laid white cups or plates of pastry on the marble tables. Old men and women read newspapers in half a dozen languages, lovers huddled and cuddled in corners. Because it was midafternoon, the café was only half filled. We found room for us and our bags and settled into the pleasant drowsiness of the place. Our beers were finished in no time, and a pair of sausages with golden rolls and bright yellow mustard being served to someone nearby looked so delicious that we ordered some and more beer and went on waiting for Part Two of *The Vienna Affair* to unfold. Neither of us said much, not even when the original ten minutes turned into twenty and then half an hour. When I got up to go to the bathroom, Sophie rose with me. "Maybe I should call her. What do you think?"

"I think you should wait a while longer and then do it. If she's as dependable as you say, there's a reason that she's not here yet. Let her do it her way."

"You're right. Oh, shit." She sat back down. "I don't want any more beer or hot dogs and I don't want to be in this café. And why don't I just shut up? Go to the bathroom, Wyatt. I'll be okay."

When I was done, I spent quite a while at the sink washing my face and hands, trying with cold water to splash life back into my body and mind.

On my way out, I collided with a woman who was in a hurry to get into the ladies' room. Those quick jarring moments of *bump, oops, excuse me* were doubly disorienting because I was tired anyway. Rounding the corner thus muddled, I saw someone at the table with Sophie, but it didn't register that it must be Caitlin Chapman. Perhaps because for a woman in the midst of the chaos of a missing husband, she looked fine. In fact, she looked better than when I'd last seen her in Los Angeles. She was speaking animatedly, one arm extended across the table, holding Sophie's wrist. She wore a black sweatshirt and jeans, a silver bracelet high up on her left arm, and her hair was combed in place. I watched them a few seconds. Both were bent forward; both appeared to be talking at once. Two nice-looking women in early middle age chatting it up in a Viennese café.

Why did I feel I would be trespassing if I interrupted them? Sophie had forced me to come with her here. Didn't that make me as much a part of the strange adventure as either of them? No. Because my blood and love weren't involved. I was doing Sophie a favor, and grudgingly at that. I was in Vienna because of a best friend. As my part of a long-forgotten deal struck on a mountaintop in Switzerland. I was here not because I was concerned or felt compelled to be here, so I hesitated to go forward and make my presence known. But what *were* they talking about so animatedly? What new thing had come up since we boarded the plane in L.A. that forced us to be meeting her here rather than in her apartment?

Trespasser or not, I couldn't stand not knowing what was up, and I walked over. Caitlin turned and saw me. Springing up, she raced over and hugged me. I knew for a fact that Caitlin Chapman was not a hugger. Normally she was a kind, albeit reserved and quiet woman who spent most of her life in the shadow of her outgoing and aggressive husband. Another thing that took me by surprise was her embrace. It went on *so* long that I started looking over her shoulder at Sophie, who gestured with her hands for me to put up with it and let the poor woman squeeze as long as she liked.

"Wyatt, it's good of you to come! So generous."

"Caitlin, what's happening? What's the problem? Is it something new about Jesse? Have you heard anything?"

"Yes, I was just telling Sophie. Can we go back to the table so that she can hear too? Jesse's back! He came home this morning."

After hitting me with that left hook out of nowhere, she took my hand, and as we walked back to the table I looked at Sophie and mouthed the words "He's back?" She nodded.

"Sit down, Wyatt. You have to hear all this because you're important to it now."

I *was* in the middle of sitting, but stopped halfway after a line as ominous as that. "More than before?" The women looked at each other. I got the hint. "Obviously more. Go ahead, start from the beginning."

Caitlin was sitting opposite Sophie and me. I still couldn't get over how neat and ordered she looked. Nothing frazzled or frizzy, not one hair out of place. I know people deal with their problems in different ways, but how could she go days missing her partner, terrified every minute that he might be seriously hurt or dead, yet still look as if she'd just come from the hairdresser's?

"Wyatt, you know my husband pretty well—"

"No, he doesn't," Sophie interrupted. "They've met only a few times. You were there when they had that stupid fight. Jesse doesn't like Wyatt because he's gay."

Caitlin's eyes widened as she snatched a quick embarrassed look at me to see how I responded to that. Sophie waved it away impatiently. "Look, there's no time for decorum now. My brother Jesse is a decent man. Too much of the time he's a stiff tightass who refuses to accept that he could be wrong about things, but that's his failing. We all have ours. What you're going to hear now you have to put in that context. What I mean is, here's a guy—Wyatt—who is the original skeptic. He believes a deal is real only when the contract is put in front of him to sign. He doesn't like French restaurants because he can't understand the menu. You get the drift. Seeing is believing. Go ahead, Cait."

Her friend looked at me and began again hesitantly. "About a week ago, Jesse got up one morning and went into the bathroom—to wash up and brush his teeth, I thought. He's almost always up before me and starts making breakfast for the two of us. This time—I don't know how long it was, but I'd guess half an hour later—I got up and went in there. He was sitting on the toilet with his head in his hands, not moving. I thought he was sick to his stomach and had been throwing up, but then I saw that the seat cover was down. I went over to ask if he was all right but the moment I touched him, he pulled back as if he'd been stabbed. And his eyes were as wild as a horse's in a fire. The only other time I'd seen him that way in our whole marriage was once when we were in a bad car accident. Jesse's the ultimate Mr. Dependable; nothing rattles him. But he was badly rattled that morning.

"When I asked what was wrong, he wouldn't say. I asked

all the wifely questions, but that did no good; he wasn't going to tell me anything. Maybe, I thought, he was too embarrassed to talk about it. Fine, leave him alone; let him handle it. I went out to the kitchen.

"Jesse is a creature of habit and always eats breakfast. One of his rules: always go out with a full stomach. I expected he'd at least have something to eat, a banana or a glass of milk to calm his stomach. But he didn't, and the funny thing is, that worried me more than anything. I didn't even hear when he left the house. A few hours later I did call him at his office and he sounded okay. And that night when he came home he seemed fine, but he still wouldn't talk about what had gone on that morning. You know how it is—life is full of weird things, and you try to let them slip by without a fuss if possible. Because if you take note or complain, they stick around. So I pushed this thing aside and blamed it on a full moon or whatever. Fine.

"Until the next night, when I woke after hearing him in the bathroom crying out, 'I don't want this! I don't want it!' Again and again. It was the middle of the night, two or three, that time when things scare you most and not just because you're coming up out of sleep. I went in and saw him standing in front of the mirror, staring at himself. Again, when I asked what was going on he wouldn't tell me. He was shocked that I'd come in while he was doing whatever he was doing, and said only he'd been having nightmares. I knew it wasn't the whole truth, but what could I do? He told me to go back to bed; he'd be in soon. I wanted to stay with him, but he wouldn't allow it. God, it was horrible and I felt so helpless . . .

"I waited for him in bed and he came soon enough. What was strange, though, was that when he got there, he grabbed me roughly and made love to me as if we were two high school kids in the back seat of a car. All kinds of fumbling, flipping around, and rough, much too hard. When he . . . when he came, he cried out again, 'I don't want this!' but before I got up the nerve to ask what, he fell asleep. Absolutely exhausted. Jesse only snores when he's totally pooped, and that night he sounded like a truck with no muffler.

"Next morning he was business as usual, although I kept waiting for him to tell me what the hell was going on. At least tell me something! But nope. He left for work and that was the day he disappeared. Walked out of the house, went straight to the airport, and flew away."

"But now he's back?"

"Yes, he came this morning. I was out shopping, and when I got back, there he was, sitting in the living room in his yellow bathrobe, drinking coffee."

"What did he say?"

"Not a thing. And I was so relieved that I didn't press him about where he'd been. He was very calm and didn't say much except that he was okay and glad to be home."

"But you did ask again?"

"Yes, finally. And then he said he'd been to London and Venice."

"Did he tell you why?"

Sophie interrupted again. "First tell him about the bandage."

"Okay. Well, the sleeves on his robe are long, but once when he made a gesture I saw all the way up the left one. There was a flash of a big bright white something. I asked whether it was a bandage, and he said he'd done something to his arm while he was away. I didn't ask about it because there were too many other questions."

I looked at Sophie. "What does it mean, this bandage?"

"You'll hear in a minute."

The waiter came by and asked if Caitlin wanted anything. She spoke quickly in German and he went away.

"What was I talking about?"

"The bandage."

"Right. The whole scene was loony, but you regain perspective fast. Okay, husband, so now you're back. It's time to answer my questions *p.d.q.* What have you been doing? Why did you go to London? Venice?

"Then I got really wound up and started ranting and

raving . . . but it was relief and fury and angst and all that stuff coming out at once. He didn't try to say anything till I was finished blowing my top. Why hadn't he called and at least told me where he was? Didn't he stop even once to think how worried I'd be? Oh, yeah, my gun was full of bullets.

"After a while, I ran out of them and we sat there, silent, looking at each other. Then he asked if I had ever had a real enemy, someone I wanted either dead or destroyed. Huh? What? The question stopped me cold. What was he talking about? I wanted to know about his disappearance; what did enemies have to do with it? When I asked what he meant, he said, "Do you remember Ian McGann in Sardinia?" Caitlin turned to Sophie and asked if I had read the letter. Sophie nodded.

"What letter?" I definitely was not tuned to their channel.

"The letter Jesse wrote me about their trip to Sardinia. Remember I showed it to you? About the man there who dreamed he talked to Death and asked Him questions?"

The two women watched me expectantly, hoping I'd make the essential connection without having to be told. A quiet fell over the three of us that lasted while I searched their faces for further hints. It was as if we were playing charades and they'd given a brilliant final clue.

"London. Venice. A bandage. The cut has something to do with all this?"

They nodded.

"McGann. His girlfriend's name was strange. She was Dutch."

"Miep."

My eyelids got it before my brain did. I felt them rising and for a few seconds didn't know why. Then my tongue knew it before my brain because *it* started saying "Mc-Gann!" a moment before all the pieces snapped together like train cars connecting. KA-CHUNK! MC-GANN!

"Jesse went to London to find McGann!"

Neither moved. Waiting to hear more.

"The bandage. A wound. Like McGann's! Oh, Jesus Christ, your brother is having those dreams too?"

"Yes."

Then I remembered with another KA-CHUNK the policeman, Death, in the Hollywood mask store saying sometimes He came early so that people could get used to Him or ask questions. He had told me Ian McGann was not dead. I'd not forgotten any of that day; I'd simply worked hard not to remember. When I was in college, someone I knew had a snake for a pet. He fed the thing mice and once asked if I'd like to watch what happened at mealtime. What interested me most was the mouse's reaction. After being dropped into the terrarium, it ran to a corner and washed itself furiously. When it was finished it stood there, motionless, and appeared to look out through the glass. Didn't it know what was in there with it? Animals have all those hyperaware senses; didn't one of them warn the poor creature that Death was nearby? Watch out! Run for your life! No. The snake oozed over, opened its mouth, and struck. The mouse got away once, but not the second time. I couldn't believe it. So calm, yet the little thing had to know somewhere in itself its enemy was inches away. Why hadn't it run or gone mad? Then again, why hadn't I when Death offered me a picnic lunch?

"What did he mean when he asked if you'd ever had a real enemy?"

"Because the minute he had the first dream, he knew the person who spoke to him was his enemy."

"Who was it?"

"Norman Ivers. Jesse's best friend when he was a boy. Norman drowned their first year in high school."

"A boy? But it makes sense. It could be anyone who's dead, right? Why not a boy? Did Jesse tell you what he said?"

"He couldn't. But he can tell *you*, Wyatt. He said he can tell you."

"Why me?"

"You know why."

"No, I don't."

"Because you're terminal."

Sophie said it. Caitlin wouldn't even meet my eye. When she did speak, she addressed the table top. "That's why I couldn't let you into our apartment. Jesse and I were arguing about how it should be done. I said we shouldn't involve you, but he insists. He said you're the only one he can tell these things to because of your condition. If he said anything to Sophie or me, we'd get infected the way he did. We'd start dreaming the dreams and get scarred when we didn't understand Death's answer."

"But what can I do? All I can do is listen."

"He thinks that's terribly important. He said—" The last word fell apart as Caitlin began crying. A silent crier. Tears rolled down her face, and her voluptuous mouth shrank into an old woman's mouth. Pinched, wrinkled, nothing but years of sadness and pain there.

Sophie got up and moved around the table to sit next to her. The silence came back. So did the waiter, who put a cup of coffee in front of Caitlin. When he saw her face, he shot disapproving glances at Sophie and me and left in a hurry.

"You don't have to do it, Wyatt. You have enough trouble in your life as it is. I told him I'd tell you but that I didn't think it was right. If you don't want to see him, he'll understand. I know he—" The tears got hold of her again and she tried to wave the rest of the sentence to me with a hand.

"Sophie?"

"Yes?"

"What do you think?"

"It's my brother. It's hard to be objective. I think different things with my head and my heart. You know what they are."

"I want to talk to him on the phone before I make a decision. Can I do that?"

"Of course."

"Then let's call right now."

Caitlin and I went to the public telephone and she dialed her home. Jesse must have picked up on the first ring because she started speaking almost as soon as she stopped dialing.

"Honey? Yes. Yes, I told him. He's right here with me.

We're still in the café. Wyatt says he wants to talk to you on the phone." She paused and gave me a small false smile while he spoke. It didn't reassure me. "No! But he—" Her mouth moved to say more but she was being interrupted and he was so loud that I could hear his flood of words coming in a jumble. "No, but Wyatt said—" Again she was stopped. She nodded, closed her eyes, tried to speak, couldn't. After many more long seconds she was able to slip in "Yes. I'll tell him. What? I said I'd *tell* him!" Putting a hand over the mouthpiece, she seemed to gather her strength before saying whatever it was to me she was meant to convey. "Jesse says he can't talk to you over the phone. It has to be face to face. It can't be any other way. You'll understand when you see him."

What was this nonsense? I reached for the receiver. She pulled it way back behind her ear, her other hand still over the lower part. "No! He said no. He can't talk to you this way. He's crazy over there, Wyatt. He's shouting at me and cursing. He never curses at me, never. And now he's shouting and . . . he's crazy. I don't care what you do, but you can't talk to him this way. I can't let you. It'll make him even crazier."

No one was crazier than Caitlin at that point. Her face was a shiny mess; she was holding the receiver so tightly that I could see the red and white of her clenched knuckles. Crazy, crazy. Everyone around me was bent in different directions.

"All right, all right! Tell him I'm coming over now. Tell him to take it easy till we get there."

She nodded like a little girl getting reassurance from a parent after having had a nightmare. Slow dips of the head, eyes wide and hungry to trust.

"He'll come, Jesse. What? No, I'll tell her to stay here. I'll bring him to the door, then come back here and stay with her till you're finished."

Sophie didn't protest. She took my hand, thanked me, and watched as we walked out. Traffic on Gumpendorferstrasse was brisk. We had to stand in front of the café a while before there was a chance to go. I wished we could run across, run to their apartment, run to Jesse, get all the information in two seconds—everything fast forward. Whether it was going to be good or bad, this was one of those times when I wanted the speed of life to double so that I could know much sooner what was next. *Zip fast boom*—here we are; now you know what's what.

"He's been talking about birds since he came back."

"Excuse me?" A long champagne-yellow Mercedes shushed by, wearing a German license plate. I was in Europe. God, I was in Europe again for the last time in my life. Last times. Days full of last times.

"Jesse's been talking about birds, but I don't understand what he's getting at."

I looked at Caitlin, but before either of us had a chance to say more there was a break in the traffic, and we scurried across the street. Once there, we walked quickly back toward Laimgrubengasse.

"What about the birds?"

"He has this book with him constantly that he brought back. He keeps reading passages from it to me."

"Are birds his hobby?"

"Not at all. That's what's strange. I've never known him to be the least bit interested in them."

"What else has he been talking about?"

"This is it—turn right here. About Venice; about how expensive it's become and how grouchy the people are."

"How long was he there? Why did he even go?"

"He got in touch with the place in Sardinia to ask for Ian McGann's address in London. He called and called, but there was no answer. So he went up there to look for him. It wasn't easy, because the people in the travel agency where he worked weren't helpful. But he did get hold of McGann's brother and learned that Ian was in Venice with Miep; they'd been there since they left Sardinia. He flew directly there from London, which, if you knew my husband, is so utterly unlike him it's astonishing. He doesn't just jump on planes and jet off to Italy or England or anywhere. It's not in his nature."

"Why is McGann in Venice?"

"He wanted to spend time there with Miep before he died."

We arrived at their building. Caitlin started to open the door.

"What's McGann's condition?"

She stopped turning the key and looked at me, poised to say something, but she stopped. "Jesse should tell you. I don't want to get anything wrong."

The door was one of those enormous wooden things you often see in Europe that date back to a time when the purpose of a door was not only to close off the outside world, but also to keep out the demons and hounds of hell. Caitlin needed both hands to struggle it open.

A lovely thing appeared—a shady silent courtyard with a marble water fountain in the center and well-kept flower beds. The centerpiece of the fountain was a child angel looking up to heaven with an impish smile on its face. Although we were in a hurry, I had to stop to have a look. The figure was startling in its mix of the sacred and the naughty, with even a bit of the sexy thrown in. A devout, naughty, erotic angel.

"Isn't she a joy? It's one of the reasons we took the apartment. We get to look at her every day. The first time we came here, both of us stopped as you did and just gaped at her. Now look up for the full effect. See how the walls of the building are brown and narrow? It's as if the angel's sitting out there in the middle of the *Hof* taking a sunbath and smiling like that because she's able to get a little light on her face."

"You think it's a girl?"

Caitlin smiled, then checked to see if I was kidding. "You *don't?* That's funny, because both of us immediately assumed it was a girl."

"I don't agree. I'd have to study it a while. But no, I wouldn't jump right in and say that."

"Oh, look, there's Jesse! Do you see? He's waving." She pointed up in a vague direction, but I saw only windows, most of them sealed to the eye by the afternoon's white sunlight. "Come on."

Walking around the fountain, I watched the smiling angel as long as I could, and then we entered a cool dark entrance-way with, far at the end, a winding staircase and a massive wooden banister. When we'd walked to it, I looked around worriedly for an elevator. There was none.

"Where's the elevator?"

Caitlin shook her head.

"How many flights up?"

"Three."

I took a deep breath and created a smile for her. "Let's go."

The steps were deeply worn stone and very wide. I watched Caitlin's feet climb and tried to match her pace because, living here, she obviously was an expert on climbing stairs. When going up Mount Everest, aren't you supposed to do what the sherpas do? Nevertheless, I was quickly winded and had to stop twice to catch my breath on the way up, while she danced her way farther and farther ahead. "Didn't I read somewhere that for every stair you climb, you live three seconds longer?"

"Something like that. If it doesn't kill you first." She smiled happily over her shoulder and kept on climbing.

The door to the apartment was high and wide and made of some impressive wood. Old wood doors and stone steps. How many people had lived in this place, come to answer this doorbell when it rang? Lived on the stone and behind the wood, planning and plotting, hopeful or weeping over things no one on earth would remember today?

Caitlin rang the bell. Short seconds later Jesse opened the door as if he had been waiting right on the other side.

"I'll go back down to Sophie now, honey." She gave him a kiss on the cheek and turned. When she got to the top of the stairs, she looked back once over her shoulder and smiled, shrugged, and walked quickly down.

He was wearing gray: pullover, trousers, socks. No shoes. He saw me looking at his feet and grinned. "Hello, Wyatt. I changed, but didn't get around to my feet yet. Come in."

Their apartment began with a long gloomy hall that led

into an equally dark living room crammed, to my great surprise, with gigantic pieces of furniture. Hanging on every
wall were corny oil paintings that hurt your eyes just to look:
mountain scenes or portraits of fat men with thick beards and
an air of dumb self-satisfaction. I knew Jesse Chapman was
square, but *this* square?

He saw me checking out the room. "Wonderful pictures,
aren't they? They're *not* ours, thank God. We discovered a
strange Viennese rule when we moved to this town. If you
rent a place that's 'furnished,' that means whatever furnish-
ings are there *stay—forever—*whether you like them or not.
We hate this trash. It looks as if someone a hundred and fifty
years old lives here. But when we asked the landlord if we
could move it out and bring our own things in, he was really,
seriously offended. So it's your home and you certainly pay
enough for it, but at the same time it's *not.*"

"Like living out your life in someone else's skin."

"Right."

"Well, what's up, Jesse? Sounds as if you've been having
an adventure."

"That's a good word for it. Have a seat on Frau Spusta's
couch." He pointed me to a plump zeppelin of a thing,
where we sat on either end and faced each other.

"What do you know about birds, Wyatt?"

"Some of them sound nice and others taste good."

"That's true. But listen to this." Reaching to the coffee
table in front of the couch, he picked up a small blue book
filled with white paper markers sticking out the top. He
counted a few and then opened the book to one. "Have you
ever heard of the ortolan? It's called *Emberiza hortulana.*"

"No."

"I guess it's delicious. Listen to this: 'When eating particularly succulent ortolans, European gourmands cover their
heads with large napkins so that oily juices do not squirt their
dining partners.' What do you think?"

"I think I don't care about ortolans, Jesse. I'm exhausted
and sick and not in the mood for gourmet fare. I think we'd
better talk about other things, because you've got two

women downstairs who are pretty damned worried about you."

"But you're not?"

"You're not my friend. Your sister is, and I worry about *her.*"

"Fair enough. But listen carefully." Annoyingly, he read the passage about ortolans again. "Ian McGann gave me this book. He marked specific passages for me to read. That was the first one. I didn't understand what it meant either. He sat and watched me but I didn't know what to say. I'd found him to ask about these dreams and what was happening to my life. He was the only one who would know. Instead of answering, he gave me a book about birds.

"He and his girlfriend—her name is Miep—are in this small hotel in Venice next to the Danieli. It has the same view of the water as the Danieli at a third the price. Nice place. Cozy, and perfect for them. He knows about it because his agency sends customers there on package tours. Ian can't move well now, so he spends a lot of time sitting at the window watching the boats and the water. Or, if he really feels up to it, they go to Caffè Florian nearby for a few hours. It's amusing, because Miep told one of the waiters there Ian is a very famous English writer who's recuperating from a serious illness. They treat him as if he's royalty. Whenever he comes in, they clear a table for him and make sure he's given the very best service. Miep's wonderful; he's lucky to have her. Funny how some people have the best things in their whole lives happen when they're about to die."

He spoke quietly but warmly, as if recounting a particularly happy anecdote that had happened long ago but was so gratifying that it was still flower-fresh in his memory. I wanted to interrupt and ask my questions, the ones that were burning up my mind, but I knew that wasn't correct. Jesse had to tell it his way. Besides, I was sure everything would come out in time. Everything I needed to hear.

"Actually, we were in Florian's when this happened— when he showed me the book and told me to read the passage about ortolans. After I finished he asked what I thought.

What could I say? It sounds funny. That's what I said. The picture of people sitting at a table with napkins over their heads so they don't squirt their neighbors with bird juice? Come on, it's a giggle." He rubbed his hands together, then held them out at arm's length and turned them up and down. "Don't you think? Anyway, I looked at Miep but she wasn't smiling and neither was Ian. He reached over and put a hand on my knee. 'It's *me*, Jesse. I did that to you; squirted my dreams all over you the moment I told you in Sardinia. And see what's happened to you now because of it. I'm sorry. I'm terribly sorry for what I did.' At that moment, even with all the terror that was inside me, the only thing I felt was profound pity for the man."

"What does he look like now?"

"Ah, that's interesting! He looks as if he's been very ill—no question about that—but not much worse than when we saw him in Sardinia. I was expecting much worse; I was sure he'd be dead. But for a time when I first saw him in Venice, I thought he might actually be getting better."

"Does he still have the dreams?"

"Yes, but recently he's been able to understand some of the answers. That's why he hasn't gotten any worse. Unbelievable, but he's actually been able to do it. He also said he's been reading all the literature he can find on death and dying. One of the things he's discovered is that sometimes the terminally ill come to a kind of peace once they accept that they *are* going to die. That was one of the fundamental changes for Ian: now in his dreams, he isn't angry anymore at Death for what He's doing to him. He says that anger wastes vital and important life energy. He's simply trying now to find the right questions to ask so that he can keep Him from taking away any more things."

I didn't say a word, because I had not had that experience. For me, Death was as viciously sadistic as the worst criminal and I hated Him more than ever. My life had become worse *and* more painfully beautiful as the end closed in. Besides the never-ending fear of the coming unknown, the details of the world I would soon leave were now more wonderful than ever. Each day I lived, my heart grew more love for what I was losing. That wasn't fair. Wasn't right. One or the other, Death. Take your pick, but don't take them both. Leave me with something at my end.

"Ian's learned, even in sleep, to ask only certain questions, small ones that'll bring answers he can understand."

"Like what?"

"He couldn't tell me. Or wouldn't. He's convinced that the more he tells, the more things will worsen. Sardinia convinced him of that."

"Why hasn't Miep been infected? Why you and not her?"

"He doesn't know, but thinks it's because of love. There is definitely a correlation between really loving someone and keeping Death away."

"So you're not worried about Caitlin?"

"She's the only thing I ever *have* loved in my life, Wyatt. No, I'm terrified for her, but I must talk with someone about this or I'll be lost. I have to believe what Ian said about love."

"Why do you want to talk to me?"

"Because McGann said you'd be coming and that we're important to each other."

I snapped to attention. "He knew? How?"

"In a dream he saw you here in Vienna with me. He also knew I would go looking for him. Besides the evil things, his dreams have become more prophetic. The way he looks and talks, he even reminds you of a Greek prophet. Like Tiresias in *Oedipus Rex*. You know, in those ancient stories seers are almost always blind or handicapped in some way. That's what allows them to perceive and understand things we can't."

"What did he say about me?"

"He described you in detail and said you'd be in Vienna by the time I returned. I swear to you I had no idea you and Sophie were coming."

"Why? Why is he dreaming about me now?"

"Because you're the only person who can save me, Wyatt. You're the only person who can stop the dreams from killing me."

"How?"

"By finding Death. That's what you want anyway, isn't it? That's why you came with Sophie?"

"I don't know what you mean."

"Sure you do." I waited for him to go on but he only looked at his bird book and slid a hand back and forth across the cover.

"What are you saying, Jesse?"

His mouth tightened, and when he looked at me, his face was set in fury. "You said you didn't want to waste time! Okay, fine, Wyatt, so let's talk about what happened to you before you came here. Let's talk about that cop you met in the store and what he said to you. Okay? Let's talk about that."

"How do you know—"

"I don't. Ian did. He knows all of it now. He's this wonderful sick man who's fighting the most impossible battle, yet has time to worry about me. And he worries about you. He knew about you. That's what I'm trying to say—he can see things now."

"He's also the one who made them happen! What about that, Jesse? So what if he can see? He's the one who infected you."

"Maybe we've got to wash our attitudes."

"Watch our—"

"I said *wash*, not *watch*. Maybe what Ian's done is save me. Maybe it's the best thing that ever happened to me."

"You'll have to explain that one. I don't see dying as being a best thing."

"Do you have courage, Wyatt? Are you a courageous man?"

"I don't know. I've never been in a position to find out."

"Neither have I. But wait a minute. May I read you something else? It's important."

"All right."

He sat unmoving for a moment, as if making a decision, then got up and took another book from a nearby table. "How's your Bible knowledge these days?"

I shook my head.

"Listen to this.

" 'And Jacob was left alone; and there wrestled a man with him until the break of the day.

" 'And when the man saw that he prevailed not against him, he touched the hollow of his thigh; and the hollow of Jacob's thigh was out of joint, as he wrestled with him.

" 'And he said, Let me go, for the day breaketh. And Jacob said, I will not let you go, except thou bless me.

" 'And he said unto him, What is thy name? And he said, Jacob.

" 'And the man said, Thy name shall be called no more Jacob, but Israel; for as a prince hast thou power with God and with men, and hast prevailed.

" 'And Jacob asked him, and said, Tell me, I pray thee, thy name. And the man said, Wherefore is it that thou dost ask after my name? And he blessed him there.

" 'And Jacob called the name of the place Peniel; for I have seen God face to face, and my life is preserved.' "

Jesse closed the book. "It's one of those famous stories we learn as kids and end up ignoring for the rest of our lives. But I think this says it all. These dreams have been forced on Ian and me. You are being 'forced' to die of cancer. They are the same thing. None of us is prepared for the challenge. One minute we're alone, the next we're wrestling with a stranger intent on hurting us. No matter what kinds of lives we've lived, we've never been forced to 'wrestle' with anything until now. Can we do it? Do we have any strength? Do we know even one hold? Who knows?

"Now look at Jacob. He didn't know either, but he dropped everything and jumped right in. One minute he's traveling with his family, the next he's wrestling with a total stranger. Then it turns out he's a good wrestler and can fight this angel or whatever it is to a draw. To *fight*. I never understood the point of the story, though I've been reading the Bible my entire adult life. Courage. Courage means facing what you have to and doing it with no hope that you'll succeed. 'For I have seen God face to face, and my life is preserved.' That has got to mean something."

"But it isn't God we're wrestling," I interjected. "It's

Death! He's not going to bless us or let us go. He'll kill the three of us. There's no way to wrestle Death to the ground or understand Him. There's only suffering and fear. We're beaten before we start."

"Not true! Not if you accept the challenge; not if you're willing to wrestle. Doesn't matter if this stranger is God or an angel or Death. If we lie down and say, 'You win. I quit!' then we *are* doomed. Look at me." He pulled his sweater over his head and pointed to a bandaged shoulder. "I'm getting the same scars as Ian. I'm terrified to fall asleep. Your wounds are inside. There's no difference; both are deadly. But what if we try to stop our fear and try instead to understand? Only by accepting the challenge did Jacob come to understand who his opponent really was. And he won! He fought an angel to a draw."

"Death is not an angel!"

"Maybe it is, just not the kind we dreamed of as kids. I saw you looking at the statue downstairs. That's what we hope for: children with haloes and smiles and blessings for us all. But what if angels are as complex as humans? Good and bad, dangerous and benevolent."

"That's clever but it's not real."

"How do *you* know? What if the whole world is Peniel? The angel changed Jacob's name to Israel. And Israel became a nation. Life is constantly wrestling with forces we don't understand. Maybe if we win, those forces have to bless us."

Almost to myself, I murmured, "The policeman in that store said there is free will. We're allowed to live the way we want until we die."

Jesse nodded. "Ian said the reason you're in Vienna now is to find Death in life. Not in sleep like us, because we don't understand the rules or the territory there so we have no control. Here in the real world, like Jacob. Because Death *is* here and only you can face Him successfully."

"What am I supposed to do if I find Him? Play chess with Him?"

"No. Ask all the dangerous questions you can imagine. See if you're courageous enough to do that. You're the only person who can save McGann and me. He said that's one of the things he's ever fully understood in his dreams: you're the one."

"Why me?"

"Why Jacob? Why are we having dreams that eat away at us like hungry mouths? Why do you have cells in your body that hate you so much they want you dead? Because everyone has to wrestle, and some do it for all of us.

"Come over to the window. Let's look at our angel again." He stood up and smiled. "Maybe she'll tell us something this time. I keep hoping."

I joined him at the window and we looked down at the pretty courtyard below. To my surprise, standing beside the angel were Sophie and Caitlin. I guess they couldn't see us because neither reacted to our presence, although both were staring up at us with almost identical expressions on their faces—worry, confusion, hope. As if any minute something would happen. As if it already had.

Arlen

April 20

Dearest Rose,

It was good to talk with you and Roland last week, although I must say again that I like talking to you in these letters just as well. Telephones make me feel so pressured to say everything fast and completely and full and precise and . . . unnatural. There's the word for it. Everything is unnatural over the phone, no matter how close the friend or how long the conversation. Don't you agree? You hear the real, wonderful voice, which is frustrating because it makes the friend almost there; you're dying to reach through the receiver and pull her through so you can have the rest of her with you too. And no matter how long the call lasts, if there's a lull or a pause, my mind starts working double-time to think up something, anything to say to fill that dead space, like a disc jockey on the radio. Even with someone like you, my other self–alter ego–soul mate, I feel the need to entertain or at least be interesting so that we get our money's worth from these transatlantic calls. I know you'll think that's stupid —the paranoid actress at work in me, because I really don't have to feel that way with you, of all people. But I do, so despite being almost with you via the telephone, sometimes I prefer writing you another of our never-ending letters. How long was my last one, twenty pages? Yummy. I love it. On a piece of paper I can take my time, stop for days or hours to think about what I want to tell you with no pressure on, smoke my cigarettes (which you so dramatically hate), and if there are no matches about, I can get up and go looking for some without worrying about irritating you with smoke in your face or leaving you (via the receiver) down on the chair too long.

Because I live so far out of town, the mailman usually doesn't arrive here till after two in the afternoon, and if he brings something interesting, I torture myself by not opening it right away. Instead, like a stoical child holding a birthday present on her lap for minutes before attacking, I put what-ever it is (a letter from you, a book I've ordered from America and am dying to read) on the couch. I go to the kitchen, grind some coffee, get out that favorite fat gray cup and the rest of the fixings. Wait around till the kitchen is filled with the great bitter smell of fresh brewed, wondering all the time what's in that letter, what's back in the other room waiting for me. Waiting, waiting. Put the coffee on a tray along with a clean ashtray and a Kipferl or a couple of slices of bread if its fresh. Take the spread into the living room. Don't hurry, go slow. Make the wait even more painful and delicious. Walk purposely by the couch and look hungrily at the white mail sitting on that fat chunk of black leather. Go out to the terrace and arrange everything just so. Only when the world out there is perfectly set up am I allowed to go back for the letter and read it.

The irony of last week's conversation was that I got your latest a day after we spoke, but was just as excited to see your handwriting as I was when I heard your voice on the phone. People will say we're in love.

Today I want to answer your question about living over-seas. You asked what it was like to live in a place for a long time where no one speaks your language. As I said, it's lonely and certainly isolating in a way. I talk out loud to myself a lot more than I ever have, but that could be a result of growing older and more—gulp—eccentric. One of the things that drove me mad about living in California was the sickening amount of talk I heard every day that added up to nothing. Everybody talks out there, especially in the business. Every-body has lots and lots to say, but too often at the end of a conversation, even when I thought hard about it, I couldn't remember what they'd said! And if you don't watch out, you become like them—both your tongue and brain click onto that deadly L.A. mental cruise control. Know what I'm talk-ing about? When you're awake and aware and not stoned and your lips are moving normally—but what's coming out of both your head and mouth is oatmeal? No, right now I prefer the rigors of this goddamned German language. It's a nice challenge, staggering around my short moronic sentences and being proud when I get them right.

I've lived here six months now and think I've convinced both my body and spirit that I *am* staying; this is not just another pit stop in the race to some finish line far away from here. I have no idea whether I'll spend the rest of my life in Austria, but I do want some years here. That's certain. At first, I didn't like the aloneness caused by my not speaking German well. Oh, sure, I could go into the local *Feinkost* and chat slowly with jolly Mr. Patzak behind the counter about this butter being more *billig,* but that doesn't count as real conversation—it's more kindergarten or beginning German class. Yet at the same time, the words you *do* know and un-derstand take on a hundred times more importance and meaning.

Put another way, living away from home is like being in a hot air balloon hovering over the ground, say forty feet or so.

Thirty—a little closer down. The perspective's completely different, though most things down there are still recognizable. You float over people talking and can make out scraps of their conversations, distinct words here and there, even whole phrases, but never the whole thing. And the world does become different when you experience it from a completely new perspective. In this case, being forty feet away from the existence you knew. In America among English speakers, I was *part of,* so I didn't watch closely. Here I'm forced to watch rather than listen, and like the blind person, I have a greater ability to "see," but in a wholly different way. Hear too, only different things now—things other than language.

On the other side of my life, I've been in and out of those depressions we talked about before. There's something terrifying about pulling up all your stakes and moving to new territory. Some days you admire yourself for your spunk and courage; others, you wake up in the morning thinking, God, what am I doing here? And there's the constant question of what to do with the rest of your life. Looking down the corridor of months and years that you hope are still left, you have to wonder sometimes, How am I going to walk all that way? You ask the question no matter where you are, but it goes deeper when you're far from home and can't lose yourself in a familiar culture and years-old daily routine. Or else I'm only being self-indulgent.

Sweet Weber has been very good about sending over books he thinks I'll like. Lots of novels and collections of poetry. I'm amazed at how he finds the time to read with the schedule he keeps. One poet he likes very much and has now addicted me to is Charles Simic. Listen to this, from a poem called "Evening Talk":

> *Everything you didn't understand*
> *Made you what you are. Strangers*
> *Whose eyes you caught on the street*
> *Studying you. Perhaps they were all-seeing*
> *Illuminati? They knew what you didn't,*
> *And left you troubled like a strange dream . . .*

That's how I feel so much of the time, especially when I'm depressed. There must be people around who know the big answers. If I could just find them I know they'd help in a million ways. Is that silly? Is it silly to think someone's out there who'll know just the right thing for me to do to find love and small peace? Sounds optimistic, yet I never think of myself as an optimist.

In one of Weber's early poems (which I've also been rereading), he wrote, "When we're old and held above the earth only by the hammock of our memories." But what kind of memories will we have if we don't live fully right now? How come so many old people look shriveled not only by age, but also by hate and failure and disappointment? And how did you, my best friend, end up with a good man who loves you and a healthy child? Was it only luck, or living correctly, or was there something else going on?

I went to dinner at the Easterlings' the other night and had a terrific time. I like them. Both have a sense of calm and solidity that's deeply reassuring. And they're funny! They told stories that cracked me up and I swore to write them down so you could enjoy them too.

Maris's first. Apparently her father was a grade A bastard and the whole family lived in fear of him. Lots of slaps in the face, mean punishments, speak only when spoken to—that sort of bully. Our dad the shit. Mealtimes were always silent unless Dad had something to say or asked you a question. Even when they were eating, the children would keep their heads down because just raising their eyes and looking at him was an act of defiance as far as he was concerned.

One night the fam sat down to dinner at the regular time, but Dad wasn't home yet, which was very unlike him. About ten minutes later he walked in, looking as if he'd been bitten by a snake or had had a religious experience. His eyes were as big as hubcaps and his hair stood straight out from his head. His lips were wet and his hands were shaking. It was so strange to see him this way that Maris couldn't resist asking what had happened. "I was just struck by lightning!" The guy had been walking down the street when it started to rain, and suddenly a bolt zapped down and sizzled him on the spot. But he was so awful that even lightning couldn't kill him! It's a terrible story, but Maris described him as such a skunk, and living with him such a reign of terror, that when I heard what happened and what he looked like that night at their dinner table, I laughed.

Later we were talking about high school and Walker said he knew a woman who went to a big gala party at the Palladium in New York for Liza Minelli. All the chic'y-mickeys were there in their finest and the place was really hopping. Scene scene scene—meet you at the bar. That sort of party.

After she'd been there a while, this woman had to go to the ladies' room. She found a toilet, did her thing, then stood at a sink putting on fresh makeup. A very beautiful woman wearing a tight, tight dress and looking totally glamorous came up next to her and started staring.

"Birgit Thiel! My God, it's *you!*" Birgit looked over at this goddess at the next sink but didn't recognize her. Not at all. To help her out, the other squealed, "It's me, Richard Randall! Don't you *remember?* Mill Valley High School, class of 'Eighty-six? We were in drama class together!"

It took old Birgit about a solid red-hot minute of staring and disbelieving and remembering to realize who she was listening to. When she did, she almost went into meltdown. Richard Randall had been a little nerd in the class no one ever noticed. Now Richard had become Rochelle and looked like a Las Vegas sex goddess. Our girl was trying to regain her balance and gravity in a world that had suddenly gone weightless, while Rochelle rattled on, wanting only to reminisce about the time they were in *Oklahoma* together. Wouldn't you have loved to be there, watching the whole thing?

Some people have to be struck by lightning; others cut up their bodies to make change happen. I was much luckier. I only had to *look* at my life to see I loved no one, had no passion for anything, didn't care what happened today or tomorrow or next week. You asked why I left all that and came here. Now that I've thought about it like this, I think the answer's kind of easy. Life has to have some geography.

Color, mountains, variety . . . If not, you're just living on
the moon or out in the desert. When you watch those nature
documentaries, you learn that only the weirdest, most sturdy
lizards and bugs can survive where it's either hot or cold and
never anything else. That's not me. Perhaps what I realized
most of all was that I was losing my geography, whatever
richness I had inside. No, wait a minute: maybe what I realized was I *was* becoming one of those nasty little desert bugs
who spend days digging endless tunnels into the sand.

Enough of this.

Ciao, Main—
Arlen

Dear Rose,

Here it is, the end of May and I haven't written you in
too long. Please forgive. The truth of the matter is, I've been
in a funk for weeks, and no matter how many Sacher tortes
or glasses of new white wine I drink, I can't seem to get over
my self-inflicted bruise. Part of it resulted from a big mistake I
made after writing to you.

When I retired and moved here, I swore I would not
"be" Arlen Ford anymore, not the Arlen that people knew
me as. Oh, sure, once in a while someone stops me on the
street to ask for an autograph, and that's nice, but otherwise I
don't want it. I recently rented an old Tony Curtis film, *The
Great Imposter,* and watched it with the greatest longing. The
character fakes his way through many different lives and pro-
fessions and gets away with almost every one because he's so
good at what he does. People don't question his authority. I
know it's naïve of me to ask, but why can't we stop living a
certain way and simply change direction without being
brought to task by others? I know it sounds bratty, but I do
not want to be an actress anymore; it left me empty and
hugely unhappy, and the time came when I realized I wasn't
a person as much as a personality. Acting is a wonderful
profession, especially when you're successful, but is it un-
grateful to say I've had enough of it and want to do something else now? What? What do I want to do? Unfortunately,

I don't know yet, but it took me half my life to decide I wanted to be an actress. Maybe it'll take the other half to decide what's next. In the meantime, the past sticks like something ugly on the bottom of my shoe.

What am I talking about? An Italian journalist appeared on the doorstep recently and asked if he could do an interview. I was surprised at his chutzpah for just showing up without being invited, but I like people with nerve as long as they aren't obnoxious. I invited him in for a cup of tea.

At first he seemed an interesting guy. He knew a lot about my films and was a good talker. A pleasant chat on a Wednesday morning. Attractive too, in a skinny way, and as I told you before, I've been celibate a long time. The fact that he was good-looking didn't hurt. I wasn't going to go to bed with him, but it's nice being in a room with a pretty boy. We talked, had a few giggles, and I thought, Oh what the hell, let's do the interview. Maybe it'll be interesting.

It started out innocently enough. Stock questions: Why did you retire? Why did you choose to live in Austria? What was your favorite role? I tried to be clever, sprightly, and amusing. But about halfway through, an ugly look came into his eye that said he wasn't having any of it. Finally, I stopped being darling Arlen and asked what he really wanted. He smiled like a barracuda with a million teeth and said he had enough material for the interview; could we now talk off the record? What do you mean, Mr. Interview Man? Well, the word's going around that the real reason Arlen Ford so gracefully stepped down from the silver screen is that she has AIDS: she's dying of the media's favorite disease but naturally doesn't want anyone to know. As if I were going to pull a Freddy Mercury and tell the world a day before I died.

Instead of getting riled, I said I'd be happy to show him the results of a blood test I'd taken three weeks before, when I'd had a full medical examination for my Austrian health insurance application. He said he'd like to see that. Still calm, I went to my study and got the papers. See, no AIDS. Next question? The son of a bitch had more!

The most disturbing thing was that I've never spoken with a journalist who had done his homework better. He seemed to know more about me than was possible. When I asked where he'd found all this information, he said he had spent a month and a half on special assignment researching my background. I suddenly knew what it must have felt like for people to go in front of Joseph McCarthy's committee in the 1950s and be questioned about meetings they had attended or people they'd talked to twenty years before. It was frightening, but more than that it was terribly, terribly depressing. Once I got used to them, his questions were really no more than annoying; but what was awful, Rose, was that I started feeling like a drowning person whose life was flashing in front of her before she went under for the last time. And what I saw, I hated.

What have we done to deserve grace or forgiveness? I gave up a career because it left me empty at the end of the day, which scared me. But have your life spread in front of you like a map, or flash in front of you as if you're a dying man, and you cringe at the mistakes, the gluttony, the waste. I desperately wanted a computer printout like that AIDS test, a simple piece of paper that said in black and white that I was all right, clean. Only this paper would testify in crisp scientific numbers and reassuring medical terms that I'd lived okay. There'd be a range from zero to ten, and if you fell anywhere in there, you were following an essentially valid path and needn't be concerned. But I didn't have a paper to shove in his face. This nasty little nematode threw details and facts at me: comments from old lovers and acquaintances (he even had a statement from our beloved eleventh-grade English teacher), reviews of my work going all the way back to the first film, ticket sale numbers on the flops . . . and it all added up to a big *so what*.

When I was a little girl, my parents were lent a summer bungalow with a big back yard. Mom invited a friend over for coffee one afternoon. While the two of them were talking, I was up in my favorite tree, practicing Indian war cries and having fun. Mom told me a few times to calm down but I wouldn't. Finally her friend got ticked off and said, loud enough for me to hear, "What that girl needs is a good inferiority complex." Well, thirty years later it's happened.

I didn't tell you about this, but I've been doing volunteer work at the children's hospital in Vienna. I said I'd do anything they wanted, so they assigned me to a special ward of terminally ill kids who speak only English. I go every day and read to them or play games—basically, whatever they're in the mood to do. I got the idea from Weber after he told me about working with cancer patients in New York.

As you'd expect, seeing those heroes battle not only for life, but for just a little peace and comfort in their day, makes me feel that my own turmoil is stupid and repellent. Every day I leave that building feeling secretly happy to be healthy and alive—only to get home and fall right back into the apathy and self-loathing that seem to be permanent guests now in my life.

The shocker came last night. I had just walked out of the hospital onto the street. It was a beautiful, rich summer evening when everything smells heavy and warm. I'd played Monopoly for three hours with Soraya and Colin. They'd screamed and argued and cheated like normal, healthy kids. Great stuff. I stood on the sidewalk with my hands in my pockets, in no hurry to go.

At that minute there was a scuffling sound behind me. I turned and saw a very attractive young couple: the woman on her knees and the man bent over, trying to help her up. Then I realized he was trying to *pull* her up, but she wouldn't stand.

She stayed on her knees and started pounding her fists into her thighs. "It isn't fair! It's not right! It isn't fair! Oh, God, it isn't fair!"

The only word for it is keening. She wasn't crying or moaning; she was *keening*. The woman sang her grief. The husband was embarrassed but was crying too. He kept tugging at her arm and saying, Come on, get up, come on. But she wouldn't. What had happened in the hospital? Had their child died? Had they been told it would die? Had they visited it for the fiftieth time and seen suffering and misery no child on earth deserves?

I ran over and asked if I could help; was there anything I could do? Both froze and looked at me as if I'd laughed at them. There was hatred in their faces. I'd interrupted their grief, so somehow everything was now my fault. The woman staggered to her feet and, pushing me out of the way, ran down the street. The man ran after her. Looking back once at me, his face said, *"You should die!"*

And they were right. If life was fair, what good do I do anyone, including myself? What good have I ever done, besides entertaining people for a few hours and then sending them back to their lives no better, wiser, calmer? I have no children, love no one special. I have more money in the bank than is decent, yet I worry that I won't have enough to live on for the rest of my life. But what life? I don't even know if I have *ever* loved anyone, and that in itself scares the shit out of me. I read my books, walk the dog, and work in a hospital where kids fight battles I cannot even imagine fighting, much less enduring, from one day to the next.

Here is my résumé: A. Ford made some movies, fucked a lot of men, worried about herself an obscene amount of time, and was discovered by an Italian journalist and a Viennese couple to be exactly what she was—a shadow, a fake, an empty pocket.

Love,
Arlen

Hi, Rose, honey. Yes, I'm sending a tape instead of a letter. I've had a *strange* couple of weeks that I want to talk about. When I sat down to write to you about them, my fingers couldn't keep up with my thoughts. I wanted to tell you everything fresh off my mind; that's why the tape. If I ramble and repeat myself, please forgive, but I'm going to try to tell all this and analyze it at the same time. You know how that gets muddled sometimes. But if I can't ramble and get confused with *you,* then who's left?

As I'm sure you got from my last letter, life on this side of the water has been very dark and full of doubt for me lately. To tell you the truth, it got so bad that I realized I had to try to get out of this black hole, or else. One way of doing it was by jumping back into the outside world, rather than hiding away on my hill like a Kafka character.

Now, don't short-circuit and call to see if I've hanged myself on one of the grapevines yet. All's well. In fact, it's so well that it makes me frigging nervous. Okay, um, how do I begin?

Well, it began with the opera. Vienna has a giant festival every May where they pull out all the cultural stops, and just about every big name in music appears here at the Opera, the Konzerthaus, Musikverein, or one of a dozen other places in this music-mad city.

I've never liked opera. Yeah, I know, it's where the human voice becomes the most beautiful instrument of all, the music is tran-scendent . . . I've heard the arguments, but it still don't grab me. Maybe because the singers don't act; they stomp around, if they move at all, flinging their arms out like Big Bird trying to take off. Nope, I pass.

But I *am* trying to turn over a new leaf here, so I bought a ticket to a première and put on a nice dress. And everything that led up to the damned thing was delightful: the grandness of the building itself, the snobby audience whose faces were all frozen with money and disdain. You got the feeling you were in a place that was best friends with history.

But twenty minutes after the lights went down and the howl went up, I got totally claustrophobic, and I was out of that seat in seconds, shoving to get outside. I didn't give a damn who I was disturbing—I had to get out of there before the top of my head blew off. Ever had a panic attack? I never did, and, boy, it scared me right down into my soul. You have absolutely no control over yourself. None! Everything's pushed aside by fear like hot lava bubbling up and there's nothing you can do to stop it. I charged out of the theater and right into a woman in front of the building who luckily was happy for my ticket when I offered it to her.

You remember where the Opera is—right at the end of the Kartnerstrasse, that snazzy walking street downtown? In nice weather, street musicians and other performers play for passersby. I was so glad to be out of that airless, stifling place that I felt like dropping money in every hat or violin case that I passed.

Ambling down the street, I stopped and watched two or

three groups play. With no plan in mind, I kept walking and ended up at the Danube Canal. It was a beautiful summery evening. People were wearing shorts, eating ice cream cones, and walking slowly. Whole families were out on their bicycles, and groups of teenagers sat around on the benches by the water, smoking and laughing ten times too loudly.

At Schwedenplatz there's a permanently docked old Danube steamship named the *Johann Strauss* that's been turned into a restaurant. I'd never been on it, but it looked great that night: warm lighting, people all dolled up and excited to be there, women holding their husbands' hands. The men acting like big shots, squiring their ladies on board. Ahoy, mateys! It was so nice. I stood around and watched. I wasn't jealous or sad. I felt like a kid watching her parents get ready for a big night on the town.

I don't know how long I stood there before this friendly woman's voice came up behind and over me like a sonic boom. "Are you with the A.I.S. prom party?" she asked in pure New York City English.

I turned, and there was the face to match the voice—a big smiling woman in an ochre party dress.

"This *is* the boat, isn't it? I'm confused. My husband shooed me out of the car and said, 'Just go down the stairs and there's a big boat. Get on it and you'll find them.' Easy for him to say; he's parking the car. But look—there's another big boat down there. I know one is the sightseeing boat and the other's the restaurant. We want the restaurant, right? Which do you think it is?"

Now I wanted to know how she knew I understood English. Then it hit me: I was standing in a formal dress next to a big boat, so of course she assumed I was with her group, whatever it was. I played along and asked for the name of our boat.

She squinted at the boat, then started waving at someone up there and said, "The *Johann Strauss*. Oh, look up on deck! There's C. J. Dippolito. This's got to be it. If that's C.J., then my son's gotta be nearby. Come on. I didn't catch your name. I'm Stephanie Singer." We shook hands and I mumbled something, but Stephanie was already moving and I was part of it. She swept us both onto the boat and right into the middle of the senior class prom of the American International School of Vienna.

I didn't go to our school prom and was always secretly sorry, although I never admitted it to you. Every girl should be granted one magic night in spring with a date wearing a new haircut, English Leather cologne, and a white dinner jacket. You get to wear something silk or floor length, a corsage, and you have your hair done. The way I see it, after that life's all downhill. I never had that midsummer night's dream, and it terminally deprived me. But now by some marvelous fluke, my opera dress and Stephanie Singer were giving it to me. A prom in Vienna on a boat on the Danube!

The *Johann Strauss* was a vision of goofy-looking boys in white dinner jackets and girls looking like angels with cleavage. You could tell under their dresses many still had baby fat around the edges, but they looked happy and proud to be with their guys. Stephanie found us a table, but before settling in with her, I excused myself and wandered around looking at the kids. Some of the couples were in love, some were showing off, others were terrified to even *look* at their partners. But this was their big night and they were all trying to do it right. It turned out that the reason Stephanie and her husband, Al, were there was that the school needed some parents to help chaperone the dance and the Singers had been volunteered by their son. A girl about sixteen told me this later. While she spoke, I realized she thought I was a parent too. That shook me up until I realized, hey, I *am* old enough to be mother to some of these kids. And that was okay because it was a special night and everyone there was looking as good as they ever will.

So Mama Arlen walked around with a glass of cheap champagne, having a great time. One of the things that impressed me was the international mix of the students. Although it's called the American International School, these kids weren't only American. Arabs and Africans in djellabahs and dashikis, girls wound in saris . . . A California blond boy had his arm tight around an exquisite Indian girl named Sarosh Sattar. Isn't that a beautiful name? There's a branch of the United Nations in Vienna and it would have done all those bureaucrats a lot of good to be there and see how diverse people really can get along.

I'd been on the boat about fifteen minutes and was sitting with the Singers when a girl came up and asked very hesitantly if I was Arlen Ford. When I said yes, things changed a little but not much. Some of the students wanted autographs, and a couple of the boys asked me to dance, but generally I was just another chaperone having a good time watching the dancers having fun and acting like adults for a night before they went back to their last days as kids.

Everyone had a camera and was taking pictures. Flash-bulbs popped and kids shuffled their friends together for shots of them laughing and holding their fingers up behind one another's head. Guys stuck flowers down the front of the girls' dresses or made silly faces. Photos you find curled in the back of a drawer twenty years later when you're doing a thorough spring cleaning. You pick 'em up, blow the hair out of your eyes, and the nostalgia from the pictures hits you so strongly you have to sit down. You remember the smell of that night in the car, driving over to the party, and the way your date kissed you when it was almost over.

I hung around another hour and was interviewed for the school newspaper by a boy named Fadil Foual. All Fadil really wanted to know was whether I'd ever met Billy Joel or Stephen King, so it was a comfier interview than the one I did with the Italian journalist.

I went back to my car feeling much younger at heart and very grateful to the Great Powers for allowing me to have the night.

A few days later, the Easterlings called to ask if I'd like to go on a picnic with them and Nicholas, their little boy. We met at their place and drove to the Lainzer Tiergarten, way out on the edge of town. It's a big forest reserve that used to be a royal hunting ground. But it was turned over to the people of Vienna and is a nice place to go if you're in the mood for an afternoon of back to nature. Animals run free, and you can take it for granted you'll see deer or wild boar somewhere along the way if you spend a couple of hours there. When we drove up, I thought that's where we were going, but Walker strapped on the carrying bag with the baby and led us on a path alongside the park to a staircase that went straight up forever. When I asked if the top was worth the climb, Maris and he said yes. Unconvinced, I asked what was up there. Maris said, "The Happy Hill." I couldn't very well say, "I'll wait down here," so I took a deep breath and followed.

The staircase *did* go on forever, and when we finally got to the top, the two of them kept going. I thought we'd at least stop for a cigarette break, but no way. We walked through woods a while until Walker veered left, and suddenly we were out on a huge open meadow with a great view down over the city. They called it the Happy Hill because it was one of the first places Walker brought Maris to when they first met. They made me promise never to go up there unless it was a great and special occasion. This was only the third or fourth time they'd been there together, and they'd decided to go there that day because they wanted to bring their baby and show him.

Their Nicholas is a cute kid, fat and robust, but he was born with a big hole in his heart. Maris said that's a relatively common occurrence and he's in no real danger. Surgery will have to be done to correct it in a few years, but now he's just a big happy baby who can't sit still and who laughs all the time.

I'd brought the wine and dessert; they had everything else. Cold chicken and salad, three kinds of cheese and crackers, fruit. Just seeing all that food spread out in the bright sun on a blue-and-white tablecloth, a breeze flicking its corners, and holding Nicholas in my lap while he patted my face with one hand and drank his apple juice with the other . . . it was sublime, Rose. I had a baby in my lap, nice people sitting near, food . . . I must have sighed fifty times, I was so glad to be there. I kept thanking Maris and Walker for inviting me, but how do you thank people for giving you peace, even if it's only for a little while?

After lunch, Walker got out a Frisbee, and we put Nicholas on the cloth while the three of us spread way out over the field. We threw it back and forth and watched it go crazy in the gusts. Right when we were growing tired, a man appeared with a beautiful Viszla that looked very much like my Minnie. Only this was a male named Red and his specialty was playing Frisbee. He caught it no matter where or how far you threw it. He was amazing. The baby was asleep by now, the dog was leaping ten feet off the ground to catch, Maris and Walker held hands . . . it was bliss. Life doesn't get better than that. I didn't want to walk down that hill again.

But things weren't finished. When we got down, Maris suggested we walk into the Tiergarten a few minutes to see if any wild boars were around. And almost as soon as we were through the gates we saw a small pack being fed stale bread by one of the gamekeepers. Have you ever seen boar up close? They're adorable, ancient-looking beasts; they remind you of what animals must have looked like in cavemen times. These guys were not exactly tame, but they'd come close for dinner. The keeper called them by name—Mickey Mouse was the biggest, the head of the clan. He got first dibs on whatever was thrown. A crowd had gathered to watch, and the gamekeeper came over and handed me a loaf of black bread. I was wary, but went close enough to smell them. Indescribable. Talk about the forest primeval! Their snorts and tusks were enough to knock you over. When I turned around, I noticed lots of people were taking pictures, but assumed they had Mickey Mouse in mind and not me. I was wrong. You'll see why in a minute.

Okay, I took a little break and now I'm back for the next installment.

Walker was going out of town for a week, so before we said goodbye, I invited Maris and Nicholas to spend a day at my place. It gave me a good excuse to do something I relish these days—clean the house. I know, I know, I used to be one of the world's great messes, but this is my new phase. Or else cleaning my house is only good therapy now when I don't have a clue about how to clean up the rest of my life. Whatever, I went at it hammer and tongs even though it was already tidy. I mean, how much is there to do when you own five pieces of furniture? The answer is if it's already okay, then polish it or get down on your knees and attack, swab, scrub it to death. Or maybe my obsessive ground assaults result from not having slept with anyone since moving to Europe. That's the truth! I told you I was going to refrain, and I have. I am gradually regaining my virginity. Someday my prince will come and this time I want it to be an *event*.

After cleaning, I went into Vienna to shop at the Naschmarkt. I'm a sucker for open-air markets. Seeing all that variety laid out in front of me, smelling the sexy spices, the spreads of strange foods you can only guess at. It makes me want to cook colossal meals that take forever to prepare. I never enjoyed cooking till I moved here. Then Weber started sending over great cookbooks, and the last few times he came we spent whole days in the kitchen while he taught me how to do things right and well. Another thing I'm grateful to him for. I'm lucky to have you all as friends.

Anyway, I drove to Vienna with a shopping list a mile long. Besides the Austrian stands at the Naschmarkt, there are Turkish bakeries, shops of natural foods, an Islamic butcher, and a store that sells the world's most wonderful peanut butter from Indonesia. Fresh fruits and vegetables from Bulgaria, Israel, Africa. Big tomatoes from Albania, Emmenthaler from the Alps . . . it's a place you get lost in for hours.

I was so involved in shopping that I didn't notice the sound till my bag was almost filled. The Naschmarkt is all noise anyway, so it's hard to pick out one as small as a camera click. But as I was squeezing a melon, I heard the sound and looked up. The woman who ran the store was smiling at something over my shoulder. I turned and saw a big man aiming a camera at me. I was in a good mood and mugged for him, putting a melon to my cheek and making a face like a girl in an advertisement. He smiled and took a few more shots. I put the melon down, waved at him, and moved off. Vienna's a town full of people taking pictures. I paid no attention.

Until a few minutes later, when I heard the sound again and saw him still aiming it at me. That time I frowned and turned away. I have too many bad memories of people who didn't give a damn about how I felt and only wanted to take pictures. At least *ask,* damn it. Remember when we were at the Sundance Festival and the lunatic from Japan did that crazy thing with his camera bag? Even if this Naschmarkt guy was harmless and just liked the way I looked, I didn't want it. I turned and walked away fast.

About halfway down the market on the other side of the street is a funky old café called the Dreschler. A lot of heavy duty characters and low-rents hang out there, mumbling into their beer. But the place has a real Vienna-1950s feel to it and I often stop in for coffee before heading home; take a window seat and watch the action at the market. I did exactly that, and instantly realized I was being watched right back by my new nemesis, Mr. Camera Head. He made no attempt to hide—he stood directly across the street and pointed his Nikon at me. It was equipped with a telephoto lens as long and wide as a weightlifter's arm.

I tried to ignore him but couldn't. And he wouldn't go away. Exasperated, I started to move to a table back from the window but then thought, *The hell I will!* Why should he ruin my peace? I was on the verge of giving him the finger but got up instead, told the waiter to leave my coffee where it was, and marched out. To his credit, the guy didn't move. Most photo creeps have no guts when you confront them. They'll take pictures of you in the nude or having sex or committing suicide, but face them off, and they run like chickens. This guy saw me coming but held his ground. In fact he kept shooting as I steamed across the street, battle flags flying.

I know I live in a Germanic country and *am* trying hard to adapt, but I still jump into English when I get mad.

I said, "What do you think you're doing?"

He had a nice face. Mad as I was, I couldn't help noticing that. Plain, but alive and amused.

"Taking your picture. I don't often see movie stars."

"Goody-goody. You've got enough, so stop now and leave me alone. Stop sticking your lens in my day."

His face fell. No, it *collapsed* in confusion. Then he asked if it really bothered me.

"More than you can imagine. If you know who I am, then you know I'm retired. No more movies, no more public face. No more pictures, okay? Be nice and go away."

He did something strange: put out his hand as if we were being introduced. He said, "My name is Leland Zivic. I'm very sorry, Ms. Ford. I'll stop. I only thought—" He was on the verge of saying something more but stopped and shook his head.

"Thank you, Leland. I'd be grateful." I started to leave, but an ugly thought stopped me. "What are you planning to do with them?"

He held up the camera. "With these? Oh, don't worry! They're only for me. I'm not going to sell them or use them. Please don't worry about that."

"Good." I turned and walked back across the street to the café without looking again. When I sat down at my table, I glanced at where he had been standing, but he was gone.

I had so much to do at home that I didn't think about him again until that night in bed. I hoped he was telling the truth when he said he wouldn't use them for anything more than a souvenir. But there was nothing I could do about it. Anyway, what difference did pictures of me shopping make?

The next morning I got up early and went outside to walk the dog. Usually we have a good long walk then because Minnie's full of energy, and if I keep her outside for a while, she'll race around till she's exhausted. Then we come back home and she curls up in her bed and sleeps for hours. We went over the vineyards and into the forest where you and I sat that day and talked. Remember?

When we were coming back up the path to the house, I saw a large manila envelope propped against the front door. I live so far away from the main routes that the postman leaves packages out in the open like that without worrying they'll be stolen. But it was eight in the morning, too early for him, so it had to be either Federal Express or special delivery. But *they* required signatures when they bring anything. I picked up the envelope, sat down, and opened it on the spot.

There were seven large photographs inside. The first one stopped the air in my throat. The second made me curse, and the rest were so startling that they zipped both my mouth and mind totally shut.

The first was of me through the dirty window of Café Dreschler. One hand's in my hair pulling it back off my face. That sounds like nothing special, I know, but the art of the picture's in the framing of the scene and the expression it's caught. You know me, Rose: when it comes to visual images of Arlen Ford, I'm the world's coldest, cruelest critic. What was so stunning here was the look on my face and the way the hand was pulling at the hair. It made you think this woman, whoever she was, was going through some heartsearing pain. The head's thrown back, eyes closed tight. The mouth's so twisted that it makes you think she's either crying or snarling. She's just found out someone she loves has died. Or the man she adores just said fuck off. She looks as if she's tearing her hair out and being killed by whatever she's heard. Even crueler, behind her in the café is an old woman walking by with a deadpan face. Outside on the street, directly in front of the window, is a couple passing in the other direction, laughing. Mystery, isolation, and pain all together in one photo! It was so haunting. If you saw it in a gallery you'd want to go forward and recoil at the same time. You'd wonder, Oh, God, what's happened to her? How was the photographer able to catch that moment of agony and the world's indifference to it?

When I saw the photo, I was so shocked that for a few seconds I didn't even realize it was *me* there; that I was the woman. I didn't remember pulling back my hair. I certainly wasn't unhappy in the café that day. Maris and the baby were coming to visit. The only memory I had was of being glad to sit down after shopping and then my annoyance at realizing the guy was still taking pictures. That's all.

I flipped to the next one. Lainzer Tiergarten the day of the picnic with the Easterlings. I'm offering bread to Mickey Mouse, the boar. We seem to be smiling at each other. Love at first sight. Maris is standing nearby with the baby in her arms. Nicholas has his hands in the air and is laughing. If that first picture was Hell, this one was Heaven. Everyone, including the boar, is happy. I'd been shaken by the first picture, but this one exuded such happiness that, despite myself, I grinned.

As I said, there were five other shots: two on the *Johann Strauss* the night of the prom, one in front of the Opera, one walking my dog down by the river. The last was of me from behind as I crossed the street back to the café. An old man in a silly hat is watching me and pointing. He's telling his wife something and they're both laughing. That son of a bitch photographer took another picture of me five seconds after saying he'd stop! But it was such a funny picture that I giggled; if you didn't know what was going on, you'd think the old man's pointing out my ass to his wife. After I'd looked at them over and over, I dropped them into my lap and pulled the dog over to hug. Who was this guy? How long had he been following me around taking pictures? And what pictures! Each one was startling, special. I was suspicious, but intrigued as hell. It was perverse and impressive.

Maris came over later that day. After she put down the baby for his nap, I got out the pictures and showed them to her without saying where they came from. I wanted her first impression. You know how famous Maris is becoming for her model cities. I wanted to hear what an artist had to say before I took any further step.

They were in the original order. She spent the most time on the first, but stopped almost as long on the one of me walking the dog. When she asked if they were done by the same person and I said yes, she said it was hard to believe. One looked like part of the series of me in *Vanity Fair* by Herb Ritts, but the Opera one reminded her of a 1920s Bauhaus photograph, something by Moholy or Herbert Bayer. The corker, though, was the café shot; it was as good as any picture she'd ever seen. Who was the photographer? She wanted to know if he had a book out because she'd get hold of it.

I told her how I'd met the guy. She shook her head but didn't stop looking at the pictures. I asked if she didn't think the whole thing was bizarre and she said yes, but they were brilliant nevertheless. Maybe it was her own strange sensibilities, but she didn't think the man who took them was strange. I rolled my eyes and said, hey, he followed me around for days, obviously, without my ever knowing it. He was James Bond and Peeping Tom rolled into one! Not to mention a good photographer. How long had he been there before I knew it?

She said if he ever came around again and bothered me, I should just tell him to go away. But she didn't think he was going to do that. Then she said something that got me. "We're afraid of everything these days, you know? Terror dominates pity." I had no idea what she meant by that and asked her to be clearer. Shuffling through the batch, she held up the picture of me in the café. "This man doesn't want to scare you. He doesn't want anything from you. If anything, he wants to tell you something. He's saying that you're in trouble."

My stomach clenched and I asked whether it was so obvious. She said, "Well, kind of."

I have that small television in the kitchen which I usually turn on to CNN when I'm in there for any length of time. Once in a while I look up if something sounds interesting, but usually it's only background noise in English.

Yugoslavia's only a few hundred miles away from here, and since it exploded, Austrians have kept a close eye on what's going on down there, for obvious reasons. Dubrovnik is the favorite target these days, and it's obscene the way they're destroying that beautiful town for no reason other than spite.

Two days after Maris's visit, I was making lunch while listening to the latest report from the battle zone. Bombs exploded and people ran for shelter. There was the sound of machine gun fire and an ambulance raced by. An old woman loomed up in front of the camera, hands to her face.

A reporter's voice came on, describing what was happening. I was chopping onions and trying to remember if I'd bought chives. The voice on TV said, "Blah blah blah Leland

Zivic." I knew in the back rooms of my brain that the name meant something, but I was too concerned about chopping and chives.

Another voice came on, this one smoother and sweeter than the other. I looked up only because someone laughed, which sounded strange in the middle of all that gunfire.

There he was! His name was written across the bottom of the screen with PHOTO JOURNALIST below it. I grabbed a marker and wrote it with indelible ink on the wood chopping block. I'd worry about scrubbing it away later.

The reporter said Zivic was famous for his photographs of trouble spots around the world. He'd been in Rumania when Ceausescu fell, Liberia when Doe was executed, Somalia at its raging worst. When asked what he thought about the Yugoslavian conflict, he said something like "Forty years of peace in this country. Then from one day to the next they're going into maternity wards and shooting newborn children. Does anyone besides the politicians understand how that happened? The trouble with wars is that they all look alike to the people who aren't involved. Only the skin color of the dead is different."

The reporter said, "If that's so, why do you keep risking your life to take these pictures?"

Zivic nodded as if the reporter had made a good point. "Because if I do my job well, people will see wars *aren't* the same; they aren't just body counts and anonymous casualties. Death should be shown in such a way that it will be remembered."

I know one of the film correspondents for CNN. After a long time on the phone, I got through to her in Hollywood. Explaining what was up and where I'd just seen him, I asked her to trace down Leland Zivic for me. Good woman that she is, she didn't ask why I was interested.

It turned out he had an apartment in London and was represented by an agency there. She gave me both of the addresses and phone numbers. I assumed if he was on television in Yugoslavia, it wasn't likely he'd be answering his phone in London, so I called and left a message on his machine: "This is Arlen Ford. Please call me when you get a chance."

I expected to hear from him soon but didn't. At first I thought he hadn't answered because he was still on assignment. In grisly moments it struck me that he might be dead. I tried to put the whole thing out of my mind, but his photographs sat on the table in the living room and naturally I looked at them a lot. His London numbers were stuck on a yellow slip above the telephone, and "Leland Zivic" was big and black in my handwriting on the chopping block. I'd give it a week or two before trying to wipe it off.

Opening the mailbox one morning, I saw it was empty except for a postcard. The writing was unfamiliar: neat block letters; postmark, Sarajevo. A 1930s' photograph of New York's Thanksgiving Day parade. Giant floats of Pinocchio, Uncle Sam, and the Tin Woodman of Oz drifted at odd angles above the street, casting huge shadows across the buildings. They were tethered by ropes to ant-sized people below.

I read: "I'm afraid to call you and will do so only if you give the all clear. Since I dropped the pictures off, I've been wearing a crash helmet in case you go nuclear. On a scale of one to ten, how angry are you at me for them? How did you get my telephone number? Is there life on other planets? Answer any or all of the above questions at your leisure."

Sarajevo had recently been under fierce attack. Was that still going on? I pictured him in an underground shelter or command post, writing the card as bombs flew overhead. How amazing of him not to mention what was going on there! People have so little courage nowadays that when we do meet someone who has it by the pound, it's hard not to be impressed. Only a little twist of fate had permitted me to know what Leland did for a living. Otherwise, I'd still have thought him just another geek with a camera who'd gotten too close. Yes, I was uncomfortable with what he had done to me, but also touched and intrigued that this interesting, modest man liked me. I called his London apartment again and said only, "The coast is clear," and then started waiting again.

Did you ever notice how life picks up when you're expecting an important or interesting call? The telephone itself starts to dominate the room. You're always on edge as you move around the house because any minute it could ring and be he. And if it doesn't ring at all, you become even more nervous. Or I do. I didn't know this guy, yet he had taken these remarkable and distressing pictures and last been spotted dodging bullets in Yugoslavia. Days went by. God knows, I wanted him to call. Then I thought maybe my phone message had been too curt and he'd been scared off. I thought about what to say if he did call. Ask about his job? Or why he took the pictures? Would he turn out to be interesting, or only brave and dull, with an eccentric fix on retired actresses? I never said his name out loud but once in a while would try it out on my mind's tongue. Leland. That sounded American. Zivic did not.

It was late at night. I was in bed, rereading *Mariette in Ecstasy*—have you gotten it yet? Please do. It makes life in a cloister sound transcendently beautiful and full of possibilities. The phone rang. I was sure it was you because you're the only person who calls so late. But I didn't recognize the voice, so when he said my name, I asked, "Who is this?"

"Leland Zivic. Can we talk?" His voice was completely different from the way I remembered it. Of course, what did I have to remember from the only time we had talked? Three sentences? Thinking about him, I must have imagined many different voices to suit the image in my memory. The one I heard now was soft and neutral. Low, but not so that it was distinctive or anything special. He said he'd planned to be witty and make excuses, but he couldn't today; he just wanted to talk. Was that all right? I asked what was the matter, and he said he was in Yugoslavia near the war. I told him I knew because I'd seen him on TV. His voice got very quiet then and, oh, wow, you should have heard it. He said he'd seen things the last couple of days I wouldn't believe. He was a photographer and took pictures of war. Normally it never bothered him because it was just a job. But maybe because his father's family came from there, this time it was bad, really bad. Wait a minute, Rose, I've got to stop and light a cigarette. Just remembering his voice gives me a chill.

Here we go. Anyway, his voice sounded scared and lost. He'd called because he wanted to talk to me. His words were rushed and breathless, like a confession to me and a conversation with himself. It took me completely off guard. I'd hoped when we first spoke that it would be interesting but relaxed. This was already a hundred thousand volts in my ear. I told him to say whatever he wanted and tell me anything. I sat up in bed and pulled my pajama top tighter. I wanted to look presentable for him even though he was a world away!

He said, "I'm in a *slasticarna*. That's a Yugoslavian pastry shop. There's cake all over the floor. Can you imagine that? Cake. The whole floor is fluffy goo. The man and woman who own the place are down on their knees, trying to clean pink and blue icing off the floor. All the windows are blown out of the shop and everything's a mess, but their phone's working and they let me use it."

I asked whether there was fighting where he was and he said yes, but it wasn't bad now. It *had* been a couple of hours before, but it had calmed down. He said it was very kind of me to talk to him so late. I told him it was nothing, that I'd only been reading and trying to fight off the urge to sneak into the kitchen for something to eat. He asked me to tell him about my kitchen, which took me completely by surprise. When I said, *"What?"* he said, "Describe it. I want to have a picture of Arlen Ford's kitchen in my mind."

"Um, okay. The kitchen. Well, it's white and wood. Very simple, but everything's there."

"Do you like to cook?"

"Very much."

"Me too. That's when I feel cleanest. Everything makes sense. A woman who smokes and likes to cook. That's good."

There was a loud metallic noise, a scraping sound, from his end.

"What's that?"

"It's outside. A woman and boy are dragging a man on an upside-down car hood past the store. There's a hospital near here." He stopped and there was a long pause. I felt I was right there and could see that man on the car hood. I asked if he wanted to talk about what he'd seen there. There was another silence, as if he were trying to decide. "No. I want to tell you why I took those pictures of you."

Naturally my heart hopped into my head and started pounding all across my temples. The moment of truth! Let me tell it to you in his words, as best I can remember. It was so beautiful and touching.

He said, "I've been down here for a few weeks. It was all right at the beginning. I was here before on vacation and on assignment for the winter Olympics a few years ago. But now the whole country's eating itself alive. When it got too much, I asked for R and R in Vienna. Give me a few days off and some calm scenery and I'll be ready again. I'll give you all the blood and flames you want for your front pages. They said okay, so I went up there and just walked around, did nothing. Went to museums, took off my watch, made no plans. But I couldn't stop thinking about what I'd seen, which is rare for me. Maybe because there are so many Yugoslavians in Vienna. I'd see them and wonder if they'd lost someone in the war, or if they were worried about family back home. Overload. Sometimes you get overloaded doing this and can't shake it off by closing your eyes or taking a vacation. It sticks like a cockleburr on your brain.

"I rented a bicycle at Nussdorf and rode it up along the river to Klosterneuburg. I was black. My thoughts were so dark and sad that day. What was I going to do? Go back to Yugoslavia and take more pictures of dead people? Blood and bodies? I know a photographer who changes the position of bodies so that they'll look more fascinating in his pictures.

"Right in the middle of that darkness, I saw you. You and your red dog. Unbelievable! A vision! As God said, There *are* nice things in the world too. Arlen Ford walks her dog by the Danube. What were the chances of that happening? Meeting up with you like that?" He stopped and said something in another language to someone nearby. They spoke quickly back and forth before he came back on. I asked what was happening. He said the guy who owned the store wanted to know when he was getting off, so Leland had just given him a hundred dollars American and would hand him another fifty if we talked much longer. I told him that was crazy, but he said it was the best-spent money in weeks.

Then he said, "Let me finish this story. I was about to take a permanent swim in the Blue Danube when you suddenly appeared, looking even better than you did in your movies. I felt like a thirteen-year-old. First, I almost fell off the bike, my eyes bulged out . . . So I stalked you. I admit it. There you were; I had a camera. I wanted one shot. One great shot of Arlen Ford to put up against all the others of Hell I've had to do recently. And then I got greedy. After that one by the river, I followed you home and staked out your place."

Naturally, I told him that made me *very* uncomfortable. He said he knew and apologized, but wasn't sorry. That's kind of ballsy, huh? I mean, especially if he wanted me to like him. But he did it because they were necessary pictures. That was his word. It wasn't only me he was photographing; he was trying to take pictures of things that would keep him alive. Good things: movie stars and their red dogs, people in wine gardens, old couples sitting in their Sunday best on a bench by the river. It became a kind of crusade for him. There's that nice *Heuriger* down the street from my place, and the *Gasthaus* that has the good fried chicken? He sat there and talked to people, then watched my house a while. I told him it was weird and wanted to go on with the thought, but his voice hardened and he said, "Wait a minute."

Lulled by our conversation, I'd forgotten where he was and what was going on around him. I heard him speak another unknown language to someone nearby. A man barked something and Leland said, "Shit! They're that close?"

I asked, "What's wrong? What's wrong?" He said they were about to be a bull's eye and he had to go. He'd call again when he could. Was that all right? I said of course, but he'd already hung up, and that was that. Imagine what I went through trying to sleep that night!

The next postcard arrived two days later from a town named Mostar, which reminded me of North Star. I went around thinking he's on the North Star now. All he wrote was:

Two friends meet on the street.

FIRST: "I just married a woman with two heads."

SECOND: "Is she pretty?"

FIRST: "Well, yes and no."

That was it. No message, no further report.

"Then I came in from shopping one day and saw the answering-machine light blinking: "Arlen, it's Leland Zivic. Sorry you're not there."

I was furious that I hadn't been home. So furious that, stopping myself in the middle of my rant, I smiled and said, Well, well, well. What's happening here, missy?

After that he didn't call for a while, which would have worried me if the mail hadn't started bringing things I'd only previously seen typed on the inside of my forehead. His post-cards and letters were full of observations, soliloquies, quotes from what he was reading at the moment, more jokes. Altogether in one. I didn't know who he was talking to, but was glad to hear what he had to say about most anything. Here's a few:

> So many soldiers are crazy—their daily life of war has kicked them in the head and crushed a small but key center of balance and longitude in there that's critical.

> Old men should have gardens. Unlike men, old women have an inner peace. They've done their job the best they can and know it; they've used their energy well and are now done. But from the look on their faces, life is never finished for old men; never enough, never complete. So put them in gardens, where they can pretend their work is useful or they're keeping order. They're pathetic; humor them.

> Seen in a ruined town: a pair of red plastic children's handcuffs at the base of a tree.

> My brother likes reading books about famous failures. They reassure him that no matter how dull his life is, at least he's safe and sound. He's in no danger of the kind of self-made catastro-

phes that destroyed the likes of Fitzgerald or even Elvis Presley. My brother is dull and unmemorable but he's safe, which is more than can be said for those other dead legends, fireworks and all.

Then this quote from Diane Ackerman's *A Natural History of the Senses:*

A breath is cooked air; we live in a constant simmering. There is a furnace in our cells, and when we breathe we pass the world through our bodies, brew it lightly, and turn it loose again, gently altered for having known us.

Cooked air? Photos that showed me parts of myself I was never aware of, letters I carried around and reread constantly . . . Who *was* this guy? I tried hard to reconstruct what he looked like, but all I ever came up with was a nice face, glasses, tall. So when he called again, the first thing I asked him was to tell me what he looked like. He said enjoyment, spontaneity, and affection. I went, Excuse me? And he said, You asked me to describe myself. I said, Yeah, *physically.* Know what he said?

"I knew what you meant. Next question."

I took a deep breath and said, "Will we ever see each other again?"

"I don't know. Do you think it's a good idea?"

I said, "Don't be coy."

"Oh, I'm not being coy. If we were to meet and it was a disaster, what then?"

"Well, it wouldn't be, because we've already had our disaster; the day we met I thought you were a camera creep." He said, "I am. I'm a professional camera creep. I don't know, Arlen. I love writing those cards to you; they're my oasis down here, but getting together . . . ahh, that's something else."

"Why?"

"Because we both have expectations. We each know how we want the other to be. But hopes don't usually work out in real life. As long as I can talk to you in postcards or over the phone, then you're the Arlen I love from the movies—Lady Cool, pretty . . . And face it: you were put off by my photos, but I was the one who saw you that way. Why would you want to meet the guy who insulted you?''

I screamed at him that I wasn't insulted. I loved most of them, and the others . . . Medusa wouldn't be thrilled to see herself in a mirror! I told him Maris saw the one of me in the cafe and said I looked like the Masque of the Red Death!

He laughed and said, "But don't you love that story? All those dumb people trying to party their way through the end of the world? Death has a sense of humor. He didn't just come in and bust up their soirée; He dressed up in a costume like them and walked in with a drink in His hand!''

I was not interested in Edgar Allan Poe and asked him point-blank when he was coming to Vienna again. He said he didn't know and wanted to think about it some more, the shit! I was dying, Rose! I was throwing myself at his feet, and he had to *think* about it some more. Talk about a smack in the face!

So fade out on that and fade in on Minnie and me sitting out on the front step, taking in the first sun of the day, when he arrived. My eyes were closed and my hands were wrapped around a hot mug of coffee. The best part of the morning. Then I felt her tense against my leg. I slowly opened my eyes when I heard the sound of a car drive up nearby and a door click open. A taxi stood at the bottom of the hill and some-one was bent into the back door pulling a duffel bag off the seat. When he had it out, he turned and waved at me. Oh shit, oh shit, there he *isssssss!* I didn't have makeup on, hadn't brushed my teeth, and had had garlic soup with dinner last night . . . Great, huh? Perfect timing. But *that's* what he looked like! Everything about his face came back in a second, and I didn't know whether to stay where I was or go down to greet him. I was calm; not one quiver or tingle of worry. He was finally here. I guess I'd been ready all along.

I stood up and started down the path, Minnie running ahead of me. While she stood at the gate, waiting and wiggling to get out, Leland closed the door of the taxi, which took off. He tried to pull the bag onto his shoulder but stumbled and let it fall heavily to the ground. I was close enough to see him lick his lips.

I kind of joked and asked if it was such a heavy bag. I opened the gate and Minnie launched herself onto him.

He said it was just a little tricky and I asked whether I could help. He said no but that he'd done something to his side. I looked and saw he was bleeding! He smiled and said *that* was the problem. He was wearing a white shirt with the sleeves rolled to his elbows. Right where the roll touched his side was a large patch of dark red. I asked him what happened and snatched the bag away.

Absolutely calmly, as if he were describing breakfast, he said he'd been hit by shrapnel and that he'd have a nice scar if he was lucky. Macho idiot. I told him to come in the house, for God's sake. He said I couldn't carry his bag because it was too heavy. Can you imagine, saying that while bleeding through his shirt?

The bag *was* heavy but I got it up to the house and put it down at the front door. When I asked if he should go to the hospital to have the wound checked, he said no, it wasn't serious, just messy. I said that sounded a little too fucking heroic.

Once we were inside, I asked if he was hungry, and as I started for the kitchen, he touched my arm. "Was it all right to come here? I know I should have called first—"

"Of course it's all right! Now sit down and take it easy. I'll make you something." But he followed me to the kitchen and sat at the table. Minnie kept right up with him and lowered herself onto his foot. I asked whether he'd like some bacon and eggs; he loved the idea. I said, Fine, now tell what happened to you.

He'd been riding in a UN convoy when some bastards strafed it. I said *that* hadn't been on the news, and he laughed. A lot of stuff isn't on the news, he said, and that's one of the first things you learn as a journalist. They say they're telling people the news, but usually it's cleaned up and defanged, no matter how gritty it looks. People say they want to know the truth, and think they're interested in seeing death and bodies, but *show* the reality, and they're horrified.

After I digested that, I asked what really was going on in Yugoslavia. He said everybody wants to be free of everybody else these days. Fifty years ago, you had wars because one country wanted to own another. Today it's because *parts* of countries want to be free of other parts. The Croatians from the Serbs, Czechs from the Slovaks, every part of what used to be Russia.

While I was cooking, I listened with my back turned. When I glanced over my shoulder to check on him, he was resting his head on his fists and seemed to be speaking to the far wall. I wanted to ask lots of things but knew he needed to talk about what mattered to him, so I kept quiet.

Minnie was lying next to him and he asked her name. I told him and said if she gets to be too much, give her a shove. She thinks everybody loves her as much as she loves them.

He nodded. "You know what's funny? When I got hit and they were patching me up, I couldn't think of where to go. I mean, I have my apartment in London and there are people I could stay with, but still. It's no big deal—it's a flesh wound, but it frightened me. When I was most scared, I realized I wanted to come to Vienna. I wanted to see you. After we talked last time, I was sure I wouldn't do that, but here I am. I hope I'm not intruding, breaking your peace . . . If I am, just say so."

"Your eggs are ready. You're not intruding on a thing. Notice how busy I was when you arrived. Here, eat." How else could I have said it, Rose? I've never been so happy in my life to see a man? That would have gone over big!

He eats just like me: hasn't swallowed a mouthful of food before the next is going in. I told him that and he said it was a habit from being in dangerous places—you eat when you can and as fast as you can. I told him he could slow down because it wasn't dangerous here. He stopped and, pointing his fork at me, said, "Wanna bet?" My heart vaulted into my throat and there was this big silence, but then I got up the nerve to ask why he *had* come.

"Because I still need to write my life in what remains of this moment." That was what he said, exactly that.

The line stung and thrilled me at the same time. What a strange, compelling thing to say! I understood it at first, then didn't. I wanted to ask him to say it again but instantly knew I shouldn't, because when he looked at me after saying it, his look said, "Understand me." I didn't, but never would have told him that.

Thank God Minnie broke the tension by biting her ass and chewing at it furiously. We both watched, smiling, and I was glad for the distraction.

He went back to his food, and when he was finished he stood up slowly and asked if I knew of a good hotel nearby. I said, "Don't be ridiculous, stay in my guest room; there's a separate bathroom, clean towels." But he wouldn't do it. The *Gasthaus* down the road has a couple of rooms above it, so I called and found the rooms were available and reserved one. I didn't know whether I was happy or sad that he'd refused. My mind was a sewing basket full of different-colored, tangled emotions. He was wounded, I wanted to talk to him, get to know him better. But his staying with me would mean a whole bunch of other things, and we both knew it.

Now, was I attracted to him? No, he's not my physical type. At first glance I thought he looked like an old college fraternity brother. Nice face, very animated when he spoke, but not one that would stop you dead if you saw him on the street. He looked like someone's likable brother, if that makes sense. So no, it wasn't that. You know I think about sex a lot, particularly when I haven't been with someone for a while. Leland made me feel that he was listening carefully to every word. He seemed a good person to confide in, but not someone you'd jump on and drag into the bedroom.

We brought his bag out to the car and I drove him to the *Gasthaus*. On the way, he said he was very tired and was going to sleep for a few hours. After that he'd be fine again; could he call? I invited him for dinner and offered to pick him up. He said dinner was great, but he'd walk over, because it would be a joy to go somewhere on foot without having to worry about being shot at along the way.

The rest of the morning I cleaned and planned. I pored over my cookbooks and came up with something delicious but easy to prepare. It needed the freshest ingredients, so I drove back to the Naschmarkt in Vienna for the things I needed. Passing his hotel, I smiled and said a quiet "Hello there." And when I got to the market I kept thinking about the time I'd met him there and what had followed.

Because I knew he'd been there and was so near now, the city itself took on another kind of pleasant weight and feel. You know what I mean? When he felt better I would show him the places I liked. We'd go there and there. I wondered how long he'd stay.

"Because I still need to write my life in what remains of this moment." Jeez, what a line!

The ride home was one of those small, wonderful half hours you later think back on and cherish. There were fresh strawberries in the bags, leeks and fresh Hungarian paprika for the soup, vegetables big enough to hold in two hands. I thought about how I'd spread them out on the white kitchen table and prepare them as best I knew how. I'd made the meal before and it was always good. A long afternoon in the kitchen ordering and anticipating. Use the good china and beautiful Czech crystal glasses. Was there enough wine? Should I buy a cake for dessert?

Standing in the kitchen again all ready to begin, I almost didn't want to start, because every step would lead me closer to completion and his arrival. In comparison to this day, how quiet my life had been recently; how peaceful yet faint. Weber once sent a postcard saying, "Live every day as if your hair is on fire." For a long time, I thought I'd had enough of that fire, with all the years of California burning up my head. But now I knew by the excitement in my heart that the months in Vienna had been too much the other extreme; too quiet, removed, and monklike. The time had made me think *too* much about life and frankly scared me with the darkness that was there. Leland's arrival was the best deterrent to biting into myself with my own poisons.

I'd only just begun to cook when the doorbell rang. He stood there, holding a bouquet of flowers.

there? How'd the spiders manage to stretch their strings all the way from there to there without breaking them? How did the webs survive all this time without someone walking through them?"

I asked what he meant by that but he shrugged, got up, and said he had to go to the bathroom. He didn't come back for a long time and I got worried. I went to the doorway and called to see if he was all right. No answer. I walked to the bathroom and saw that the door was open and the light was off. Where was he? I scooted around the first floor of the house looking for him, sure he was collapsed on a floor or leaning against a wall with his eyes closed, barely able to stand. I scolded myself for not remembering that he was wounded and that talking had probably tired him out terribly. There was a decent hospital in Klosterneuburg and I could have him there in ten minutes if necessary. But where was he?

"Arlen?"

I stopped and realized that I was so worried, I hadn't noticed the front door was open.

"Leland? Are you out there?"

"Yes, come quick. Look what we found."

This is what I saw when I rushed out—but there's no way in the world I can ever do the picture justice with words. He was sitting on the front step with his back to the house. Exactly where I'd been that morning when he drove up. Minnie was against him with that wonderful full-bodied lean she uses when she loves someone and wants to be as close as she can possibly be. Just the two of them sitting out there on that stone step together, looking like drunken sailors, was enough to make me put a hand over my mouth and almost cry. Then I noticed she was craning her head up as far as it would go to see whatever it was Leland held in his cupped hands. The picture reminded me of a parent and child, or a teacher showing a student something interesting. I walked over and came up right behind him. Before I focused on his hands, Minnie looked at me not with her normal crazy excitement, but with calm love in those golden eyes.

There was a small gray-and-brown fur ball in Leland's

"I thought you were going to sleep!"

"I did a little, but it's too nice outside to sleep. May I take Minnie for a walk?"

I suggested he take her up to the vineyards and she'd show him her favorite path. I stood at the door and watched them head out. She ran a way, then turned to see if he was following. He ran after her a few steps and I worried that he might hurt his side. Oh, God, Rose, I was so happy watching them. So happy and excited!

The rest of the day was great too. The meal didn't turn out as well as I'd hoped, but he devoured it and complimented every dish. The conversation filled me much more than the meal did. You think you've led a zippy life till you meet someone like Leland; after hearing *his* life story, you feel as if you've spent all your days in a mouse hole.

He dropped out of college at nineteen when he realized the only thing he wanted to do was take pictures. Went to New York and worked as an assistant to Ovo, the fashion photographer, but the glitzy scene disgusted him. He quit and went on vacation to what was then Rhodesia. Their revolution began about five minutes after he arrived, so he was stuck in the country with little to do but take photographs of what was going on. That's how he got started in photo journalism, and since then, it sounds as if he's been in every ugly and dangerous place on earth. I asked if he was ever scared. He said all the time, but fear made the experiences richer and more satisfying. For fun, I started naming odd places, and he'd either been to most of them, or his plane had touched down in their airport on the way to somewhere even closer to the end of the world. He rode in a camel caravan with Mauretanian slave traders, saw a ghost hovering outside a Buddhist monastery in Nepal, was in Beijing when the Chinese army cracked down on the students. Stories on top of stories. He's been in remote jungles and seen animals named the bongo and the armor-plated pangolin . . .

What do you ask someone who's done all this? I wanted to know if he'd come to any conclusions. He said, "You know those strange spiderwebs you run into when you're walking down a major street sometimes? What are they doing hands and I was about to say something when it slowly un-coiled from its protective tuck and stuck a tiny, shiny black nose off the edge of his fingers. Kilroy was here. That time I couldn't stop an *oh!* from jumping out of my throat. It was an igel, Austria's version of a hedgehog. It's the cutest animal in the world, and sometimes at night, if you're lucky, you see one tiptoeing slowly across the ground, stopping here and there to look around and sniff. Minnie isn't interested; if she does come across one, she'll nose it and move on. But when you touch one, it normally tucks itself into a tight ball like a porcupine and stays there till the danger has passed. Here was my dog looking at the adorable thing as if it were a friend. And the igel was unafraid enough to come unwound and snoop around in Leland's hand.

I asked where he found it and he said it'd been on the step when he came out. I was amazed—who was this guy? Robert Capa, Indiana Jones, *and* Saint Francis of Assisi? He asked what the creature was called, and I told him and said I'd always wanted one for a pet. Did I want that one, he asked, but I said no; I just liked the picture of the three of them together. He turned around with a beautiful smile, then put the igel down on the ground. The little thing just waddled off in no big hurry. Minnie didn't move, but looked back at me as if to say, "See? Did you see that?" I asked Leland how he felt and he said fine. He put a hand on Minnie's head and she leaned into him even more. The sound of a plane swept over us, and a few seconds later its flashing lights and dark shape moved across the sky. Leland took his hand off the dog's head and reached up. He pretended to grab the fist-sized plane and bring it down slowly. Then he opened his hand to me and said, "It's for you."

Wyatt

My second day in Vienna I raised the dead.

Jet lag set in right after Sophie, Caitlin, and I had dinner at a restaurant near our hotel. One minute I felt fine; the next, I was so exhausted that I didn't know if I'd have the energy to get up from the table and stagger back to the room. I did, but once there I simply dropped my clothes on the floor and fell into bed.

At six-thirty the next morning I was wide awake and on the phone to Jesse Chapman, telling him to come get me in his car because we had to go someplace right away. He didn't sound surprised. The only thing he asked was if it had to do with what we'd discussed the day before. Yes, it did. Come get me.

I was standing in front of the hotel when he pulled up half an hour later.

"Hi, Wyatt. What's up?" There was an eagerness on his face and in his voice that hadn't been there the day before.

"Do you know where the Friedhof der Namenlosen is?"

"Cemetery of the Nameless? No."

"Do you have a map of the city?"

"Yes, in the glove compartment. What is the place?"

"I don't know. I've never been to Vienna before, remember? I just know we have to go there now. Is it this one?"

He looked at me a long second, then nodded. "What's going on?"

Without knowing anything about the city or this place we had to visit, I looked at the map for no more than a few seconds before finding the cemetery. "Here it is. I don't *know* what's going on. Do you know how to get here?" I pointed. He took the map and looked at it for a moment.

"It's out by the airport. Yes, I can find it."

There was a great deal of traffic, so it took us half an hour to get there. The only time he spoke was to point out certain famous sites—the Hofburg, the Prater, a building where Freud had lived early in his career. It was a clean, orderly city that didn't strike me as very interesting. There were other places I would much rather have visited before I died. I'd always wanted to go to Bruges; always wanted to see that spectacular view of the sea from Santorini.

We rode for a while beside the Danube Canal. The water was brown and slow. There were no boats on it, not one, which I thought strange. Fishermen stood on the bank with their shirts off; bike riders pedaled by. A high summer day in Vienna. Jesse said they were in the middle of a drought—every day at least ninety degrees and no sign of rain. Trees drooped and the grass near the water was spotted with brown. A news broadcast in English came on the car radio and the commentator went into long details about the terrible war in Yugoslavia. Thousands dead, concentration camps; no one had any idea of how to make peace.

Jesse switched off the radio as soon as the report was finished. "Can you tell me anything about this, or do I have to wait till we get there?"

I ignored his question and kept looking out the window. How could I explain? I hardly understood it myself. I did *not* understand it.

We were on an autobahn a few minutes, then off and winding over back roads that bordered a giant oil refinery and gray block housing. More back roads. Billboards advertised familiar things in an unfamiliar language. Orange soda lived here, as did panty hose and Bic pens. I wanted to be home, seeing these products advertised in my language. I wanted to be home. Warehouses with trailer trucks parked in front with bold Cyrillic writing on their sides. Russian and Bulgarian license plates.

I said, "This really *is* the East, isn't it?"

We slowed, bumped across railroad tracks, and stopped. He took the map from me and checked where we were. "We should be almost there. It must be just up the way a little."

We drove a bit farther and then I knew before he did that we had arrived. "Here, stop the car on the other side of the circle. It's up that hill."

He parked and we got out. On our left was a high warehouse with many broken windows and giant cranes in front that leaned out over a spur of the canal. The top of a black barge peeked over the edge of the pavement.

"There. Go up those stairs."

He didn't move. "How do you know, Wyatt?"

"Austria's a Catholic country. If you're Catholic and kill yourself, church law prohibits your being buried in consecrated ground. City officials put this cemetery here for two reasons. They needed somewhere to bury their suicides, and when they were building the canal, many of the workers drowned or were killed on the site and they needed a nearby place to put them."

Instead of asking how I knew these facts, he started up the narrow staircase. At the top was a strange building that looked like a stone beehive. It was the chapel for the burial ground. The light switch was on the outside wall. When you pressed it, you could see behind an ornate locked gate a small but gaudy altar loaded with fresh flowers and one lit candle. Whose job was it to come out here first thing every morning to check on the candle and light it?

Down another short set of steps to a waist-high cement wall with FRIEDHOF DER NAMENLOSEN in thick block letters. On the other side of the wall were perhaps a hundred graves. Almost all had identical black metal crosses at the head of the humps of earth. At the bottom of each cross was a square that looked like a small chalkboard for something to be written, but only a handful had names and dates recorded in white script. The rest were blank. Nevertheless, there were a surprisingly large number of flowers and wreaths on these graves. It touched me to think that people came out here to pay tribute to the anonymous dead. What inspired them to do that? Someone kept the candle burning in the chapel; someone brought fresh bouquets of flowers. Was it someone's job? Did the city of Vienna pay salaried homage to a few dead no one knew or cared about? Or was it simply the kindness and respect of some good souls? I hoped it was that. A sudden rage in my chest hoped it was that. Here and there stood a few regular stones with names and dates and the causes of death. But they were rare and looked out of place among all the other black crosses.

I walked to one anonymous grave and, putting a hand on the marker, looked at Jesse. "This was a man. His name was Thomas Widhalm. Committed suicide in 1929 by jumping into the Danube. His body washed up, as did a lot of the others, right over there on that hook of land that divides the canal from the river. He was from the town of Oggau but came to Vienna to study medicine. The great pride of his family. But he was gay, which nobody knew of course, and when he found out he had gotten syphilis from sleeping with a fellow student, he killed himself. After the family hadn't heard from him for two months, they sent his younger brother Friedrich to Vienna to find him. But Friedrich hated Thomas, and after a week of halfhearted searching, he went home and told their mother her favorite boy had run off to

Germany. At the end of the war, Friedrich was killed by the Russians when they invaded Austria. They shot him when he tried to keep them from a cache of Nazi bicycles."

A couple of feet over, I touched the top of the next anonymous cross. "Margarete Ruzicka. She came from Czechoslovakia. From Bohemia." I closed my eyes and thought a minute until I saw her face clearly and knew everything about her. It was like driving through thick fog into clearness. One moment nothing; the next, a view that went on for miles. She had been hired by a wealthy Viennese family with a villa in Hietzing and a summer residence in Meran to take care of twin baby boys. I saw her packing her cheap suitcase, saying goodbye to her family, riding the train to Vienna with her head pressed to the cold glass window. Trying to see everything at once. She said to herself a hundred times, "I'm going to Vienna; I have a job in Vienna." Then her shy dip of the head and curtsey when she was introduced to the master of the house. Her terrible claustrophobia that first week away from home. In her tiny room at night she tried to read the Bible but had no heart for it; she tried chanting "Vienna" to herself as she had on the train, but nothing helped.

Things slowly got better for her, but what she *didn't* understand, because she was naïve and silly, was why the master, who smelled of würst and '4711' cologne, was around too much of the time, watching her, watching her constantly. Then that night in spring when he came to her room and took her for the first time. She thought, There is nothing I can do now. Nothing I can do about this. I'm not pretty; why does he want me? For the first time in her life she began looking in mirrors whenever she got the chance. Rape had made her vain. He ignored her after that, stopped looking at her altogether, except when he took her. His breath was always bad, his skin always cool. She would look at him, thinking all the time, What will I do if he tells? What will I do if he tells my mother? And then her period didn't come and another maid who was kind and jealous told her she must run. So she left the house and disappeared into the city.

One afternoon a customer wouldn't pay her for the ten minutes of sex he'd just had, and when she complained, he slit her throat as neatly as if he were opening a letter.

"How do you know?"

I blinked and realized my mouth was open. I closed it and looked down at her grave. "Because I had one of your dreams last night. I dreamed I met Philip Strayhorn. Do you know who he was?"

"No."

"He was a well-known actor who killed himself a while ago. We were lovers once for a short time, but that wasn't what we were about. He was my friend and I admired him."

"Can you tell me what happened?"

"Come on. Let's go sit on the wall there. I could tell you the names and histories of every person in here. All their hopes and hatreds; the secrets they thought were so important but weren't . . . Not that it matters. Did your person glow?"

We were up on the wall and he turned to me, confused. "Glow? What do you mean?"

"The dead person you talked to in your dream. Who was it?"

"A kid I knew in school. What do you mean, glow?" His voice was testy and suspicious.

"Strayhorn glowed. Not like a lamp, but there was a definite . . . illumination to him. His whole body.

"I dreamed I was sitting in a steak house I like in New York. Gallagher's. I was looking at the menu and Phil came in as if we had a date for dinner. We shook hands, and he sat down and asked what was good here. It was all very calm and comfortable."

"Were you surprised?"

"No. I understood immediately why he was there and what was about to happen, but it didn't bother me. We both ordered sirloins and mashed potatoes. Dinner with a dead man."

"What did he say?"

"He asked if I had any questions. I asked why he glowed. He explained it to me and I understood."

"*What?*" Jesse's eyes widened, and, sitting up straight, he pushed himself forward with his hands. "You understood? What did he say?"

"I can't tell you. You know that. But I *did* understand."

"I can tell you anything I heard, Wyatt. I can tell you anything you want to know about my dreams. Ask whatever you want."

"*I* can't. My situation is different from yours."

"Why? Well, what the hell *can* you tell me? Did you learn anything that'll help us?"

"Yes. I understood every answer he gave to my questions."

"No!"

"Every one. But I was careful. Most of the time we just chatted. I'd ask him something only if I thought I could understand the answer, and it worked."

"Was he surprised?"

"No, he seemed pleased, even congratulated me once."

"What can it do for us?"

"It means that for the time being you and McGann will be all right. Nothing more will happen and you will not dream again. Strayhorn specifically said that—you two are okay as long as I continue to understand his answers."

"Then McGann was right: you *are* the one who can save us."

"Save? I don't know. At least for now. But who knows what will happen next? It reminds me of the Arabian Nights. But instead of having to tell good stories night after night to keep from being killed, I have to understand a dead man's answers. So far, so good after one night. What'll happen in the long run? Anyone's guess."

"But you're sure for now that McGann and I will be okay?"

"*You* will, yes. I don't know about me. He didn't say anything about that. Plus, I didn't ask to be saved—I asked for knowledge. He asked whether I'd rather survive or *know?* I said, 'Won't I be able to protect myself better if I know some things?' He nodded and, well, that's when he congratulated me."

"I don't understand this. What do you mean, know or be saved? What is there to know? You mean the big questions? That's stupid! You'll get all those answers when you die, if there's anything *to* know! What's more important for any of us now than surviving?"

"When I knew I was terminal, I told Sophie the only thing I wanted before I died, if it were somehow possible, was to meet Death and ask Him questions. Phil did that for me. I don't know if he *is* Death, but he's close enough. He obviously speaks for his Boss." I smiled while Jesse shook his head disgustedly and mimicked the word *boss*.

"But what does it do for you, Wyatt? Give you the ability to recognize bodies in a graveyard? So what? Does that give you new insight into the way God works? Huh? Is that helpful?"

"It might save your life for now."

He put a hand on my shoulder. "I know that. Please know I'm grateful. But I'm thinking of you now. I don't want anything to happen to you."

"Thank you, but it already has—I've been dying for a while. That's a big difference between us."

"He can stop it!"

I shook my head. "Maybe, but you've got to realize that there's another big difference. You and McGann both have partners who love you very much. You also have Sophie. I don't. I'm alone and have been dying alone a long time. I don't love anyone the way you love your wife. I wish I did. That's the heart of the matter. Since there's no one to love, I've got to love myself the best way I know how.

"Listen, when my father died a few years ago he went out in the worst possible way. No heroics, no last-minute grace. Just pain and suffering all the way down to the end. Worst of all, he made those of us who loved him suffer too.

"One day toward the end, when he was still coherent, I sat with him and said, 'Dad, even with the agony, you're still much luckier than most people. Mom and I are here and we love you, there's enough money in the bank to pay for your care, and you've lived a wonderfully long and full life.' I know it's easy to say those things when you're not in another person's skin, but it was the truth. I really believed that if he could somehow turn his mind's eye toward that truth, it would be easier for him to let go. You know what he said? 'Wait'll you're where I am, buddy boy; then let's hear you talk about a good life.'

"Well, here I am, Pop, right behind you on the oblivion express. On my way to knowing *exactly* what it's like to be there. But you know what? My opinion hasn't changed, and I'm dying a lot younger than my father. He had a great life, so he felt cheated by what was happening to him at the end. How dare things go bad! They had a deal: he'd live, and life would be good to him. How dare his health fail and all those strengths and fail-safe systems stop? He'd always ignored final things because he had no use for them, and when they started arriving, he only knew how to be bitter and confused. Not me. Not if I can help it.

"If you have someone loving you, then it's different. That gives you all sorts of real reasons to go on living, but I don't. I *don't* want to die, but when Strayhorn offered the choice between possible understanding and survival, I thought, What's surviving if you don't understand anything? Better to know something about it. Isn't that what religion teaches? Christ was at peace and so were Muhammed and Buddha, the saints . . . That peace can come only from understanding, not from living another ten years. If I can learn something from these dreams, then I'll be all right, no matter what happens. Maybe it would be different if I had a great love like you, but I don't. Whether it's now or later, I would love to learn enough so that when I saw Death coming, my only reaction would be to say, 'Okay.' "

"No one does that! Forget the saints. No one ever reaches that kind of final peace. It's not peace when people give up because their bodies are exhausted and anything has to be better than all that fucking pain and fear!"

"A week ago I would have agreed with you, Jesse, but today I'm not so sure."

"But you can't trust these dreams!"

"Why not?"

"Because it's Death talking. Death's the *enemy*, Wyatt.

Why should He make deals, give you a peek into the cosmic consciousness, when He holds all the cards? You *can't* trust Him."

"I agree, but maybe I can find enough so that I only have to trust myself, and that'll be plenty."

There are times, maybe once a month, when my mind goes absolutely blank. For several seconds I truly do not know who I am, where I am—anything. When I was younger, these forced visits to the outer limits scared me, because I thought I was going mad. But over the years I've learned almost to enjoy them. Before, when the spells came, I would become petrified and think as hard as I could: Who am I? What's happening? Find the thread, damn it, find the thread! Now that I'm older I know my mind is only taking its foot off the gas and coasting. It'll start again in a minute, so I don't worry.

The first time I saw Emmy Marhoun in Vienna, I had just emerged from one of these lapses and my head was readjusting to the world. Jesse and I had left the cemetery after arguing some more about what to do with the powers my dreams gave me. I had no idea what else I was capable of now, but we both stuck to our beliefs, and the discussion degenerated into his anger and my stubbornness. We drove back to the city, with him doing most of the muttering. Back at the hotel, I didn't want to see Sophie yet and have to explain where we'd been, so I waited till Jesse pulled away and then I went for a walk.

There was a small pastry shop across the street from the Opera House and the aroma drifting out of it was so delicious that I went right in. The place was jammed but luckily one small table in a corner was free. I ordered my cake and coffee and sat down, feeling happy for the first time that day. No desire to think about anything. I wanted only to be in that hot little shop full of ambrosial smells, surrounded by chattering old women, and eat an *echt* piece of Viennese torte. Afterward I'd . . . I know someone who signs all his letters *After Words*. That's exactly how it would be now. I was past words and wanted to let my tongue and senses have rein for a little while.

As if in agreement, my mind went into a full-fledged zone-out and I was suddenly nowhere in particular. It lasted long enough for the waitress to bring my order. Coming back to earth, I blinked a few times at the black cake on the table. Then while my head continued to clear, I looked at the people standing at the counter. Up there waiting for an order was Emmy Marhoun.

But that was impossible. Emmy Marhoun had been dead for at least three years. I knew her when she worked as an editor at a New York publishing house. My television show was at the height of its popularity then, and we met when she wrote to ask if I'd be interested in doing a book for her company. We had dinner a few times and I liked her. She was smart, witty, and the kind of aggressive, enterprising woman who usually gets what she wants. It didn't hurt that she was also quite beautiful. If I were straight, I'd probably have fallen in love with her. As it was, I did fall in love to a certain harmless degree, and that was why we continued seeing each other after I said no to the project.

One day someone told me she had died. Fallen off a horse and been kicked in the head. There are many strange ways to die. As we grow older we become accustomed to bizarre accounts of how So-and-So went. Still, there are times when you hear something like Emmy's story and your only reaction is "What do you mean, kicked by a horse?" I didn't mourn because we hadn't been close, and it was a long time since we'd seen each other. But I had loved her a little, and it was surprising how much I thought about her after hearing the news.

Today she stood ten feet away and even touched her hair in that showy pat-pat way I remembered. I got up and went over, but she didn't see me until the last moment. Then she turned away from the counter, and we were face to face.

"Emmy?"

Her eyes narrowed suspiciously, then widened. "Oh, my God, Wyatt Leonard! What are *you* doing here?" She brought her hands together in front of her face and clapped them quickly like a delighted little kid. I had to touch her to see if she was real. I did. She was.

"Do you have some time?"

"Of course! It's so good to see you! Where have you been? It's been so many years!"

While we were sitting down at the table, my shock left, and one word came to mind that explained everything: *Strayhorn*. Last night's dream. Knowing the names in the graveyard had been Part One of whatever was going on. This was Part Two. Everything was happening at once. Dinner in a dream with a dead man; breakfast in real life with a dead woman.

I was astonished, but I knew since last night's dream that my life had shifted into high gear, at which any speed or event was possible. Now it was up to me to handle it. So instead of running away or going mad because I was sitting down to coffee with a dead friend, I spoke as normally as I could and did okay. Now and then I caught myself hyperventilating or wetting my lips for the hundredth time, but generally I was all right.

The greatest horror was that she didn't know. The woman did not know she was dead. We talked like old pals catching up. About mutual friends, evenings shared, what we'd been doing since we last met. She filled me in on everything but what was most important.

How then did I know for certain that she was dead? Because I had read accounts in different newspapers of her accident. Because I'd actually heard the funeral described by two people who were there and saw her body in the open casket. What other proof was there? The most important of all: she glowed, exactly like Philip Strayhorn. Was I the only one who saw or noticed it? I don't know. Certainly no one in the café seemed to take any special notice, except for one young man who couldn't take his eyes off her and was clearly smitten. I wanted to go over to him and ask, "Do you see it coming off her skin? That faint blue? The slight shimmer like a road mirage in summer?" But he wouldn't have seen it. These things were only mine today because of the Strayhorn dream and because I was dying.

While working for the publisher in New York, Emmy had met a man and fallen deeply in love. He was the most extraordinary person she had ever known and she was convinced he was the one for her. She lived on the top floor of joy for a few exquisite months. Then this special man told her she bored him and he was leaving. I admired her for admitting that; it would have been easy to say only that they broke up, and left it at that, but she didn't. "He said I bored him and told me exactly why. You know what the most painful part was? He was right. I *was* a bore."

What followed was a wretched series of exaggerated, supercharged affairs with men she initially welcomed but quickly grew to despise. She slept with them to try to find some kind of replacement for the one she could never replace. She was destroyed and knew it, but because she was beautiful there were always men around who were eager to try, and she let them. She let too many of them try, and their touching enthusiasm and desire only made things worse. She felt that she was suffocating inside her own life; as if it were one of those plastic bags dry cleaners put over clothes. When she breathed, she inhaled herself and her failure. There was no more air.

"It was becoming all bad, Wyatt, so I decided to cut everything loose and travel a while. That's when I came to Europe."

"How long ago was that?"

"I'm embarrassed to say. Almost three years ago."

I needed a moment to let my heart slow before I asked the next question. "Emmy, what was the last thing you remember doing in America before coming over here? The very last thing."

"I remember very well. I went horseback riding with my brother Bill. Why do you ask?"

Smiling, I tried to think of something logical to explain the question but couldn't think of anything. Luckily she made a little face of dismissal and sipped her tea. "Not that it's been much better here. I just don't have any urge to go back to America. Does that make me an expatriate? I need to be something these days."

"What have you been doing since you got over here?"

"I take a job when I have to. Nothing spectacular. You glide over the days and from city to city and nothing much happens, but you're basically all right. You live in this strange state of *okay* most of the time. You get by. There aren't a lot of highs or lows. Nothing really memorable or perfect ever happens, but nothing bad either. Livable. Halfway between blah and hooray."

"Are you with anyone?"

"No, not for a long time. That's what I mean—I'm not closed off to men, but I haven't met one I want to be with. It's all right, though; I'm content being alone."

"And you live in Vienna? What do you do here?"

For an instant, half a second, it was plain she didn't know. Her face went blank. She didn't know because there was nothing but memories and vague shadows left.

"Um, I've been working as a secretary at the American embassy. It pays the bills."

I have never read Dante's *Inferno* but vividly remember looking through an illustrated copy and seeing a picture of two people floating in the air, reaching out desperately to touch each other. As I remember, their sin had been that they were illicit lovers in life and were now condemned to this situation in Hell—close enough to see, smell, hear the other, but never for eternity allowed to join again.

Emmy Marhoun was in exactly the same place. For whatever reasons, in death she was damned to existing so close to life that she thought she still was alive. Never again allowed to touch the fullness and pulse, the body of real life, she nevertheless recognized and remembered it completely. Hell for her was walking around in life almost alive but not knowing the difference anymore.

Is that what Death would be, not knowing? Strayhorn had said nothing about that, but Jesse insisted Death wasn't to be trusted. My mind was exhausted, overflowing. I could no longer sort or decipher, and it wasn't even noon yet. I had raised the dead and met the dead and had hundreds of new questions, but now I had no more energy and felt close to collapse.

As calmly as I could, I told Emmy I had to go. I asked her to call me at the hotel so that we could meet again while I was in town. She said I looked washed-out and should take it easy. I paid the bill and we left together. On the sidewalk we kissed, and her cheek on that summer day was neither warm nor cold.

Luckily there was a taxi stand nearby and I was home in a few minutes. When I asked for the key to my room, the concièrge handed me several messages, which I ignored. It was time to rest, and if that meant seeing Philip Strayhorn again, fine. But at the moment sleep was more important than answered questions.

I am running across a bridge. I know this bridge but cannot remember why. It's very long—goes straight into the horizon. I know I'll never be safe unless I get to the other side. But the wolf is very fast and is catching up. This wolf which comes after me so many nights. It does not have eyes but, rather, two large X's where eyes should be, like the ones you make in a tic-tac-toe game. It's mouth is gigantic, full of white pointy teeth, a rubbery red tongue that goes up and down and around its lips in circles. When not drooling, the wolf grunts and growls or laughs like a hyena, because it's getting closer and closer. When it catches me it'll kill and eat me. It's wearing orange overalls that are buttoned across one furry shoulder; the other flap is broken and jumps wildly as the wolf comes full killer-speed at me. He also wears a black stovepipe hat that slides back and forth across his head as he runs. Behind me are big brown puffs of dirt to show how fast I'm going. Both of us make the sounds in a cartoon—screeching, bells clanging, brakes screaming—but none of this is cartoon for me. It's real and terrifying, my world when I was seven years old, scared awake night after night by the same dream: the wolf chasing me across the endless bridge, me always knowing I'd be caught. The moment that happened, he would whip out a cannibal's pot and logs from some deep pocket, start up a snarling fire, and throw me into the pot, now magically filled with water. I usually awoke, petrified, just as the final water started to burn me. I can't begin to express how frightening it was even though I knew the dream by heart, having had it over and over again.

I awoke this time too, engulfed again by the identical terror in head and heart I'd known as a boy. The churning gut, my fingers clawing, my tongue too enormous in my mouth. Exactly the same. A middle-aged man knowing seven again as it truly was.

"It's not the way you remembered, is it?"

I turned my head and saw Philip Strayhorn sitting on the corner of the bed. It took time to regain my senses, but he seemed content to sit and wait. I looked blankly around the room and finally realized where I was—the hotel room in Vienna.

"It was so clear! I remember the dream. I've always remembered it, but never this vividly. It's frightening!"

"No one remembers what childhood was really like. They only think they do."

"Phil, what are you doing?" I sat up, leaning back on my elbows. "Is it allowed? Can you be here like this?"

"Don't worry, this is still part of your dream. But, yes, I can go over to the real world if I like. It's no big deal. No one sees me there but the dead, and you."

I fell back onto the bed. "I can't get over that dream. How incredibly strong! I don't remember its being anything like that. Not that intense. Were things really so frightening when we were kids? How did I survive night after night?"

"You didn't—the kid died and became an adult. Life isn't learning; it's forgetting. That dream's just a small example. You needed to know that."

"Speaking of forgetting, will you tell me about Emmy Marhoun?"

He wrapped his hands around a knee and cleared his throat. "Is that a formal question, Wyatt? You know the rules."

"Yes."

I went everywhere and saw astounding things, always accompanied by Strayhorn. He was my guide and instructor. I thought I understood his answers. He always appeared pleased with me and, as reward for my understanding, gave me more and more insight, perception, powers. He called them "gifts." For a while I felt like a prodigy and was supremely hopeful. Why did other people have such a hard time understanding Death's answers? To me they seemed logical and down to earth. I could not talk to Jesse Chapman or Ian McGann about what I was learning, but I secretly began to feel that perhaps they were both dense.

My health stabilized, and so did theirs. With Strayhorn I visited wars and weddings; I walked through people's minds as if they were museums. I walked through my own, alternately aghast and delighted. Did I live here? Is this how it really was?

Besides being shown sides of life I knew few had ever seen or experienced, I was given more and more information as well as answers to my questions. I understood and ingested as much as I could, but taking it all in was impossible. There was too damned much.

Outwardly, I made it look to Sophie and Caitlin Chapman as if I'd grown keen on Europe and, because I was feeling so much better, wanted to stay a while before returning to America. Jesse was reassured to hear I'd be around and found me a good, reasonably priced *pension*. He was also heartened to hear that Strayhorn said it would be all right for him to return to his job.

One night Sophie and I went out to dinner alone. Afterward we walked to the Volksgarten and sat in the warm dark. We talked a long time. She asked me to fill her in on what had really been going on since we'd arrived. I said as much as I could, but after a while she knew I was holding important things back. Her silences became longer and longer. "Sophie, don't be mad at me. You've got to understand—this stuff is so far beyond me and I'm terrified of saying the wrong thing or taking one wrong step. You know me; I'd tell you everything if I could, but I can't."

"Is it good or bad that I got you involved in it, Wyatt? I worry about that all the time." She put her head way back and closed her eyes.

"I honestly don't know. I *think* it's good, but when I was first sick and had a remission after the early chemotherapy, I thought I was going to get well then and didn't."

" 'How Much Can a Rabbit Pull?' " She brought her head slowly down and looked at me gravely.

"What are you talking about?"

"My friend's daughter is in fifth grade and had to do a science project. She made a kind of little wagon that fit onto the back of her pet rabbit, and kept putting more and more stones into it and giving the rabbit a pinch to see how much it could pull. That was her project. Now it's yours. How much can Wyatt pull? I don't know what I've done to you or whether I did anything at all. My brother's back and is all right, but you're staying here because now *you're* having the dreams. God, I wish we were back in Switzerland together. I want to be on that hill we climbed, watching those skiers fly by." She sighed and took my hand. "I love you, Wyatt. I want you to live a hundred years."

In life, Strayhorn had been the most well-informed person I'd ever known. In death he continued to be, but now he was also terrific company. Brilliant yet easygoing, he was happy to talk about anything. My general impression was that he most liked just hanging around and chatting. I didn't know what was going to happen to me, but his calmness seemed proportionate to my understanding the answers. So long as that continued, both of us could take it easy for the time being.

I couldn't have been more wrong.

His casualness threw me off and lulled me into thinking things were somehow going to work out. His friendship, gifts, and frequent wonders sometimes let me not see the real circumstances of my life in the gloss and glare of all I was

experiencing. His cosmic show-and-tell stopped me from remembering what was important or being vigilant about essential matters. He seduced me with charm, and like the most
innocent, greedy child, I fell for it one hundred percent.

Until I learned Ian McGann was dead.

I had spent the night on Santorini, or rather my dreaming
self had. At sunset Phil and I sat at an outdoor restaurant,
drinking ouzo and eating freshly fried calamari, entertained
by a staggeringly beautiful view over the purpling sea. The
view was as rewarding as I had always imagined. My friend
spoke of the volcano that had exploded here long ago, what it
had done to the people, and how it had affected the way of
the world for centuries afterward. My dreams were now so
all-encompassing that I could smell the spicy evening air and
feel rough pebbles under my bare feet. Strayhorn seemed as
content as I to sit there silently and listen to the only sounds
around us—the clank of silverware on plates, the sad faraway
call of a single gull out over the water.

As we were finishing, our waiter came up and spoke
quietly to Strayhorn. I thought he was asking who should be
given the bill, but Phil said nothing, just nodded once, and
the waiter walked away.

"I have to do something. Stay here as long as you like.
You know how to get back." He winked at me and walked
up the steps out of the restaurant. I tipped my glass to him
and called out a lazy goodbye.

I don't know how much longer I was there, but the
sound of the ringing phone woke me. Opening my eyes to a
pitch-black room, I looked at the green glow of my watch
and slowly understood it was three A.M. Jesse Chapman was
calling, his voice very high and fast with fear. Ian McGann
had died half an hour before. His girlfriend, Miep, had gone
to the bathroom. When she got back into bed, she leaned
over to kiss him. His arm was thrown across his forehead; his
eyes were open, staring at nothing. At first she thought he
was joking. Before notifying the police, she called Jesse. She
didn't want to talk about it, only wanted him to know. When
he asked what she was going to do, she said she'd lie in bed
with Ian and tell him goodbye. Then she hung up.

Jesse was calling from his living room, his hand cupped above his mouth so that he wouldn't wake his wife. He said, three times, "You said it was all right! You said he told you everything was okay for us!"

"What difference does it make what he said? All bets are off now. You were the one who told me not to trust him in the first place, Jesse! Why are you surprised?"

"I'm not surprised. I just don't want to die, asshole!"

"Asshole doesn't want to die either."

"Then what are we going to do? Can you find Strayhorn? Talk to him?"

"I think so. No. I don't know. This may change everything. Why did he do it? What was the point?"

"*Point?* For God's sake, he doesn't have a fucking point, Wyatt. He's Death! Death comes and kills you. Period. I told you that."

In the background I heard a woman's voice. Jesse's dropped to tenderness as he told his wife not to worry, everything was okay. I waited while they spoke, then he said he'd have to call me back and abruptly hung up. I put down the phone and lay down. Closing my eyes, I fell instantly asleep.

Immediately I recognized where I was, though I'd not been in the room for almost thirty years. It was the basement of my hometown church where, at Mother's insistence, I had spent years going to Sunday school. I was sitting at that familiar little round table along with the other kids who had been in my classes there. However, the teacher was not bad-tempered Mr. Crown or nice Miss Turton; it was Woody Woodpecker.

In that famously crazy high-pitched voice, he said to me, " 'I desire to be present with you now, and to change my voice; for I stand in doubt of you.

'Tell me, ye that desire to be under the law, do ye not hear the law?' "

I said nothing, though I remembered the words exactly. Galatians 4: 20 and 21. I had been made to memorize them for this class, though the teacher at that time was Miss

Turton, not a cartoon bird. He gave that annoying laugh again and continued.

"'I am the light that shines over everything. I am the All. From me the All came forth, and to me the All has returned.' Finish the passage please, Wyatt Leonard." His voice changed to a perfect imitation of Miss Turton's.

Without a moment's hesitation I said, "'Split a piece of wood, and I am there. Pick up a stone, and you will find me there.'"

"Very good, Wyatt!"

"Why are you here like this?"

"I told you, 'I desire to be present with you now, and to change my voice—'"

"Phil, why did you kill McGann? You said it wouldn't happen as long as I understood your answers!"

"Don't be naïve, baby; I have a job to do. Sometimes I can put it off for a while, and that's what I did with him. He got to live a little longer and had a lot of joy. That's good, isn't it? Would you rather he be hit by a truck? The man was supposed to die a long time ago, but I let him see Venice with the woman he loved. It was the best time of his life. He even died with a hard-on!" Winking at me, he pushed back from the table and ran a hand over the bright red comb on his head.

"Phil, tell me what's going on. How does this thing really work?"

"Formal question?"

"Yes, damn it, just answer!"

"All right. It's simple—I have a job and have to do it to everyone sooner or later. It's my decision how. Naturally, I like some of the people; others I don't. The ones I like, I try to do it to as easily and comfortably as possible: let them die in their sleep at eighty, or have a stroke on the tennis court so they're dead before they know what hits them. That sort of thing. The people I don't like, suffer. Too bad for them.

"I like you. I liked McGann because the man showed real courage. Even Jesse's okay when he's not being a pompous ass. He'll be all right for a while longer."

"You said that before, but now McGann's dead!"

"But weren't you all happier with that lie? Are you sure you really want the truth? I doubt it."

"That's all? It only comes down to that? Children fall out windows or starve in Somalia only because you don't *like* them? I don't believe it! What have they ever done? They didn't get a chance to live! How can you do that to kids?"

"Because I do. It's not hard."

"And good people die in misery and pain and confusion because you don't *like* them? What about all the good they do in their lives?"

"You and I have different reasons for liking and disliking people, Wyatt. And be careful of the tone of your voice; I don't like being lectured."

"Who are you? You look like Strayhorn just because it's easier for me to understand, right?"

"Right! In my time I've been . . . let's see"—crossing his arms, he tapped a finger against his beak and looked thoughtfully at the ceiling—"Humbaba, Grendel, Old Toast, Cold Storage, the Cop in the mask store . . . whatever you want. Whatever you understand."

"Are you the Devil?"

"Nope. He doesn't exist. Just Life and Death. It's so simple, no one's ever wanted to believe it."

"But there's a God! Don't say there isn't!"

He started to speak but stopped and smiled instead. "That's one answer I guarantee you wouldn't understand, so I'll spare you a scar. Believe what you want."

I love doing this taping, Rose. *I hope it's not boring you.* I'd give so much to be able to tell you these things face to face, but since there's no way that's possible now, this is a pretty good second best.

So I spent the next three days taking care of Leland—or as much as he would allow it—and showing him the Vienna I love. Unlike Paris or Venice, this is not a city for lovers. It's too sedate, too formal; it has *no* passion or spontaneity. None whatsoever. To me its greatness is its dignity and beauty. Like an illustrious old statesman who's lived a long and worth-while life, its history is its identity. Like the old gent, it sits in its perfectly tended gardens, content to live in memories for the rest of its days.

We went to museums and some touristy things, but spent most of our time taking long walks on the Ringstrasse and Prater Allee or deep in the Wienerwald. I was amazed at how much Leland knew about Vienna—a hell of a lot more than I do. At Freud's house he got into a long discussion with one of the curators about Anna Freud and Ernest Jones. Then only a few blocks away from there he stopped and pointed to a church where Beethoven's funeral was held. Standing in front of the building, he described the funeral so fully that I was totally engrossed. It was like being with a Beethoven scholar and social historian in one. I don't know about you, girl, but to me one of the sexiest things in the world is a man who knows things but makes no big deal about it. Leland's knowledge always came out as sheer enthusiasm—wow! Look at that! Guess what happened here? Can you believe we're actually here to see it? I tagged along with my mouth open, feeling so lucky to be along for the ride.

Once in a while we'd stop because he was tired or un-comfortable, but even then it was a treat because he'd go on with stories about his life. I couldn't get enough of them. Did you know the Chinese eat more watermelon than any other nation? They love it so much they actually have a watermelon museum? Or that Ceausescu had a limousine only for his dog? I was completely captivated and didn't want the meals or the walks or the days to end.

And as you can guess, my feelings toward him got warmer and warmer. Even his nice plain face gradually started look-ing like Gary Cooper's. I wanted him and wanted to tell him that. No ties were necessary, no commitment—just I'd like this day to go on into the night and see what you're like there too. Because if it's *anything* like now, then I'm yours, brother. But he didn't make a move, not one, not even for a shivery second. Didn't accidentally touch my arm or brush my hand when he was making a point in conversation. God knows I wanted him to, and started feeling that maybe I had cooties or something, because there wasn't even the slightest any-thing to show interest on his part. No quick look at my chest, or bumps-into when there were plenty of good chances for them. I even tried bumping into *him* once when we were on an escalator, but when I moved, he moved faster. It got so frustrating that I even caught myself thinking, Hey, I'm Arlen Ford the glamorous movie star; don't I interest you at all? Or maybe he was gay? Uh-oh. That thought loomed gloomily over me for a whole day until he made some reference to a woman he'd had an affair with a year ago. Luckily he was looking away, because my face lit up like a sparkler when I heard that, and I almost started whistling. Since he'd put the subject on the table, I breezily asked if he was involved with anyone now. He said only that he was, but it was over.

We went to the casino on Kartnerstrasse and he won a thousand schillings. When we were walking down the street later, a really good South American band was playing. We stood and listened a while. Then Leland went over and put all of the money he'd won into the guitar case the players had open for donations. When the guys saw that, they started playing so fast that they sounded as if they'd overdosed on Dexedrine.

Wherever we went, he took pictures. Many of them were of Vienna, but most were of me. I didn't mind. This time he was my friend and I looked forward to seeing them when they were developed. When he was walking around, he carried two little cameras in his front pockets—one loaded with black-and-white film, the other with color.

After the casino we went to the Café Hawelka to watch the late night scene there. After we'd settled in with our coffee and cigarettes, he asked me why I had really stopped making movies and left L.A. He said he'd read the stories and interviews, but not many people just stop in the middle of their lives like that, especially when they're successful, and run away.

I said I'd quit for two reasons. The first was that I woke up one morning with a bad taste in my mouth and a bad guy in the bed next to me. If the acting had been going better, that would have been basically bearable: I'd have thought, Oh, this is just a rotten time and things'll get better. But the other reason for quitting blended in with that in the worst possible way. I've tried to describe this to you, Rose, but never had a good way of putting it till now. It came to me when I was talking with Leland.

I've finally realized I'm one of those people who peak early in life and then go down just as fast. Or part of us does.

You know how awful and confused and strung-out I was before I left? I believe it's because I unconsciously realized I no longer had the ability to be a good actress. I'd done all of my best work, and from there on out, if I had continued, it would have been impossible to do anything well.

Leland said he read a review of a famous dramatist's newest play. The critic said the play was terrible and what the writer should have done was stopped writing twenty years before—after having had a couple of flops—because by then he *must* have known somewhere in his soul that he no longer had the magic to do great work. If he'd stopped, then we'd know him for his masterpieces, and not the embarrassing shit that came afterward. He should have just stopped.

I said *exactly!* That's exactly what happened to me but I wouldn't admit it to myself. Down deep I knew I'd reached my peak and it was over. Maybe I had enough to . . . maybe I'd end up in some cheesy TV series making lots of Joan Collins faces and saying godawful lines. But I didn't want to end like that. The last film made me reach down too deep into myself to find a good performance . . . It was brutal, Rose, harder than anything I've done. Weber helped a lot with his direction, but every day after work I was totally exhausted, because I was squeezing out whatever last drops were still there. Talent drops. When the movie was finished, there wasn't one left in my tank. Like it or not, I was done as an actress. End of a career, crummy men, a house I never wanted to go home to because there was nothing there . . . That's why I came here. Because Vienna was one of the few things I really did love.

Right in the middle of that conversation, a hundred-megaton brunette swept up to our table as only an egregiously gorgeous woman can—head thrown back, tits pushed forward, a smile that says of course everyone in the room is watching me, but don't they always? I saw her before he did and watched as she tacked through the tightly bunched tables over to ours.

Her face got happier and happier the closer she came.
And it was real happiness—nothing fake or put-on about it.

"Leland!" she shouted. He looked at her, but instead of
being thrilled and leaping to his feet because Miss Lalapalooza
was trilling his name, he only smiled and stayed where he
was. He didn't even attempt to get out of his seat when she
was standing on the other side of the table, obviously dying to
get her mitts on him.

"Hi, Emmy. Emmy Marhoun, this is Arlen Ford." That
stopped her. She looked at me for really the first time and
there was a *glumph* of recognition in her eyes. Also, the cour-
teous coolness of Leland's voice said a lot. Her reaction was
very strange—she shrank down into herself. But she was val-
iant and tried again. "Oh, Leland, it's been so long! What
have you been doing?"

She wanted to talk but he didn't. He was very pleasant
and polite, but gave her nothing to grab on to. It was as if he
were a sheer mountain face of glass she desperately wanted to
climb but couldn't get a handhold on. When I realized what
was happening, I sat back to enjoy the show. Her eyes
jumped between Leland and me. After a few embarrassing
minutes of getting no further with him, she began speaking
directly to me, as if I would understand and be able to trans-
late her better to him. Fat chance, Emmy.

She was in Vienna on business. How long would he be
staying? Could they meet for a drink . . . it'd been such a
long time. It was so wonderful to see him again . . . but
nothing doing. The pleasanter he was, the more desperate she
became.

At last she understood this meeting was all she was going
to get, and even Miss Self-Adoring realized there was no way
she was going to get what she wanted from him. So she tried
to back away gracefully and wave beautifully and be gone in
another romantic *sssswi*rl. But there was a pathetic falseness
in her gestures and the kind of hurt in her voice and around
her eyes that said she'd been snapped in half.

I asked who she was, and he said a woman he was crazy

for a few years ago. He thought she loved him too but she didn't. Seems she had her own heartbeat to attend to. He said the ironic part was that a week after they broke up, he saved her life and she never forgave him for it, but he wouldn't explain that.

I shook my head and said, "You know, Leland, after hanging around with you these days, I'm beginning to feel that, in comparison to your life, I've lived mine on a microscope slide. What *haven't* you done?"

His answer came very quickly. "I've never had a child. Never written a book. Never really got lost in sex. I've never learned how to sit still. I'm scared I'll end up being one of those old men who'll need a garden or a dog to boss around because there'll be nothing else left at the end of my life.

"That's why I'm envious of you, Arlen, and the way you've chosen to live now. Your life used to be the way mine is now. All crazy running around, no real substance. But you stopped and got out. You've got so many things, qualities, I wish I had."

I couldn't believe he was saying that after I told him what a screwed-up mess I was. I don't know what I'm doing with my life these days. It's like an instrument I used to play pretty well but don't know how to even *hold* anymore, much less play.

He said, "Many have life left over when luck runs out. They waste their happy moments and farther down the road would like to turn around and return to them. There are more days than luck." That's a line from the writer Gracián, and right after saying it, he quoted another: "Two kinds of people are good at foreseeing danger: those who have learned at their own expense and the clever people who learn a great deal at the expense of others."

All the bustle and noise of the café fell away. We looked at each other so sadly. He was lost in his chaos; I was afraid mine would return the moment he left town. So I took a deep breath and just said it. "You know what I'd like to do more than anything else in the world right now? Go home and make love with you."

He looked away and my heart fell. Then he looked back and said, "I can't do that. I'm HIV positive."

I grabbed his hand and squeezed it as hard as I could. He squeezed back. It was the first time we had ever touched.

"They discovered it when I was here last time. That's really why I came to Vienna. I had this cough that wouldn't go away and was losing weight . . . Can we leave now?"

Oh, Christ! Jesus, you can't imagine how I felt. I put money on the table and we left. I walked in front of him, paying no attention to anything but the door. I went through it and held it for him. When we were outside, we stood there staring at each other.

He touched my shoulder. "Three people said your name as we were leaving."

I shook my head and began to cry. I put my arms around him and wept. He patted my back but then stopped, and he wept too.

He said, "I was never going to tell you. I made a deal with myself. If I ever saw you again, I wouldn't tell you. But then I got shot and was really scared. I'm really scared."

I feel such knots in my stomach even telling this now, Rose. It was so hard. So hard!

I got him to come back to the house with me, and we talked for a couple of hours, but when we were exhausted and there were long silences between us, he said he wanted to go back to his place. I pleaded with him to stay—in the living room, the guest room, with me if he wanted—but he said no. I had no right to insist, so we woke Minnie and walked the half mile down to the *Gasthaus* in silence. We held hands, but I was the one to take his, which lay completely dead in mine. I wouldn't let it go for an instant.

When we got there, he brought my hand to within an inch of his lips and kissed the air near it. Then he thanked me for being so kind. The tears started down my face again. There was nothing else to say, so I lamely asked what he'd like for breakfast. He tried to smile but couldn't. "Bacon and eggs again, if you still have some." He moved toward the door but turned back to me and said quietly, "Be sure to wash your hands as soon as you get home. I don't know anything about this disease and who knows how you can get it."

Back at the house I sat down on my front step and, with Minnie sniffing around, looked up at the stars. A story he had told me came to mind. It struck some chord I couldn't name, but still it gave me a feeling of hope and possibility.

He and a bunch of other journalists were in Rumania a year before the fall of the government. The living standards were horrible and it was impossible to get a decent meal, even in the supposed best restaurants in Bucharest. But one guy had heard about a place, and they all went. They almost fell over backward when they saw what was offered on the menu. The most exquisite French cuisine—escargots, white truffles, and a wine list that was amazing. What a find! Was this the end of the rainbow? Whatever it was, first they feasted on the possibilities the menu offered, then very carefully made their selections. The waiter nodded and disappeared. They were the only customers in the place but thought that was because the food was obscenely expensive by Rumanian standards. An hour passed but nothing came. They hadn't even seen the waiter in that time. By then they were getting suspicious. Finally he reappeared, very upset, and said unfortunately none of the things they'd ordered was available tonight. What else would they like? He offered menus and they chose again —lovely second choices. Another hour passed and the same thing happened—no food, no sign of the waiter. When he appeared he told them again he was sorry, but these things were also unavailable tonight. They were on the verge of killing him by now. What *was* available? He said pork. Pork? That's all? Yes, that's it. Why? Why hadn't he told them that two hours ago and spared them the wait, rather than offering the menu that had them all drooling with anticipation?

After much hemming and hawing and throat clearing, he admitted to being both waiter and cook. In fact, he owned the restaurant too. As soon as a customer gave an order, he ran out the kitchen door to scour the city for the necessary ingredients. The man really *could* make all the dishes offered on the menu, but it was more a question of what was available at the markets that day. Which usually meant next to nothing in that desperate city. So each night he had to return empty-handed and, as waiter, go through the charade of telling the customers such-and-such was "unavailable." What else would they like?

I told Leland I'd always believed a good story is better than a good time, since you have the story to tell again and again but the good times tend to be forgotten. When I asked if the pork was good when it was finally served, he said terrific.

Thinking through what had happened that night and over the past days with him, waves of different emotion poured over me. But in the end, that story kept coming back. It seemed the moral was, Look, we don't have escargots but we *do* have pork, so let's make it the best goddamned pork ever cooked. I couldn't decide whether the waiter's refusal to admit to an empty kitchen was good or not. At first all that pretending looked sweet and optimistic, but there was also something pernicious about getting people's hopes up, then, after making them wait hours, serving only pork. And not just one night, but every night. So there's only pork. So what? If that's all there is, then admit it and do magic with it. Make it the best pork ever eaten.

As far as Leland's health was concerned, he lived in his own Rumania now but that shouldn't stop us. In the morning I'd go down and tell him even if we only *did* have this and this, we'd do whatever we could to make it work. Simple as that. I'd invite him to come stay with me as long as he liked, or whenever he liked. Then we'd work with the materials at hand, whatever they were, from day to day. If AIDS developed, I'd try to help and comfort him as best I could. He was a remarkable, heroic man. It would be a privilege to be his friend and support.

I went to my desk and spent a long time making lists of things to do, questions to ask, people to call or see. I knew next to nothing about AIDS or HIV. How had he gotten it? Was he bisexual? Did he do drugs? Did it matter? There was only the disease now and however we could deal with it. Only the "pork."

I woke early the next morning though I'd gone to bed very late. The moment I opened my eyes I was ready to get ripping. Take Minnie for her walk, prepare the bacon and eggs so the minute he walked through the door I could get him going, make more lists . . . How would I ask him to stay without making it sound like pity or the wrong kind of concern? What would I do if he said no? I didn't want to think about that. Get books, get information on living with someone who has AIDS. But he *didn't* have it yet! Don't even think in that direction. There's all kinds of things that can be done, looked into, tried out, before that actually happens. That was the absolutely worst way to think. Just the other day I'd read an article about a virologist who said he was convinced there was no genuine link between those who were HIV positive and those who had full-blown AIDS. Over coffee, in between articles, I found the piece holding my attention for a few minutes, but then I turned the page. Now it was the most important article in the world. Where had I read it? Who was the scientist?

I raced around the house trying to do everything at once, trying to figure out what I could realistically do and what was in the hands of the gods. The gods? God? No time to think about that, GOD, now. There'd be plenty of time later. As that thought crossed my mind, I half-raised a hand, as if asking for His patience and understanding.

I waited two nervous hours before beginning to worry. Where *was* he? Why hadn't he come or at least called? Leave him alone. Let him do things his own way, on his own schedule. But maybe he thought he couldn't face me after what he'd confessed last night. Too bad, Arlen, leave it alone. It's his decision. I waited and talked to myself until I couldn't stand it anymore. Then I hooked Minnie up again and hotfooted it down to the *Gasthaus,* hoping to meet him coming up. No such luck. When we got there, we stood outside a few minutes while I tried to decide what to do next. I finally got up the nerve to go in—and was told the gentleman had checked out earlier but left no message.

I went home and sat like a stone, most of the time blank, but now and then something inside me bellowed, "Do something! Get up and find him!" But putting myself in his place, I realized why he'd taken off. The shame, embarrassment, the doubt that any person can help in a calamity. Still, why hadn't he said anything this morning before leaving? Had I been so unsympathetic last night? I carefully ran through what we'd talked about ten times but came up blank.

As the despair was peaking, the phone rang. He said, "I'm at the airport. I'm going back to Yugoslavia. Thank you for being so kind—"

I asked him, please, just let me talk a few minutes, but he didn't want that. There was too much going on inside him. He asked for some time to think and said he'd be in touch.

I took a deep breath and closed my eyes. I wanted to yell, "I think you're wrong," but there was nothing I could say except please call me. Please come back whenever you want because I'll be waiting. Whenever you want.

I'm going to stop here, Rose. You understand.

I worked in the garden, walked the dog, kept the television tuned to CNN day and night. I don't remember many details of those days except that whatever I did, I did as hard as I could, completely concentrated, so as not to think too much about the silent phone or the frightening reports from the battlefront in Yugoslavia. I knew he'd go straight there and was afraid this time he'd be killed. Or would try to be killed rather than die the ghastly slow death of AIDS.

I went to the children's hospital every day and spent more time there than ever before. I remembered the woman on her knees in front of the hospital screaming that it wasn't fair. One night I saw an igel crossing the road and immediately took it as a good sign. I wanted to call Leland and say only that—ten seconds in his ear: "I just saw an igel and I know it means something good." Then in one of the few happy moments since he'd left, I realized I *could* call him—in London and leave messages on his answering machine. The idea was so exciting that I spent the better part of a morning in the garden on my knees, digging and thinking about exactly what I'd say if I got up the courage to call. I wondered how long his tape was and how many times I'd be able to leave messages before the thing was full.

Small things, hedgehogs and answering machines, were the tiny shots of light and hope across the horizon of those days.

Sarajevo got worse. Thousands of people were dying. I cringed at the television footage, but was always alert for his face or anything that might have to do with him. I bought a map of Yugoslavia and studied it, trying to say the names of towns and cities. Where was he today: Trebinje? Donji Vakuf? Pljevlja?

You and Roland called and it was the first time I've ever been disappointed to hear your voices. I wanted to get off the line so that it'd be free, just in case. The things we talked about were all background noise to me, whereas any other time I would have cherished our conversation.

Immediately after that the phone rang again and it *was* he. He was in Sarajevo, conditions were desperate, but he'd called to say he was all right and still thinking about things. Most of all, don't worry. Don't worry? Was he nuts? But you'd be proud of me; I held my tongue. I didn't push him about anything—not to come back, not to know *what* he'd been thinking. I treated him like . . . like the igel that had allowed itself to be held. I was so glad to hear his voice that I let him talk and asked only questions that might make him talk more and stay on the line. When he hung up, I put the phone down but kept my hand on it, as if to get whatever echoes of him it still might hold.

Coincidentally, *Standing on the Baby's Head* was on TV that night. I watched it because I'd never seen one of my films in German. The woman's voice they chose for mine was eerily similar, making me sit way forward in the chair and pay complete attention. Listening, I could understand some of what she—I—was saying, but it was like having the oddest German lesson ever, with me both as teacher and rapt student. Was the story the same in translation? Was it better or worse with Weber's original words inverted, emphases altogether different? Could a story ever be the same in another tongue? I thought about Leland telling his life story in a language I considered my own, but I wasn't a man, wasn't HIV positive, hadn't experienced what he had, although the way he told it brought it vividly to life. So is there any language common to all of us? For a while I thought the language of the human heart, but no way. That's *the* most complex and diverse, you know? Is there any way to fully grasp another's story without actually being that person? Doubtful.

When I'd almost gotten used to those strange anxious days, almost gotten used to worrying and wondering and not hearing from him, I got a telegram from someone in Yugoslavia saying Mr. Leland Zivic was coming to Vienna. His train would be arriving early the next morning and could I possibly meet it.

Rose, I folded and folded the piece of paper until it was impossible to bend anymore. I put it on the table and watched it slowly try to uncurl itself and tell me the blessed news again. Minnie was asleep on the couch. I lay down next to her and put my arms around her warm body. She lifted her head and looked at me to see if everything was okay. We lay there a long time: she snoring gently, I knowing tomorrow was going to be the beginning of something extraordinary.

What I didn't know was the *way* he'd chosen to return. In one of the innumerable cease-fires that had been negotiated by Lord Carrington, it was agreed by all the warring factions to allow those who wanted to leave Bosnia-Herzegovina to go to other countries. Hungary, Austria, and Germany agreed to accept most of these poor people, but there were so many who wanted to leave that not even the experts knew what to do with them once they'd made their way to safety. It was the largest exodus in Europe since the Second World War and no one had any idea of how to handle it.

In keeping with his adventurer's way of doing things, Leland chose to ride back to Austria on the first refugee train out of Sarajevo. There were literally thousands of people on that train, and being in the *Südbahnhof* when it arrived was one of the most harrowing and electrifying sights of my life, so help me God. It was like hell on earth.

I got there half an hour beforehand. Since I didn't then know anything about the significance of the train, I thought because it was so early in the morning few people would be around. But the platform was overflowing. Large families, singles, old, young, well dressed, tattered . . . every type you can imagine had gathered.

The mood of the crowd was just as mixed. From what I could see, half of them were carnival-happy, festive; the others looked worried or terribly, terribly sad. What was going on here? Children were everywhere, darting in and out, wrestling down on the ground and being shouted or laughed at by their families. Old women wrung their hands and rocked back and forth as if praying. Men with two-inch-thick mustaches looked down the tracks with thousand-yard stares.

Amazed and utterly baffled at both the turnout and *variety* around me, I stopped a railroad workman and asked why they were all here. He smiled and touched his head in the familiar Viennese gesture that says everyone is crazy. "The war train from Yugoslavia's coming in. They're all waiting for their families. As if we don't already have enough damned *Tschuschen* in this country!"

Hearing him call them "niggers" made me frown and pull back. He sneered and slowly looked me up and down as if I were for sale. I walked quickly away. When the loudspeaker announced the train's arrival, I found a place to wait that wasn't too crowded.

Slowly the locomotive came around the last curve and moved toward us. When it was closer I could see all these heads sticking out the windows, lots of hands waving, faces beginning to take shape as the train loomed larger. The crowd on the platform drove forward, some of them waving back, others talking excitedly and pointing as if they'd already seen the person they'd come for. The engine gave two short hoots and came hissing into the station, brakes squealing.

If I'd been shocked at the turnout at the station, that was nothing compared with what arrived. Long before the train stopped, passengers were leaping, dropping, pouring out of the cars. If you'd just arrived, you'd have thought there was a fire on the train and these poor people were trying to escape.

But no, they were only getting off. There were businessmen in suits, women in high heels, peasants, farmers with dirt all over their clothes, women in babushkas with babies strapped on like backpacks . . .

Window after window passed me, and the faces still on board were another show of every emotion possible. Flat-out, hand-waving joy; one whole compartment was holding hands and dancing; hysterics—Happy? Sad? Who could tell? —crying. The last thing I saw go by was a young woman slapping a man so hard that his head hit the window with a big thump. All passed in seconds. One picture after another, a living mural of humanity.

When the train finally stopped, people spilled out in a riot of shouts, gestures, flying colors. In an instant I was engulfed by at least a thousand people. Workers wearing Red Cross armbands and speaking different languages at the top of their voices tried to organize them, make some order out of the chaos, but it was nearly impossible. These people had been through months of war, praying for a way out of it and a chance to live another day. Then suddenly they were all cramped into a train with nothing to do but think about what they'd lost, what little they had left, what they'd do now so far from what could never be home again.

I looked for him from face to face, around heads, bundles . . . but everything was all right up in my face; everything was too much for me to be able to see clearly and make out one man in that great explosion of people. Panicking, I pushed forward into even more. No luck. There were so many eyes and smiles, arms, words, packages, children . . . I pushed harder and was pushed right back.

This didn't work, and the crush scared the shit out of me. Maybe if I returned to the gate, I'd find him there. He knew me and knew I'd come for him. But how could we find each other? I turned around and bulled my way back. At the exit I stood on tiptoe to look for him in a mob that never stopped or thinned, so many of those people looking lost and scared and totally alone. God, it broke my heart.

At last, after about three lifetimes, things did get calm and only small groups were still on the platform, most of them sitting forlornly on their bags, talking among themselves or to the Red Cross workers. But no Leland. Had he missed the train? Had something happened to him before he left Sarajevo?

But then there—oh, God, oh, God—way down at the front of the train, walking slowly, carrying that big red knapsack over his shoulder and waving when he saw me . . . Oh, Rose, I started running. But then immediately I dropped my purse, and everything spilled across the whole ground. I bent and scooped as fast as I could, looking up constantly to check that he was still coming. I finished, zipped up the bag, and tried to run. Then my left leg buckled and I wobbled, but straightened out and was off. He was much closer now and was smiling. He was smiling at me! At me! At me! Ten feet away he dropped his bag and, throwing his arms out, shouted my name so loudly that it owned the whole station: *Arrrrlennn* Everybody looked at him and then at me and started smiling. One little boy screamed it out too, and their voices hung together for a few seconds, and it was the most wonderful sound.

By the time he stopped, I was hugging him as hard as I could. We stayed there so long. And then he said, "I want to go to Italy. I want to go with you. Will you go with me?"

Wyatt

and Arlen

I looked at Wyatt and thought of him for a moment as Finky Linky, the vibrant, funny man who'd made a million kids laugh and think. More than anything in the world, I wanted him to *be* Finky Linky now—full of magic and solutions, capable of flicking a wrist and saving both of us from what was already happening. His eyes met mine but fell away quickly, as if he were guilty of some crime. He was only a man, a sick man who had come to my house because he was as scared and confused as I was about what had happened. I sighed and worked up as much of a smile as I could find.

Before the conversation began, I'd put things on the table. I wanted to look at them as I spoke so that I'd remember everything. The brown leather dog leash, the blue baseball cap, and of course the photograph. Where would my story be without that? I'd brought it to the table along with the other things, but turned it face down so that he couldn't see what was there until I was ready. "Wyatt, do you remember the first time I saw you at the Hilton? The day you arrived in Vienna with your friend?"

"Yes. It was such a surprise to see you."

"That was the happiest time of my entire life. Forget the career, the fame, and all the rest. Right then was *it*. I've thought about it so much since, and even with everything that's happened, that was the best. My heart was full of absolute pure joy. I've never been more exactly where I wanted to be. With a man who was compelling and marvelous. I totally believed in him and what was possible between us, even with his sickness hanging over us like a black radiation cloud. Still! We were going to Italy because he wanted to be with me. Finally. When I saw you I wasn't surprised at all. It was just *another* great thing. Hey, there's Wyatt Leonard, isn't that nice? Know what else? Know how sometimes when you're having a great time, you can't help wondering when it's going to end? When's the bad going to come back? That never happened. For, I don't know, two weeks, I was utterly fulfilled and satisfied. There was nothing more I wanted from life. And I didn't wonder whether I was worthy or when it was going to end, or why this wonderful thing was happening to me. It just *was* and I flowed with it and thanked God twenty times a day."

"God?" Wyatt snorted and said the word archly.

I looked my friend in the eye. "Yes. You want me to say there is no God after what's happened, but I won't. I don't understand any of it, but I do believe that if there's one of them, then there's got to be the other."

"Strayhorn says there is only Life and Death."

"But Phil's not a very reliable source, is he?" I tried to keep my voice steady but it cracked at the end of the sentence.

"Tell me the whole thing, Arlen. I want to hear it all. I have to."

"I know, I'm getting there. But I've got to tell this my way, or else I'll get confused. So, we met you at the hotel and then took the bus to the airport. We would've taken my car, but Leland said we shouldn't because he had no idea when we'd be back, and parking might end up costing a fortune. Such a zip of electricity went up my back when I heard that! He didn't know when we'd get back. Everything was up in the air, everything up for grabs. Neither of us had any plans beyond each other, and we were pushing everything else away. People talk about just picking up and going, but they never do it. Too dangerous, too much at stake. But the hell with dangerous! We were going to try, so don't take the car to the airport 'cause we don't know when we'll be back. Moments like that make you want to shout and throw your arms in the air. And there were so many moments those days when I'd really gasp at the intensity of something, or a chill would freeze me with excitement and anticipation.

"The things Leland said and the way he saw life got more and more interesting the longer we were together. The man knew things, and you wanted to hear all of his opinions. On the plane to Italy we talked about politics and love, food, travel. Every time we got talking, it just got richer and fuller, no matter what. He knew so much and could express it so well; put a whole new spin on a subject so your head would be vibrating and reeling at the same time.

"Another thing was his incredible ability to listen and retain everything you said. Do you know what a compliment it is when someone brings up something trivial you said but forgot four days ago? The man remembered it all! Even the *way* he listened . . .

"There was a beautiful young stewardess on the plane who was obviously interested in him, but he didn't even tip her a nod. She kept trying to bat her big eyes and make contact, but it was funny, because he ignored her and kept listening to me."

"Well, you're also known by half the world as a pretty good-looking woman yourself, Arlen."

"Sure, but this was different. He wasn't paying attention because he wanted to seduce me. He knew he had that if he wanted it. No, he was interested in what I was *saying.* He wanted to hear. That's a whole other thing and such a compliment! Anyway, isn't that what love boils down to in the end? I want to listen to you; what you have to say matters to me. I believe it is. I even started laughing once and told him the way the two of us were always head to head gabbing away must make us look like two little kids sharing secrets. And who listens more carefully to a kid than his buddy?

"Florence was lovely, but it didn't matter where we were. We went sightseeing and ate in restaurants Leland had heard about. My main memories of those days, though, were walking and talking and the *heat.* It was so hot that we'd walk a while, then plop down in outdoor cafés and order ice-cold Cokes. I've never liked Coca-Cola so much in my life. Usually they brought it to you by the glass, but if you were lucky they gave you the bottle and a glass. That way, before you poured it out, you could roll the cold bottle across your forehead or up and down each arm first. It was as refreshing as the drink itself. Walking and conversation and cold Coke.

"One day we took a bus to Siena. It was overcast and cooler. By afternoon it was misting rain. We climbed to the top of the fourteenth-century tower in the middle of that incredible town square, and no one was up there but us. Leland described the famous horse races they hold there every summer. The Palio. How Siena's divided into districts and each has its special name for the race—Eagle, Giraffe, Caterpillar, Goose."

"Did he ever touch you when you were there?"

"Never. He wouldn't even hold my hand unless I took his. Ever since he told me about being sick he'd been wary of any kind of physical contact between us. That was the strange part—there was so much passion and intensity crackling between us, but so little physical contact. As if we were both naked and mad to touch, but separated by a thick piece of glass. Frustrating, but in a way delicious too. I felt like a virtuous teenager in love for the first time and dying to do it, but the boy respected me and agreed I should be a virgin when I get married. That was mostly from his side; I wanted the contact bad."

"Would you have actually slept with him? A man who was HIV positive?"

"I don't know, to be totally honest with you. Pure suicide, huh? I thought *if* it happened, we'd deck ourselves out with double condoms and spermicides . . . maximum safety, but who was I kidding? It *was* insane, and so was I for him after a while. Who knows."

"You loved him that much?"

"Sometimes I'd look at him and couldn't breathe. Sometimes I felt I was being crushed from inside by my swelling heart.

"Anyway, after Italy we flew to London because he wanted to show me things there he loved. It was terrific. More bliss, more great days together.

"Only one curious thing happened while we were there, which didn't amount to much, so I basically ignored it. I love roses and somehow that came out when we were in London. One day we split up to do separate errands. When I got back to his apartment, he wasn't there but a giant bouquet of yellow and white roses was sitting on the kitchen table. Propped against it was a note in his handwriting: 'I think we are not only a secret place but also a dangerous place. It's a world so beautiful, so pure, that now that we've gone inside, we have two problems. First, how can we bear all this beauty and stay alive? And second, how will we ever manage to get out and keep living in the ordinary world?'

"Any other time, flowers and a note like that would have sent me over the moon. Instead, I put it down, frowned, and didn't know whether to be upset or feel even sorrier for the guy. I stared at the gorgeous flowers and, after a while, walked into his bedroom for the proof I knew was there.

"As I'd expected, he lived very modestly in London except for the books and music. His entire apartment was floor-to-ceiling shelves for the most colossal collection of books, records, and CDs. They were done in this beautiful honey-colored oak, and he must have spent a fortune on them, because the apartment was oddly shaped in many places and the shelves were custom-fitted into just about every available nook and cranny. And *needed* to be, because they all were packed to the brim. There was no order either, which surprised me, because other book collectors or audio freaks I know are absolutely gaga for order. But Leland's collection was everywhere. Books, records, and CDs were all together helter-skelter and since there were so many—thousands of each—it would have taken a hell of a long time to find something. When I asked him about it he said he rarely wanted to read or listen to specific things. He was a browser, responded to a mood, and liked nothing better than roaming around his shelves and discovering what was there. He chuckled and said sometimes he'd even buy something, bring it home, put it on the shelf, and forget it. Then he'd rediscover it with new delight days or even weeks later. It made sense. His life was spent going from one deadly situation to another. At home, why not relax and let everything have its spontaneous way? He'd known so much horrible riot; at least here the riot was enjoyable.

"But I knew what *I* was looking for and exactly where it was. A few days before I'd been looking through the books and come across a novel called *Minotaur* by Benjamin Tammuz, a writer I'd never heard of. It was short, and since I was waiting for Leland to come home, I'd sat down and read it straight through. I liked it very much, and one memorable passage in particular: the one I had just read on the note pinned to the flowers. Having received his many postcards from Yugoslavia, I was used to his quoting from things he was reading. But he always put the name of the work and the author's name afterward so that if I liked it, I could read the book too. I took it for granted that anything else on those cards were Leland's own thoughts, which was great because I usually liked them more than the quotes.

"I remembered where the Tammuz was and took it down from the shelf. Skimming through, I found the passage. With the exception of a few words, the lines were exactly the same as on his card. I put the book back and went into the kitchen to cut the stems on the flowers and place them in a larger vase. After that, I kept trying to push the thought away but couldn't. When he came in a few hours later, the first thing I said was how much I loved both the flowers and *his* quote.

He said he was glad. That's all. It made something in me cringe. What if everything he'd written to me was someone else's? What if *none* of those canny, moving, funny lines, insights, observations were his? The possibility made me feel sorry for him, then ashamed I'd ever asked. But I had, and that was that. I remember looking at one of the bookcases as if it were to blame, as if it held the real culprit. I'm sure too that on my face was the blush of a person caught looking through a keyhole or going through someone else's drawers."

"Arlen! Why would *you* feel guilty? He was the guilty one. He was lying."

"That's a big word. And come on, Wyatt, you know the rules—whoever says I love you first, loses. This was a double whammy—I told him I loved him first, but then was also the first to discover he *was* lying in a pathetic way. I felt guilty and hurt but didn't know if I had any reason to feel either. It was all very strange.

"Anyway, maybe because of that, I started feeling itchy to get back to Vienna and quietly suggested it to him. He could do whatever he wanted—come with me, or stay in London and then come over. But he seemed to like my suggestion, and a day later we flew back. Neither of us knew how things would work out or what exactly we were going to do, but I fully believed that our being as happy as we were with each other would take care of problems. He agreed. We'd do it one day at a time and whenever there was even the slightest *anything,* we'd face it square on.

"I've never had so much fun hanging around with any man. We cooked together and walked and watched TV and he told me anything I wanted to know about him. We talked about high school and old flames and what we felt about our parents. He said just when we grow up enough to begin forgiving them for whatever happened when we were young, we have to get used to pitying them. I thought it a strange comment, and then the question raced nastily across my mind: Was it his thought or something he'd read? I said nothing, but it returned later to hit me on the back of the head like an iron boomerang.

"Every morning we followed the same routine. He'd get

up first and wake me. Then he'd take Minnie out for a walk in the vineyards while I made breakfast. At his request his breakfast was always the same—bacon and eggs because that was the first meal I'd ever cooked for him.

"Usually they came back in a fluster because they'd had an adventure—seen a deer grazing, or Minnie had taken off over the hills and Leland had had to chase her. He never seemed to mind. They loved each other, and whenever he sat down on the couch, she'd follow and climb right onto his lap. He was very sweet to her, and sometimes when I was out of a room I'd hear him talking to her as if she were human. I liked that too about him—liked knowing he enjoyed the dog as much as I did and didn't see her as any kind of imposition.

"And then she . . . died." My throat closed quickly and I had to stand up. My chest heaved and in a second I was crying hard. "She just died."

Wyatt got up and put his arms around me. Such a nice man, but no arms would have done any good then. All I could think of was that dear, dear animal and what a good friend she'd been. How she brought her chew bone to my feet and said with happy eyes, "Let's play! Throw it!" Or the time she was sleeping on the couch and, shifting, slid slowly down and onto the floor without ever waking. How slobbily she ate food but didn't like to be watched when she was outside doing her business. How gentle and sweet she was.

"That sunny morning she had staggered through the door, blood pouring out of her mouth. She collapsed on the floor and had one last, agonizing seizure. It was over so fast.

"As Leland ran in shouting for her, she twitched a few times and then was still. She'd been nosing around something, he said, but then she'd put whatever it was in her mouth and began eating it. Seeing that, he went after her to get it away, but she ran off toward home, delighted to be naughty right in front of him.

"Poison. Poisoned meat. The veterinarian in Klosterneuburg, the man who'd given her her rabies shot and told me what to feed her, pulled off his rubber gloves and threw them onto the examining table in total disgust. Sometimes it happened. Sometimes an animal hater bought a nice piece of meat, laced it with poison, and put it where he knew it would be found.

"I was destroyed. Yet even in the darkest, saddest moments I thanked God Leland was there. He took over everything and gave me all the space and time I needed in which to grieve. And though he was wholly *there,* most of the time he stayed invisible. But somehow he also sensed when I needed him in the room with me. Then he'd hold my hand and talk to me, and from the things he said, I knew her death was as terrible to him as it was to me. I had nothing but pain inside, so he supplied all the other necessities for both of us—love, strength all around, and a solidness that I couldn't get enough of. What must it be like to lose a *child?* How in his own fear and failing health did he find the strength and goodness to keep me afloat? Are there really such precious people on earth? Here was one. He was proof.

"I thought I'd loved him before, Wyatt, but after Minnie died and he saved me, whatever I felt before was absolutely nothing compared to this. Do you know what a *shochet* is?"

"A what?"

"A *shochet.* That's a kosher butcher. You know, the Jews do their slaughtering very differently. The whole procedure is done in a way so the animal feels no pain. They use a knife called a *chalef,* which means 'sharp-no-nick.' Another way of translating it is 'that which from life to death transforms.'

"What are you talking about, Arlen?"

I could see concern in his eyes, as if he were afraid my sanity had begun to wobble.

"They're important words, and they'll mean a lot when I've finished telling you the whole story. '*Shochet*' and '*chalef.*' "

"*Shochet* and *chalef.* Okay."

"You know the saying 'Never get comfortable till you hear the other shoe drop?' I was still staggering from Minnie's death when Leland came in a few mornings later with the mail. There was a large manila envelope from my uncle Len Mira in West Lafayette; he was my mother's brother, and I hadn't heard from him in years. Inside was a small, thick leather book with the word DIARY in gold letters on the cover.

There was also a note from Len saying it was Mother's. Dad had sent it to him years before, right after Mom's death. He said he was getting on now, and though he'd never read it because he didn't think it was any of his business, he thought I should have the book."

"Why didn't your father keep it?"

"Because Mom and her brother were extremely close, and Dad probably thought it was the one thing of hers he could give Len that mattered. Len's a shy man and I believed him when he said he hadn't read it. But *I* did and instantly suffered another death—my own. How about some coffee?"

I started to get up but Wyatt pulled me back down. "Come on, Arlen, you aren't leaving after that. What are you talking about? Forget the coffee."

"All right. My mother and I were real pals. She died when I was a teenager and it was one of the worst traumas of my life. I never got over it. There were so many things I needed to do with her and tell her. But one day she was just gone. I wasn't even around—I was away at school. I loved and trusted her more than anyone because, most important, she was my friend. The Girls. That's what Dad called us, the Girls. We were always together, and I think he was often jealous. But she died just when I was beginning to become a woman. You remember what those first teenage years were like—so much coming at you at once and you had no idea how to handle it. Sex, figuring out who you are, what you want to do—all the biggies. Suddenly my only guiding light was dead, and who was there to turn to? Definitely not my father, who was a good guy but very straight, and totally blind to who I was. My friend Rose became a good substitute later on, but for a few years I was on my own after Mom's death, and I did a lot of wrong things.

"I'm getting off the track. I thought we were as close as a mother and daughter could be. At least that comforted me when I thought about her dying so young: at least we loved and appreciated each other when she was alive. She was my biggest supporter and believed in me no matter what. In return, she knew I told her everything and was as honest as I could be. It was a good relationship, Wyatt. I don't know many kids who get along so well with their parents. When I was still famous, an interviewer once asked me what I'd wish for if I could have one wish and whether I'd give up my career for it. I immediately said yes, because my wish was to bring Mom back to life. That would have been worth ten careers.

"So you can imagine what a wonderful, unexpected treasure it was to suddenly have her diary in my hands. It was that great woman alive again. Now I could hear, across all the lost years, what she had to say about things we'd known and shared. It was a remarkable thing to possess, a real gift from God. And coming so soon after Minnie's death, it instantly lifted a whole ton of the weight off my soul. I would read it in little bits, savor each piece, do a page a day, and that way stretch it out a long time.

"The first entry I read said, 'The best thing about fall is that Arlen leaves for school and I don't have to be around her for a while.'"

"What?" Wyatt sounded as surprised as I felt the first time my eyes read those words on the diary page.

"That was the first entry. It almost didn't bother me. I thought she must've been depressed, or whatever, and didn't really mean it. I could remember times when she got on my nerves. So what?

"But this was different and she meant it, all right! Because there were other sections, too many of them, that said the same thing. I've memorized them. Like 'My daughter keeps telling me things about her life that I don't want to hear and that make me like her even less.' And 'How many times have I written in here that I would give anything to leave my husband and daughter, go off, and start again? Have a second chance to try and make another life that means something?'"

"Oh, Arlen! God, you poor thing. What did you do?"

"Wept. Stared at the wall and felt my whole history slipping away from me. Then I made myself read more, hoping for some light, for a change in her feelings, but it was all, all the same. No let-up, no change. I read the whole book in an hour and a half. Those years. All those years I thought we were so close, but page after page in that sweet handwriting I remembered so well . . . They said the same thing: she hated her life. She thought my father and I were selfish boors and she'd have given anything to escape us. The only time she ever had any peace was when I went away to school.

"And then she died. It was horrible."

"Did you tell Leland?"

"Yes. He was superb. Told me to put it all into perspective. Talked about how proud she would have been if she could have known me now. How happy she would've been to know she'd been so wrong about her daughter. Lovely things, but they did no good. And the fact it happened so soon after Minnie died . . ." I closed my eyes tightly. "How can these things hurt us after so many years and changes?"

"Because memory keeps them fresh. That's the trouble with memories—they've got a half-life of a thousand years, whether we like it or not."

"You're right. But can you see how the whole thing was collapsing? Leland's sickness, my mother's diary, the dog. Where was the other side, damn it? The things that might have balanced these horrors? It should have been the love for Leland, but he was a time bomb, a time bomb on the other side of a piece of thick glass. It felt as if everything I knew and loved was either gone or exploding. It was a fucking nightmare.

"What it ended up doing was making me love him more. I thought, Okay, maybe there's only so much time left for us together, but he's all I have and the best I've *ever* had. He grew in me till I almost couldn't stand it anymore."

"How did he take that?"

"Beautifully. I kept thinking, How can he stand me now? How can he want to hang around someone who's all pain and has nothing to give?

"But he did, and there came a point when I knew that if he died, I'd kill myself. There was no other way." I said this calmly because the real truth, however painful, is always calm. "The last blow, the knockout punch, came in a telephone call. You know my friend Rose Cazalet. Next to Leland, she's my only other real friend. We've known each other more than twenty years. Her husband was my agent; I'm godmother to their child. We're like sisters. Years ago she was raped and badly beaten by a guy she was going out with. It actually happened twice, but the second time she saved herself by knocking the guy's eye out with the heel of a shoe."

Wyatt's hands flew up to cover his face.

"And thank God she did, because she was sure he would've killed her otherwise. The guy went to prison, but you can imagine how long it took for her to recover.

"In the same week as the dog and the diary, her husband called me. He said that guy had gotten out of prison, found out where Rose was living, and come for her—"

"Stop! That's enough! Come on! One week? It's not possible."

"The world's full of people suffering every day of their lives." I said it so angrily that I shocked myself. Wyatt looked at me and we were both silent.

He sighed and shook his head, then rubbed his hands briskly up and down his legs as if he had suddenly gotten cold. "I know, you're right. What happened to her?"

"He cracked her skull and broke her arm. She was unconscious, and he must have thought he killed her, because he ran away."

"Was she—Will she recover?"

"She's in the hospital in stable condition. She has trouble remembering things. The doctors think it will take some time before she's all right again."

"What happened to the guy?"

"He's still on the loose. Roland called me right after it happened, and I was ready to fly over, but he said I shouldn't for the time being. It might excite her and that would be bad. I've been calling every day, and he says she's a little better.

"I was so shook up. One week. Everything together in one week. The only thing that kept me sane was Leland. I was terrified, truly terrified, down deep in my bones. What next? What could happen next? And you know what? You start creating things in your head that scare you just as much. Maybe this'll happen now, or this. You get sick worrying

about what little you have left. I didn't want him to go anywhere without me. I was sure something would happen to
him.

"The night before you called I asked him to make love
with me. I didn't care about anything else anymore. Nothing.
I just wanted him. He was safety, the only good left. Even
before I met him everything was slipping away, only more
quietly, like a pulse going out of a body. Now everything in
the body was dead except for this one shining light that kept
me alive. And that's all I wanted; that light inside *me* for a
little while so that I could be sure there was goodness in life.
What else was left? What else did I have to hold on to, to
know being alive wasn't just . . . *shit?*" I sighed and pulled
a pillow into my lap. "We talked for hours about it. At first he
wouldn't even listen when I tried to bring it up, but I insisted. He had to listen, had to do it. If he cared for me at all
he had to touch me. It was the first time we'd ever fought
about anything, but I didn't care. We both cried, stomped
out of the room, came back. At one point he even said yes,
but a moment later he slapped his head and said it was crazy.

"It *was* madness, it was murder, and not in any way necessary, because he'd promised he would stay with me. I said
that wasn't enough. Finally there was nothing left in either of
us and we went to sleep."

"Together?"

"No. He said he had to think and even being in the same
bed with me would confuse things. I was too empty to argue.
In fact, I was so tired I just put this pillow under my head and
stretched out here. He slept on the floor next to me. The
next thing I knew, the phone was ringing and it was you,
calling in the morning."

"Great time to call, huh?"

"Yes, it was. I was glad you did, very glad to hear your
voice. Hearing it reminded me that there were other good
things out there in the world—Wyatt Leonard and *The Finky
Linky Show,* kids, life. No, I was very glad to hear from you.
And I was happy when you asked us to dinner. As soon as
you did, I knew that was the best thing for us; I'd take a bath,
put on some makeup, and we'd go out to dinner with you."

"What did Leland say?"

"Oh, he seemed very glad. And when we saw you in the restaurant, all my spirits lifted. I had a nice time." It sounded so poor, a "nice" time. "So we had a nice dinner with you and I felt much better. I didn't say anything to Leland about sleeping with him, but it was in the air as soon as the two of us left you.

"When we got to the front door of the house, he put his hands on my shoulders, looked me in the eye, and said, 'All right.' Just that. I closed my eyes and said, 'Thank God. Thank God.'

"I went straight into the bedroom to get ready. I had a special nightgown I wanted to wear for him. Halfway across the room I looked at the bed and saw it was completely made up with new red-and-yellow sheets I'd never seen before. They had a pattern on them. Roses. Exactly like the ones he'd given me. Obviously he had made up his mind earlier and gone to the store to buy them without my knowing.

"On my pillow, that spanking new, fresh pillowcase, was a big envelope. I recognized it as one of his. The kind he used for his photographs. I was so touched by the sheets and excited about what was about to happen that I wanted to push the envelope away and *get going*. But I knew that for some reason he wanted me to see what was there before we began, so I sat down and took it onto my lap. He came into the room then and I thanked him for the sheets. I thanked him for being my friend and for whatever was in the envelope.

"He put his hand to his waist and bowed very deeply. It was a wonderful gesture—silly, cute, and kind of shy. I gave him a little round of applause and opened the flap.

"And screamed. *What?* What was this? Why was he showing it to me now? Why at all? At first I didn't recognize myself. There was a shrunken, diseased, hairless thing propped in a white chair, its mouth open and curved down as if it was gasping for breath. The eyes were so deep back into the skull that you didn't think they were eyes at all. I shouted at him, 'What is this? What are these? War pictures? Why now, for God's sake, why show them to me now?'

"Without knowing what I was doing, I let the photo slip

out of my hand, but there was another, and it was worse, because then I recognized who was there. In spite of my horror I looked, then I threw down all the pictures and jumped back across the bed away from them, away from him.

"The second was clearly of me, this monstrosity, lying on my bed in the beautiful nightgown I was planning to wear for him that night. And she was dead. Shrunken and diseased and emptied of anything that had ever been human. Me. It was me there. The nightgown, my bed, and just enough of something in the face to show it was a picture of me. Yes. Yes. *Me.* No one else could have looked at it and known, but I did."

By then Wyatt had lowered his head to his lap. I leaned down over him and put my arms over his back. I smelled his cologne and felt how tense his muscles were. I spoke almost in a whisper.

"Leland walked over and picked them off the floor. He paid no attention to me as he went through them. There must have been ten. He'd hold one out and say, 'I think this one's good. Shows all the delicious wrinkles in your skin. *The National Enquirer* would love it. "Sex Goddess Dies of AIDS! Exclusive pictures inside."'

"When he was done going through them and admiring his own work, he dropped them on the floor and sat on the edge of the bed. 'That's what you'd have looked like, Arlen, give or take a few months. Hey, remember what your favorite poet Charles Simic says? "Death has a cock that is always erect." I stole lots of lines from him, and you thought they were so cool. Dumbass ditz.' He lay back on the bed and yawned. I didn't move. 'But to tell you the truth, Arlen, the thought of fucking you and having to stick around here any longer bores me. *You* bore me. Call your pal Wyatt if you have any questions. He knows who I am.' He stood up, and the last thing he said before walking out was 'If you ever want to kill a dog, use strychnine; it's much more *vivid*.' "

Wyatt groaned and slowly straightened up. "The moment I walked into that restaurant and saw who was with you, I almost died." He looked at me and laughed, a real laugh, deep and full. "I wanted to meet this guy so much. The man who stole Arlen Ford's heart. I remembered him from that one meeting, but it was all so quick that I only vaguely recalled what he looked like. But this time when I saw you, you were at the table with Philip Strayhorn."

"It was Phil? You actually saw Phil with me?"

"Yes. And when you introduced him as Leland, he looked at me and smirked as if we were in on the joke together. I guess we always see the person from our dreams."

"But I didn't have dreams like you and the others!"

Wyatt shook his head as if I were missing the point. "I know. It's worse for you because he's been here in real life for you all along."

"So, he kills you with a disease and me by destroying anything I've ever loved or believed in. He joked once about how I was always cleaning. Said I seemed to be in a constant state of getting ready for company. But I was never neat before I moved to Austria. I just wanted to keep the few things around me in order. For once. Don't you think it's better that way, knowing where things are? I guess I was getting my life in order so that I could give it up. But I still have a lot of questions to ask you, Wyatt."

In an instant his face went from sadness to great anger. His normally pale cheeks flushed bright red. "What can I tell you that you don't already know? Death's here. What could be simpler? He's probably in this room somewhere listening to us, but what difference does it make? To me He's Strayhorn, to you He's Leland whatever his last name is. The people He likes, He kills nicely. No muss, no fuss. That's for me, you see. I wanted to know answers, so my 'pal' gave them to me. Result? I'm so scared, I don't even want to get up from this couch. His answers don't mean anything. They didn't help me understand.

"He *doesn't* like you, for some mysterious or stupid reason, so He tricked you into loving Him as you've never loved anyone. When you got to the point where you were willing to die for Him, really *die*, first He killed your dog, then He showed you your mother's diary, then hurt your friend. As you said, everything you loved. Result? It only made you need Him more, because He was the last thing left. Am I right? Then He showed you those pictures as His coup de grâce. He didn't want to waste the time sleeping with you and infecting you, because you're a bore. A bore!

"What other questions do you have, Arlen? Oh, that's right, I'm the guy with answers to the big questions because I've talked to Death. And you think that means I know something? I know nothing. None of His answers helped because none of them applies to *now,* this minute, when we're still here and alive but down to nothing. Don't you see? He begins by giving you everything you want—love and hope, or answers when you're scared, but none of it helps or protects you. Maybe you *think* it does for a while, but it doesn't. He's insidious. Look at us now. We're both finished. What was that word you used, *chalef?*"

"That which from life to death transforms. He's the *shochet.*"

"Right. Get a coffin. Write a will. It's over."

That afternoon while Wyatt sat with a drink in his hands and didn't want to talk anymore, I took my bicycle and went out riding. It was something I'd often done in California when life got to be too much of a pressure cooker. I'd get on the bike and ride until I was physically exhausted and I had no more energy to worry about what I'd been worrying about. Because I'm so hyper, it sometimes took hours, but it never failed to work.

This time I rode down to the Danube and flung myself into *pedaling pedaling pedaling* until the fire in my legs and pumping of my chest took some of the fear and confusion out of my heart. I knew I couldn't escape, but I could turn the volume down, and maybe that would help me think more clearly. I hoped so.

I rode beside the water, watching barges from Russia and Bulgaria go by, bicycles and laundry lines on their decks, people moving about their lives out there on that famous water. I thought about Leland and my life and what was happening, what Wyatt had said, and what little could be

done now to turn any of this away. I passed old couples
walking arm in arm, pointing to things along the way. I
passed families and knew I would never have a family. I
passed kids, dogs. My dog was dead. He had killed it. What
had I done to deserve His hatred? What did anyone do to
deserve Death? I rode and rode.

I rode into Vienna and then out again, still along the
water. There were people sunbathing and throwing Frisbees.
I remembered the time with the Easterlings up on their
Happy Hill and the red Viszla that liked to catch the Frisbee.
I thought of Minnie. I thought of Him poisoning the dog.
What had she done to deserve that? What had I done? Was it
just hatred? Did Death just hate, and that was the final an-
swer? He just hated and there was no other reason for what
He did to all of us?

I was way out of town by the time I began to tire and
knew I'd have to stop soon or I'd have no energy left to get
home. There were few people that far out, and I started
looking for a place to rest. The path next to the water there is
rough. Huge trees and wildly overgrown shrubs are everywhere. No one lives there. People venture out that far only to
take long Sunday walks or fish.

Suddenly I saw a big group of sunflowers planted in the
middle of nowhere, and for some reason the sight heartened
me. The only way they could have been there was that someone had purposely planted them for no good reason other
than beauty. It made me like that person very much, and it
seemed a perfect place to lie down a while and maybe take a
little nap. I fell fast asleep.

I awoke when I felt something warm on my face. It was a
hot day anyway and I'd really worked up a sweat on the bike.
I'd also fallen very deeply asleep, so the heat on my cheek
must have been great. When I came to, the first thing I saw
was an enormous penis. It was resting on my cheek and
besides being terribly hot, it was also very heavy. I've known
my share of dicks, but this one was shocking in its size and
weight. Imagine coming up through the fog of sleep to see a
thing like that an inch from your eye. You try to jump up, but
are held down by an iron hand that you cannot move, no

matter how strong you are. Imagine these things. And the shock and fear explode, because a second after sleep clears you *know* who it is up there, looming over you, the sun over His shoulder. You can see enough of His face to see He's smiling.

"I don't think you heard me the other night. I said, 'Death has a cock that is already erect.' I'm here, honey. We're out in this sexy glade and your big chance is *now*. Don't you want some?"

I pulled away. He let me pull away, I guess. I stood up but He stayed squatting near the ground, smiling, His *thing* still sticking out the front of His jeans. "You looked like Sleeping Beauty, Arlen. I thought I'd do a little twist on the tale and let it kiss you awake."

I didn't hurry. I was proud of myself for that. I only picked up my bicycle and started to push it away, never once looking back. I wouldn't give Him the satisfaction. He yelled at me, but I wouldn't turn around. He yelled, "I stole all those lines. Everything I ever said to you was someone else's. Did you really think you deserve anything original? Did you?"

I got on the bike and slowly pushed off. I almost fell once, but I wouldn't hurry. I refused to hurry away from Him. Somehow, somewhere that mattered very much.

Nothing more happened after that, and we did not see Leland. A few days before Wyatt was to fly back to America, I convinced him to go with me to the children's hospital. What else was there to do until the end? I believed that Wyatt's leukemia would now set in in earnest, while my fate would come from something outside—an accident or a sickness too. But besides the confusion and fear that ran wild through all the halls of my heart and mind, much more quickly than I would ever have thought possible, hate had also been born. Hate such as I had never experienced before.

What right did Death have to strip us bare of everything that mattered, and then kill us? Whether it was the failure of our bodies to the point of absolute weakness and humiliation, or the total loss of anything that mattered or had the simplest value. To reduce most of us to concentration camp victims standing naked, with our heads newly shaven, in front of leering soldiers before being sent off to our deaths. It was not only wrong, it was unnecessary.

So Death turned out to be like the Greek gods—resentful, playful, hideous. I had never liked the Greek myths for that reason alone. If those gods had such awesome powers, why did they need to come to earth and sleep with unsuspecting women or torment a decent man who was utterly helpless against them and their might. Why *bother?*

I told all of this to Wyatt, but his mind was constantly in ten places at once and it was hard to get him to hear what I was trying to say. I told him we should see it like this: Leland will kill us, sure, but until then we go forward for no reason other than to use the last days the way *we* want to, rather than letting him have even them by beating us into submission with fear. Wyatt said that was bluffing, that Leland would know we were just making busywork to try to keep our minds off the inevitable. Maybe that was true, but my way was better than nothing, and he finally agreed.

I arranged with the hospital to give us a large room so that Wyatt could put on a kind of small, multilingual *Finky Linky Show* for whatever kids were well enough to attend. On the morning of the performance, he came into the kitchen looking very wan and tired. When I put some breakfast down for him, he took my arm. Smiling, he said he had a feeling this would be the last Finky show he ever did. I said off the top of my head, "But you never thought you'd do another one anyway, so you'll be one up on Him, won't you?" He liked that and said, "I guess that's true."

We stopped at a trick store I know in Vienna. He bought hundreds of dollars' worth of rubber balls, masks, colored scarves, card tricks, and other things I didn't understand, but he and the store owner hit it off beautifully once the old man realized he was talking to a real master of the art. He even went into the back of the store and the attic and twenty other strange places to bring out things only Wyatt and he knew how to use. Both of us were loaded down with packages when we got to the car. Once there, he turned to me and said, "Thank you. I forgot how much I loved doing this." I wanted to cry but knew that would upset him, so I made the only funny face I know and told him it was purely selfish on my part—I wanted to see him perform as much as the kids did.

No one at the hospital knew who Finky Linky was, but they were glad for the diversion and did everything Wyatt told them. A few of the nurses spoke good English, and between us we translated whatever he said to the others and thus had little problem getting him set up.

As I so desperately hoped, he was magnificent. The minute the children came into the room he was "on," dancing from one to the other, pulling rubber creatures from their ears and hair and then giving them to the kids, singing songs in a nonsense language and making the children sing silly with him. He changed costumes and masks, made fire appear in his hand and float up in the air before it turned into multicolored smoke with special shapes and sizes. He pulled razor blades out of his mouth and grew a flower in the middle of his open palm.

The children were ecstatic and clapped for encore after encore. He never failed them. He juggled balls and used me as his ventriloquist's dummy at the same time. He did brilliant pantomime and coin tricks . . . He stopped only when it was obvious that the stimulation was tiring the kids out.

He finished with a line I had never heard before which he then repeated in three different languages. "He whose face gives no light shall never become a star." When I asked him about it afterward, he said it was from William Blake and that the only other time he had ever said it to someone was the love of his life. I asked what happened to him and he said only, "He went away. But to this day I'm still hoping he'll come back."

We had a glass of wine with the nurses and doctors who'd attended and then it was time to go. Just as we were on our way out, I suddenly remembered that one of the kids I had always read to when I visited the hospital hadn't been at the show. When I asked a nurse about the girl, her face fell and she said, "She's almost gone." Why should I be startled by that, here in a place where there was so much death every day? But I was. I asked the nurse if it would be possible to see her for a short time. The woman went to check, and Wyatt sat down and took a deep breath. "Are you sure you want to do this, Arlen? It's not going to make things any easier."

"I know, but I have to."

The nurse returned and told me to follow her. Wyatt got up to come along, but I asked him to wait. He said maybe he could make her smile a bit. I put my arm around him and kissed him on the ear.

We walked down several corridors and took some turns. I was breathing hard and told myself to stop it. We'd go in and if she was happy to see us, we'd stay a little while and maybe that *would* make her smile.

But it was worse than that. Far worse. When the nurse slowly opened the door, the room was almost completely dark except for light from the window, which fell halfway across the bed.

The little girl, Uschi Soding, was a tiny, almost un-recognizable curl under the stiff white sheets. She had stomach cancer, but I had known her before as a bald and jolly little naughty thing who liked to come up and sit under my arm when I was reading to the children. Once she had reached over and tweaked one of my nipples with her fingers, then laughed uproariously when my mouth dropped open in shock. Today there was almost nothing left of her. If she was still alive it was only in her pulse and the slow opening and closing of her eyes. The nurse whispered that they expected her to go any time.

That should have torn me apart except that by then I was watching her hands and what they were so slowly doing. I don't think Uschi knew we were there, and even if she did, she was so tired that she couldn't have done anything. Instead, her eyes and all of her concentration were on the small figure she held in one hand, just barely propped on her chest. It was a little shiny silver windmill, the kind you buy in a souvenir store in Amsterdam. The light from the window flooded over her hand and only after a while did I realize what she was doing with the last strength she had in her body. Slowly, she moved one finger across the windmill so that it would block the light. Then she took the finger away. Over and back, over and back. Light and dark, light and dark. I whipped my head toward Wyatt to see if he saw, but he had turned away and was looking at the floor. The nurse touched my shoulder and signaled that we should go. I was scared. I had to stay and watch her do this more to make sure it was for real, but the next thing I knew, the woman had taken my arm and steered me back into the hall.

We left all the things we'd bought at the magic store there for the kids and walked out of the building wrapped in our separate silences. I wanted to talk about what I'd just seen but needed to think some more before saying anything.

As we started toward the car, Wyatt spoke but didn't look at me.

"Do you know Claire Stansfield, Harry Radcliffe's girl-friend?"

"Sure. I used to buy things in her store."

"You know she moved to South Africa recently. Harry told me the last time they spoke, he was all ready to plead with her to return. He'd do anything, just please come back because he couldn't live without her. Anything. Well, as soon as she said, 'Hello, Harry,' he knew it was finished. There was no chance. She'd always been happy and peppy when she knew he was on the phone, and her hellos were always packed full of love. This time, though, he said it was the deadest, most regretful word he ever heard her say.

"The girl in there, Arlen. I know what's happening to me and I've known it a long time, but just seeing that little . . . it was like Radcliffe hearing the 'hello.' The other kids were great. You can see they're suffering, but they're still kids and have life in them. Not that one. God, I wish I hadn't seen her. It reminded me of when I was last in the hospital. And where I'll end up."

"But wait, Wyatt, I have to tell you something."

"Emmy!"

I turned before he said her name because the look on his face went from bitter regret to instant, big-eyed amazement. When I saw her, I understood why. In the time we'd been together since Leland's last visit, one of the things Wyatt told me about was this woman Emmy Marhoun and what Leland had done to her. She was dead without knowing it. I remembered her from the day in the café and my being jealous that my man had been involved, however long ago, with this great beauty.

"Wyatt, hello! I'm so glad to see you. I have to tell someone. The greatest thing has happened!" She was all dolled up and looked as if she was going to a party. Wyatt introduced us, and I think she might have remembered who I was but I wasn't sure from her expression. Anyway, she was too excited to be interested. "Do you have time for coffee? There must be a place around here."

Wyatt looked at me and I nodded. I wanted to ask her questions, now that I understood what had happened to her. Maybe there were things she could tell us. I prayed there were things she could tell us.

There was a small espresso bar down the street from the hospital. Inside, we saw the usual midday workers and low-lifes hanging around with their glasses of wine or something stronger, talking quietly and then not talking at all for a moment when they saw us. Emmy paid no attention and pointed gaily to a table. We sat down and she started talking immediately.

"This is so wonderful. You're the first people I've seen and I've got to tell you. The man I was in love with, I mean *really* in love with, is back in my life. Isn't that incredible? I haven't seen him since we broke up, but today, two hours ago, I was walking down Obere Donaustrasse and who comes strolling up in the other direction but him. I mean, is that absolutely incredible? In Vienna? And he wasn't fazed at all about it. Came up, gave me a big kiss, and said, 'How're you doing?' As if we'd seen each other yesterday." She giggled and then, oddly, patted her nose a few times. "It's been I don't know how long since we saw each other and, believe me, that was a truly awful time. I cried for six months afterward. But there he was today and, best of all, he was glad to see me! Asked if I wanted to have dinner with him tonight."

"Emmy, do you know who I am?"

"Excuse me?"

"Do you recognize me? Do you know who I am?" I leaned forward and glared at her. She *had* to know.

"Well, yes, it'd be hard not to. You're Arlen Ford. Why?"

"Do you remember when we met?"

"No. Have we met before? I think I'd remember meeting *you.*"

Wyatt and I looked at each other and then at her.

"What's the name of your boyfriend?"

"Leland. Leland Zivic."

"What does he do for a living?"

"He teaches literature at Grinnell College." She frowned, her eyes going back and forth between us. "Why do you want to know?"

Wyatt looked at me. "Why would he use the same name with her?"

"I don't know. Maybe it means something to him."

"What do you mean, the same name? What are you two talking about? Do you know Leland?"

A phone rang somewhere in the background but I barely noticed it. My head was buzzing with questions and possibilities. But before I had a chance to say anything, a waiter came to our table and asked if there was a "Frau Marhoo" here. Someone was on the telephone for her. Emmy stood up quickly and, with an uneasy look, went to get it.

"Who would know she's here?"

"Guess, Arlen. You've got one guess."

We watched as she picked up the receiver, spoke a few sentences, and then put it down. She waved both of her hands at us in a gesture that clearly meant she had to leave immediately. She was out the door before either of us could do anything.

"What's going on?"

"He's playing games. He wanted us to see her and now she's served her purpose. Poor thing. Why doesn't he—"

"Hello, kids. Anybody seen the lovely Emmy?"

He must have come from the bathroom behind us. He was wearing a blue baseball cap that said "Japan Professional Baseball—Hanshin Tigers," and a black-and-white shirt that was designed to look like a crossword puzzle. Both of them were mine.

He pulled out a chair and sat down. "We had this dinner date, but she didn't show up. I just called and she said she was here. Missed connections, I guess. I loved the show, Wyatt. I was the kid on the left with the colostomy bag."

"Why did you make her meet us?"

"I didn't make her; I steered her. Because it's her time and I thought you three might like to get together for a last drink."

"Isn't she already dead?" I tried to say it with venom but it only came out scared.

"She is, but today's the day she finds out. Big difference. We'll have dinner, I'll take her home to bed just like old times, and guess what'll happen when she hits orgasm— *kaboom*. Is that how you'd have liked it, Arlen? Our first big time in the sack, but instead of catching AIDS and getting to go out slowly and dramatically like Camille, your last great performance, you'd go right home? It's not too late. We can still work something out."

He said it in a relaxed, joking voice. I wanted to reach over and slap His face but that was stupid. Slap Death in the face? He held all the cards and we were only two of them.

"Why are you here? Is it our time too?"

"Nope! Plenty of time to enjoy yourselves yet. I came to show you something I think you'd both like to see. At least I *think* you would, so I'm going to show you anyway. It's original. I get so bored doing this the old ho–hum ways that I keep trying to challenge myself to come up with new ideas. Some are good. Not all of them, but some.

"Now, Arlen, I know you. You're wondering why you got it your way and Wyatt his. So I'm going to show you. I'm going to show both of you."

"Show us what?"

"The true yous."

"What does that mean?"

"Come on, don't be impatient. Wyatt got to put his show on his way. Now it's my turn." He sounded irked, as if we weren't an appreciative enough audience for Him. How human. But I kept forgetting that it was fun for Him to play human, to have the kick of *being* irked. Before continuing, He hailed the waiter and, ordering a beer, asked if we wanted anything. Wyatt said, "Ten more years?" and Leland laughed so hard all His teeth showed.

"Terrific, Wyatt. That's what I love about you. Finky Linky at his best. That's not on my agenda but, hey, who knows, right? Life's funny. No, I'm going to give you two something much better than ten more years. I'm going to give you your lives."

Both of us must have stiffened at that, because He put up His hands as if He were trying to hold us back. "No, no, I don't mean *that*. I'm going to give you your lives as they really have been.

"Arlen, you're the big poetry buff. Remember Delmore Schwartz? Come on, the book's on the third shelf from the bottom of your library. I liked him. Guy went crazy with all the knowledge he had but no one knew it. There's one poem in particular that's great. I'll have to paraphrase it because I didn't get a chance to memorize it the way the great actress does. 'No one really knows themselves because they don't know what the rest of the world thinks of them.' Hits the nail right on the head. We're all friends here, so I can tell you a secret. The trouble with people is, no matter how well they think they know themselves, they never *really* do because they have no idea what other people are thinking of them."

"You just said that." I couldn't stop it. The line popped out by itself.

His face flashed mean, but then He smiled. *"I* didn't; Delmore did. And he was a hundred percent correct. What I'm going to do right now, this very minute, is let you both relive your lives with genuine and complete knowledge of what everything and everyone around you is thinking. About you, about their lives, the works. I'll even let you in on the conversations of plants and other surprises."

Without an instant's thought, the idea terrified me.
"What's the point?"

"The point is to show why I don't like you, and Finky why I like him. That's what you wanted down deep in your little secret heart, wasn't it?"

"It's more than that."

"It's always more than that, honey, but I want to do it, so that's that."

The waiter brought the beer and Leland thanked him. He took a long drink and licked the shine and bubbles off His lips. "It's enlightenment. Guys go and live on top of mountains their whole lives to attain it, but I'm giving it to you for free."

"So I can know more about what my mother thought of me?"

"Partly. Partly. But there were good things too that you didn't know about. Now you'll know them too."

Wyatt reached over and put his hand on Leland's arm. "I don't want it. Please don't do it."

"It's done."

This is what I learned.

First the cells spoke. They sang to each other as they moved and divided and grew together. They were sure of what they were doing. Workmen, they knew their tasks and relished the building of whatever it was they were there to build. They had no idea what it would finally be; they knew only their specific jobs, and they did them and spoke to each other of alignment, angles, space, and distance. If they were dumb, they were dumb with a purpose and weren't sorry they knew so little. They were here to do this and it was enough for them. It was their life. They died easily because they had no idea of death. It came and they were gone. They had no names, no specific identities. Others were born and replaced them and did the same jobs. Their work was impossibly difficult but they did not know those words, so it was simply work and they did it. Slowly, over months, their labor came together and grew, filled with billions of voices talking, always talking about the job, about what came next, who must move where or what else must be done.

Awareness came slowly, like honey dripping off a spoon. Sensations. Touch. What is this? Awareness comes, but it is not here-I-am so much as the discovery of connected parts. This is here now, but a moment ago I didn't know that. It belongs. The honey spills onto the table and spirals around, forming a hill that melts down when more honey falls on it, and the hill begins to rise again, over and over. When the drip stops, the pool slowly takes shape and, if allowed, has its final form. This is the finish. This is what it is.

I was born on September 1 under a full moon, and every tide on earth, including the press and heave of my mother, knew each other. Like the cells, they worked in magnificent concert. Off the Cape of Good Hope, they pushed the great fish toward shore and it was a battle of love and esteem between the water and them to see who would win. A young woman in Morocco looked between her legs and ran screaming to her mother, terror-stricken by her womanhood, which had just begun. In Turkey, a man named Haroun watched a woman sleep and said yes to her in his mind because the decision belonged to the moon and not to him.

I knew all this. As I came into the world bathed in my mother's blood and cries, I still knew that there was no difference between anything but soon there would be because already my brain was bursting and winking, splitting itself into a million distinctions; the awe and flood of the opening moment in life when you learn first of all that you are alone now forever and what you were together a second ago is forgotten.

Mother hated me from the beginning. It was almost soothing to know. She hated the weight, the bad complexion and strange moods, the tension of her belly against her favorite summer dress, and the constant need of her body to give all for two now, always two.

She had been wrong. She had thought this child would save her life, give it purpose, show her who she was. But all it did was make her responsible for one more. She felt she had been tricked. Love was to blame, or my father, anything, me most of all. I was proof of the trick, demanding, selfish proof she had chosen wrong and would never now be given a chance to correct it.

As I grew older she forgot that this was at the center of her despair and thought different things about me. Almost all of them tentative, as if she were trying to learn to skate again across the surface of her life after a near-fatal fall.

The cells continued to sing, but I was a child and my confusion and great joy came together somehow and drowned out their more subtle music. Love came and defined itself to me differently every day. I wanted it but it was as elusive as a fly. It constantly buzzed louder in my face, a new sound in my head, but when I looked toward it, it was always somewhere else. The world I was coming to know was both enthralling and treacherous and made me want to be in every part at once, as I once had been with no effort at all. Effort. I learned what that meant but it did me no good. Everything was so separate now, singing its own distinct song that was sometimes beautiful, sometimes hideous but very loud and hitting against me with tremendous force.

The first person I knew I loved—*knew* it—was a tall woman with a short man's face who was my mother's best friend. The first time I hurt and knew it was when I reached for her earrings and discovered I couldn't touch them.

My life spun through its days, and I was bombarded with things I had not known but were now clear and understand-able. *That* was Leland's cruelty: What good did it do now? If only I'd known then, *would* life have been better? Would I have loved people and things that loved me; would my life have been infinitely better had I known the value of these great gifts?

As I made my life, ignoring what I didn't know or under-stand, I was carving myself down into a distinct form, yes, but the pieces and chips that fell away were so necessary.

Leland's "gift" was only a trip to a hell that was wholly and hopelessly my own. The torment there was not from knives into flesh or bodies in flames, but from neglect and disregard, underrating and blindness to so many things that could have been mine and made me whole but never were.

I have no idea how long the experience took, but when I returned to my life now, the three of us were still sitting in the seedy espresso joint and the only different thing was that Leland had a frankfurter in his hand and was dipping it into a small pile of yellow mustard on a white plate. I looked at him, but his eyes were on his food. The return to *now* was firm and immediate, yet the sense of loss filled every part of my being.

When I slowly moved my eyes to Wyatt, I saw him looking at the table with what, I was sure, was the same facial cast as mine—bewildered, lost, light years away. I wanted to say something, or wanted to hear his voice first and not Leland's blithe menace.

Wyatt did speak first, but he said something which, after that experience, was wholly unexpected. He looked up from the table and his face cleared to wonder. "I had forgotten all about that. Completely."

"What's that, Finky?"

"The last days of my father. I'd forgotten that whole time right before he died."

"Was it nice?"

Wyatt opened his mouth and started to speak but stopped. "It—yes, yes, it was. It really was."

"See, I told you there'd be nice things. How was your trip, Arlen?"

I had nothing to say. He knew.

Wyatt spoke again. "I can't believe I forgot that. Right before my father died, I stayed with him and my mother. He was in very bad shape and the only energy he had left was for anger. Anger at life, my mother, and me. Anger at everything."

"The guy wasn't very happy, was he?"

"He wasn't a happy man his whole life, so what could we expect at the end? When I got there, I tried to lift him by being funny and lively, but he wasn't having any of it. I talked to him and read to him from his favorite books, but every few minutes he would cry out his pain or anger. After a few days it became very difficult, and my mother and I talked a long time about taking him to a hospital, but neither of us had the heart. At the end that's what happened, but it didn't come for a while.

"One night very late I woke up when I heard him cry out. I went to his room. My mother was exhausted, and when I met her at the door I told her to go back to bed; I'd take care of him as long as he needed me. He heard that and laughed and said, 'I don't need either of you. I need to die and get it over with.'"

I looked at Leland. He shrugged and said, "His pop was right—he wasn't doing anyone any good."

Wyatt went on as if the other hadn't spoken. "So I sat down in that dark room next to his bed and said, 'Pop, I want you to tell me about the best day of your life. Tell me everything. I want to hear every detail you can remember.' Woo! That pissed him off! He didn't want to talk about life; he wanted sympathy and some way out of his pain. But I coaxed and cajoled and after a while I could almost see him settling his body into a more comfortable position. His voice started out rough and nasty, but as he went along it softened, and the more he got into the story, the quieter it got.

"Funnily, it wasn't a particularly interesting story. It was about a day he had spent on the island of Peleliu during the Second World War. He was young and knew the world would be waiting for him when he got home. He described the island and what was going on that day, the job he had there and other things. Just a day in the life of a young man who figured himself lucky, and after all those years he remembered how good it had been. I milked him for every detail, and maybe he knew what I was doing but went along with it because remembering was pleasant, and the only other things he had left were his pain and that dark room. When he was done he tried to slough it off as if it'd been nothing, but I wouldn't let him do that. I asked about other things that mattered to him, other memories stuck in his mind that some part of him was happy to look at again and talk about. I don't think I ever felt so close to him in my life."

"But two weeks later you *did* put him in the hospital and he died."

Wyatt looked at Leland and then away, as if what He had said was embarrassing. "Yes, that's right."

"Ah, I'm just being mean. Sorry. Memories are nice things. Sometimes they almost fill the holes."

"May I ask you something?"

"Uh-huh."

"I don't know if you can do it, but I have to ask."

"Go ahead."

"Can you show us God?"

Leland put the meat down and wiped his fingers on a paper napkin. "I can, but I'd have to do it in a way you'd understand. Otherwise it wouldn't mean anything to you."

Wyatt put his hand on his neck. "Please. Please show us God. If we're going to die, I want to know." He turned to me, his hand still there. "Do you want that, Arlen?"

"Yes."

"Okay, but let me finish my hot dogs. It's better to do this on a full stomach."

We sat and watched him finish his meal. He didn't do it slowly but wasn't in a hurry either.

"But it will be true? What you show us will be the absolute truth?"

"The absolute truth. You're not the first ones who've asked, you know. It's no big deal." He took a few more bites, then dropped what was left on his plate and wiped his hands on his trousers. He'd always called them pants, but I'd taught him to say trousers. He bent to one side and slid a hand into his pocket. He brought out a postcard and put it down on the table in front of us.

It was a photograph of the earth taken from high in space. Before either of us could say anything, there was noise. A hum, a kind of distant rumbling. The table and the room faded, disappeared, and I knew I was suddenly *in* space looking down on earth.

It was immense and took up my whole vision. The blue of the seas and white of the clouds, the brown land and curves of the continents this close, from this vantage point, were transcendent. For the first time I understood the wonder of astronauts, the love of people who spent their lives studying the heavens.

When that first miracle passed, I was able to listen, and realized the noise I had heard at the beginning was the sound of the earth from very far away. No, that was not completely true. Much of the sound came from the murmur of airplane engines as they cut their arcs and passages across the skies. Thousands of airplanes moving here and there filled with people and cargo, hope and destinations. Stately and slow, they went from day to night and back, secure in their act. The sound grew and I heard the voices from within, the conversations of people five miles above this earth. Engines and their voices, the keening of air across the metal bodies, the excitement of arrival, the warmth of expectation. These small lights against the black sky, moving across the night, emerging silver and fragile yet whole again into the light of day. The earth crisscrossed in every direction by planes. I saw it all from such a distance that it enabled me to understand.

For perhaps God *was* this, the earth and the lines of azimuth and the lines of planes and the lines of talk and the lines of everything crossing from one end to the other, forever.

"You kept your little house so clean and orderly, Arlen. Down on your knees scrubbing away at the floors, everything perfect. But in the end all you've got are chaos and connections you don't understand. There is no order, even with Him; only takeoffs and landings."

This time I was not surprised to be back. Rather than look at Him, I reached across the table and picked up the fork the waiter had brought for His meal.

"Did it help, Finky? Did it help to see God?"
Silence.

I didn't look up. I put the fork flat on the table and moved it back and forth. I put my finger on top of the stem and moved it on and off.

"I have to go soon and meet Ms. Marhoun. Are there any more questions or requests? How about some more God?"

When my finger was on top, it blocked the light from the bar. When it was off, the old fork shone dully.

"Hmm? Nobody has any profundities?"

Shine. No shine. On and off.

He must have been looking at what I was doing because, when he spoke again, his voice was irritated. "What are you doing? Remember your mother telling you not to play with the silverware?"

"Winning."

"What?"

On and off. Light and no light. "I'm winning, Leland. I've won."

"Really? What are you winning, Arlen?" His voice was amused.

"This." I held it up and, still not looking at him, turned the fork in the air so that the light went across it at every angle. Then I looked. He was sitting with his arms folded over his chest, smiling.

"Hit me, sweetie. I'm ready for your revelation. This time you'll get your Oscar. Roll 'em."

I would not look at Wyatt because I was scared that if his face said anything wrong it would throw me, and I couldn't have that happen now.

"I figured it out. I don't know when, but I figured it out. It may have been what Uschi was doing in the hospital with the little windmill. Or Wyatt's story about his father or even . . . or even because of what I felt for *you* before. It wasn't the earth; it wasn't seeing the earth, although that helped.

"Leland, you're so wrong. And that's what's pathetic about you, power and all.

"Are you the Devil? Or only Death? Or something else? I don't care. No matter what you are, you're jealous. You're jealous of every human being who has ever lived on earth. Know why? Because you've got *limits* and we don't. With all the power you have and all the fear you put in us, there's really only one thing you can do and that's to scare us. You have your infinity of ways to do it, but *that's all*. I remember reading that Lucifer fell from Heaven not because he challenged God, but because God told him to worship man and he wouldn't. I know why He told you to worship us. Because we have the capacity to create and forget."

"Oh, honey, I'm *very* creative."

"Yes, but in only one thing, which has a lot of variations. If we make pictures or bake cakes or fall in love, we can do the same things you do—use them to create chaos and sadness. Look what you did to me and Emmy.

"But you're limited, Leland, and that's the whole point. Just when you've taken everything in the world away from someone like Uschi, there she is in bed playing with light and totally *absorbed* in it. If you had come into the room at that moment, she wouldn't have recognized you. And you know that's the truth. You don't know what it is to be absorbed. You can kill her but you can never know the feeling of loss she had *in* that light. It's beyond you. That's why God, whatever He is, wanted you to worship us. But you didn't understand. Just by something as little as moving a finger back and forth like this." I moved my finger on the fork. "You hate us so much because there really *are* times when we completely forget you. Forget the pain and the loss . . .

"The traits we love best in others are the things that make us forget you: they make us laugh, they make love to us, they bear our children, they make us feel important and immortal. That's all eternity is—the moments when we're alone with our joy in life and you're forgotten.

"But we always exist for you. We're the *only* things that exist for you, and you hate us for it. You hate us more because we can make you go away with things as small as a silver windmill or a perfect memory, a really good hump or a meal under a tree on a checkered tablecloth. You win, yes, but we're always on your mind. You're *not* always on ours. Even when you're only this far away, we can still play with light and forget, and you hate that."

One breath. For one breath I saw in his eyes that it was the truth.

"Fuck you, movie star." He scraped his chair back, stood up, and left.

I put my hands on my cheeks. Hot cheeks, cold hands. I looked at the table and saw the fork. I wanted to touch it but didn't dare.

"Do you think that's true, Arlen? It's as simple as that?"

I looked at Wyatt. His face was full of hope.

"Yes, I think so. That's not to say He won't always try to make it harder. But we got Him this time, didn't we?"

Both of us burst out laughing.

"What happens now?"

I kept laughing. "I don't know. We keep asking each other that question. I don't know. I don't know. I don't know, Wyatt. We go on trying to forget him and get lost in our lives. Or what's left of them."

He straightened up. "I want to go home now. I want to talk to Jesse and Sophie about this and then I want to go home."

"May I come with you?"

"To Los Angeles? You want to come with me?"

"I'll cook you soups and hold your hand. And I want to see Rose. Maybe that's what I've been meant to do all along —take care of the people I love."

He reached across that scarred, tired table and took my hand. His was so warm and mine was so cold. We could help each other now and perhaps, when we were very lucky, forget him for a while.

"I'll cook you soups and hold your hand."

"Amen."